Praise for

Vulnerable

Here's what some readers have to say about the first book in the McIntyre Security Bodyguard Series...

"I can't even begin to explain how much I loved this book! The plot, your writing style, the dialogue and OMG those vivid descriptions of the characters and the setting were so AMAZING!" – Dominique

"I just couldn't put it down. The first few pages took my breath away. I realized I had stumbled upon someone truly gifted at writing. " – Amanda

"*Vulnerable* is an entertaining, readable erotic romance with a touch of thriller adding to the tension. Fans of the *Fifty Shades* series will enjoy the story of wildly rich and amazingly sexy Shane and his newfound love, the young, innocent Beth, who needs his protection." – Sheila

"I freaking love it! I NEED book 2 now!!!" – Laura

"Shane is my kind of hero. I loved this book. I am anxiously waiting for the next books in this series." – Tracy

Praise for

Fearless

Here's what some readers have to say about the second book in the McIntyre Security Bodyguard Series...

"Fearless is officially my favourite book of the year. I adore April Wilson's writing and this book is the perfect continuation to the McIntyre Security Bodyguard Series."
– Alice Laybourne, Lunalandbooks

"I highly recommend for a read that will provide nail biting suspense along with window fogging steam and sigh worthy romance."
– Catherine Bibby of Rochelle's Reviews

Books by April Wilson

McIntyre Security Bodyguard Series:

Vulnerable
Fearless
Shane (a novella)
Broken
Shattered
Imperfect

Imperfect

McIntyre Security Bodyguard Series
Book 5

by

april wilson

This novel is a work of fiction. All places and locations mentioned in it are used fictitiously. The names of characters and places are figments of the author's imagination. Any resemblance to real people or real places is purely a coincidence.

Interior book design by April E. Barnswell

Wilson Publishing
P.O. Box 292913
Dayton, OH 45429
www.aprilwilsonauthor.com

Visit www.aprilwilsonauthor.com to sign up for the author's e-mail newsletter to be notified about upcoming releases.

ISBN-13: 978-1974442638
ISBN-10: 1974442632

Published in the United States of America
First Printing December 2017

Dedications

To my darling daughter, Chloe.

To my sister and BFF, Lori.

And to all the wonderful people around the world
who read my books. Thank you for making
my dreams come true!

1

Jamie

"You sure you're ready for this?"

I'm sitting with my brother Shane in his vintage Jaguar, parked outside a four-unit brick apartment building located in Wicker Park, just northwest of downtown Chicago.

My new home.

Shane's not happy that I'm moving out of his house, as evidenced by the creaking of the leather steering wheel cover as he tightens his hold on the wheel. I don't have to be able to see to know my brother is on edge. He's afraid his blind brother can't hack it on his own. I'm ready to prove otherwise.

"Yeah, I'm ready," I say. I'm more than ready. I've been planning this move for a couple of months now.

Shane's fiancée, Beth, helped me pick out this apartment. It has everything I need: convenient access in and out, an easy-to-navigate floorplan, the basic amenities, and two bedrooms, one of which will serve as my home office. The apartment is within easy walking distance to restaurants, bars, the post office, and a grocery store... everything I'll need is close at hand. Anything else I need, I can order online or grab an Uber.

I can do this... with a little help from my service dog, Gus, a yellow Lab, and a high-tech electronic cane that allows me to navigate on my own.

"You can still change your mind, Jamie," Shane says, his voice laced with frustration. "It's never too late. Just say the word, and I'll take you home."

Home.

For the past several years, home has been Shane's 30-acre estate in Kenilworth, an affluent suburb north of the city. The estate offers everything I could ever want or need: a movie theater, an indoor Olympic-size swimming pool, a professional-grade workout room, staff to wait on me hand-and-foot. And that right there is why I had to go. Shane had made everything too comfy for me, a little too easy. A man has his pride, you know.

I need to do this.

I'm not surprised my family hates the idea of me moving out on my own. They want me to stay put at the Kenilworth house, safe in the lap of luxury, with Shane's housekeeper, Elly, anticipating my every need. Being waited on like an invalid was a hard pill for me to swallow. Overnight I went from a man serving his country as a US Navy SEAL to a man who'd lost both eyes. One close-range explosion had put an end to my military career, not to mention by ability to see. I didn't just lose my eyesight that day; I lost my independence, my sense of self. My self-confidence. In a bid to get it back, I decided a few months ago to move out, to find my own place and stand on my own two feet.

Today's that day. It's moving day.

I reach across the console and clasp Shane's shoulder. "Don't worry, I'll be fine." Then I steel myself to face the unknown. "Let's do this."

I push the passenger door open and swing my feet out to plant them on the sidewalk. This neighborhood is still new territory to me, filled with unfamiliar sounds and smells. All of my senses are on high alert, and it's a lot to take in all at once: a cold November wind; the hum of congested traffic on the main thoroughfare; the faint strains of live guitar music, probably coming from a tavern that's open for lunch; the pungent aroma of roasted coffee beans from the yuppie coffee bar down the street; the sweet tang of Chinese carryout. In the distance, car horns compete with the wailing sirens of an ambulance. And from the park across the street come the sounds of a barking dog and children squealing with delight on the playground.

Yeah, it's a lot to take in all at once, but I'll get used to it.

My new neighborhood.

My new home.

A moment later, I hear the sound of car doors opening and closing in proximity to us. Jake must have parked his SUV directly behind the Jaguar. Then I hear heavy boots hitting the pavement and Gus's eager bark. When Gus reaches my side, he brings with him a bitingly cold rush of air. He sticks his nose inside my leather jacket.

"Hey, buddy." I stroke his big head, scratching him behind a soft ear. "You ready to check out our new place?"

Skimming my hands down his back, I locate his harness and grab the handle. Shane's Jaguar is a tight fit for my over six-foot frame. I step out of the car and straighten, finally able to stretch my legs.

Shane comes around the front of the vehicle to join me on the sidewalk, just as our two younger brothers reach us.

"You guys go on up," Jake says. "Liam and I will bring in Jamie's stuff."

Truthfully, there isn't much to bring in – just some boxes and my laptop. The apartment's already furnished with items Beth helped me pick out – a sofa, recliner and coffee table; a dining table and chairs; kitchenware, linens, and towels; a bed and night-stands; a desk and sofa for the office; lamps.

No rugs, though. The apartment has hardwood floors, but I'll have to live without rugs. Those are a tripping hazard, as I've learned the hard way.

All of my worldly possessions are packed into five cardboard boxes and a laptop bag, which are all stowed in the back of Jake's SUV. I really didn't have much to bring with me. Life in the Navy kept me on the road for the most part, stationed overseas either in the Middle East, Africa, or Afghanistan. After I lost my sight, I donated all of my books to a literacy program in the city and switched over to audiobooks, which I carry on my phone. So, I really don't have much, or need much, beyond my phone, clothes, and computer. I earn a pretty decent living as an author, so the computer is a must.

Well, it's showtime.

"Gus, find the steps," I say pointing him in the general direction I want to go.

Gus's harness pulls taut as he guides me across the sidewalk to the smooth stone steps that lead up to the apartment's main entrance. *One, two, three, four, five* steps from the curb to the base of the stairs. I already have that distance memorized. Gus stops when we reach the steps.

"Gus, find the door."

One, two, three, four, five, six. Six well-worn stone steps lead up to the front door. I punch in the access code on the electronic keypad to the right of the door and a beep signals success.

I hold the door open for Gus and he precedes me into the building's small foyer. Shane comes in behind us, conspicuously quiet.

Is this a test? Mentally, I shake my head. If I'm not capable of letting myself into my own apartment building, what the fuck am I good for? Jesus, I used to jump out of airplanes at twenty-thousand feet, free fall until I was just a couple thousand feet above the ground before deploying my chute. If I can't handle steps and a security keypad on my own, I'm screwed.

Inside the building, it's cool and quiet, and smells of lemon-scented floor polish.

"The mailboxes are to your left," Shane says, sounding resigned. "Yours – apartment 2A – is the third box. The staircase is straight ahead. There are two apartments here on the ground floor, and two upstairs."

My apartment is upstairs, to the left. "Gus, go upstairs."

Just as we reach the top of the stairs, the door to the apartment on the right opens. I catch a faint whiff of vanilla and peppermint. The jingle of keys tells me someone is locking a door. Then light footsteps head in our direction, eventually coming to an abrupt halt.

"Oh, hi!" a woman says, sounding surprised. "You must be my new neighbor."

Guided by the sound of her voice, I turn to face her and give her what I hope is a friendly, reassuring smile. Beth tells me that my dark glasses, combined with my 'imposing' height and size – her words – make me look intimidating. I certainly don't want to make a bad first impression on my new neighbor. "Hi. Yes, I'm Jamie McIntyre."

I offer my hand, and she takes it after a brief hesitation. Her hand feels slight in mine, but her grip is dry and firm, confident. I like that in a woman.

I detect that same combination of vanilla and peppermint. *Hand lotion maybe? Shampoo?* They're definitely girly smells, and I mean that in a good way.

"I'm Molly," she says. "Welcome to the building."

"Thanks." I like her voice. She sounds straight-forward, and her voice is warm and smooth. I'd guess her to be around my age, mid-thirties. As she releases my hand, my fingers graze against hers momentarily, just long enough for me to notice faint callouses on her fingers. She must work with her hands. I wonder if she lives here alone, or if she has a family.

"Well, have a nice day." She skirts around us and heads down the stairs and out the front door.

"Blonde or brunette?" I say.

Shane laughs. "Brunette. Why?"

I shrug. "No reason. I just wondered." Suddenly, the idea of meeting new people holds a certain appeal. I've been so isolated for the past few years, I've rarely met anyone new. "Gus, go left. Find the door."

Twelve steps down the hall to my apartment door.

A moment later, I've got the door unlocked, and the three of us step inside. The apartment smells like lemon-scented cleaner and new furniture.

"Well, what do you think?" I say, knowing my brother had better say he liked the decorating since it was his fiancée who picked out the furnishings.

"Nice," Shane says, sounding sincere.

I elbow him. "Good answer, since it's all Beth's doing."

Shane chuckles. "I figured as much. Don't worry, she has really good taste."

"Who has good taste?" Liam says, as he breezes through the open door, a little out of breath. He sets a stack of heavy boxes on the floor.

"Beth does," I say.

"I don't know about that," Liam chides. "She agreed to marry this oaf, didn't she?"

"Hey, where do you want these?" Jake says, entering the apartment.

"All the boxes are marked," I say "Three go in the bedroom and the other two go in the office, along with my laptop bag. You can just set everything down here if you want. I'll put it away later."

Five boxes. That's it. That's all I have in the world.

"Nah," Jake says, heading for the hallway. "I'll put the boxes where they belong. You can sort it all out later."

Liam runs out and returns a few minutes later. "Here you go," he says, shoving a cardboard carton into my hands. "It's a house-warming gift."

"Thanks," I say, directing Gus to take me to the fridge so I can chill the case of beer. "Now I have all the comforts of home."

Jake returns to the living room. "You're all set," he says. "The boxes are where they belong, and I hung your cane here on a hook beside the door."

"All right, how about lunch, guys?" Shane says. "I've got a little time before I have to get back to the office for a meeting."

"Sounds good," Jake says. "I'm starving."

2

Molly

I'm in my art studio applying a final coat of protective sealant to a commissioned painting when my phone chimes, reminding me I have a lunch date today. Perfect timing! I skipped breakfast this morning, and my stomach's been growling for the past half-hour.

After cleaning my paint brushes, I grab my coat and head to the front of my shop to hang up the OUT TO LUNCH sign. It's been a slow morning, probably thanks to the frigid weather, so there haven't been many customers coming into my art gallery.

I lock the door behind me and head toward the neighborhood sandwich shop, which is only two blocks away. The sidewalk foot traffic might be lighter than usual today, but the street is bumper-to-bumper vehicles, as usual. Cars, taxis, Ubers, buses, delivery trucks… the street is a slushy, hot mess of folks in a hurry.

The restaurant isn't as crowded today as it normally is, perhaps thanks to the season's first snowfall last night. This late in November, the temperatures are really starting to drop at night, and the wind can be downright frigid.

Stepping inside the restaurant, thankfully out of the cold and the blowing wisps of snow, I scan the small dining area for my friend Chloe, but I don't see her yet.

"Just one today?" says the cheerful young woman standing behind the host's podium.

"Two," I tell her, holding up the same number of fingers. "Thanks."

Miss Cheerful hands two menus to another young woman who shows me to a table in the center of the room.

"Here you go," she says, laying one menu in front of me and the other at the seat across from mine. "Your server will be by soon to take your drink order."

While I'm waiting for Chloe, I scan my menu. It's completely unnecessary, as I practically have the menu memorized, but it gives me something to do and helps take my mind off the significance of today.

It's not long before the bell hanging over the door jingles, and I glance up just as Chloe walks in. She flashes me a brilliant smile as she waves off the hostess and makes her way to our table.

"God, I hate snow," she says, whipping off her oversized parka and hanging it on the back of her chair. She unwraps the black knitted scarf from around her neck and tucks it into the hood of her coat. "Please tell me it'll be spring soon," she says, settling into her chair.

She pulls back her long, wavy hair, which is the color of the finest dark chocolate, exposing an impressive collection of ear piercings. Every time I see her, she has a new piercing. Some of them I can see, but some of them aren't visible to the general public. I never knew the human body could be pierced in so many places.

I laugh. "It's not even officially winter yet. I'm afraid it'll be awhile until spring gets here."

"Ugh!" She shudders as she picks up her menu. "I hate this cold. I'm moving back home to Miami."

"No, you're not. I need you here. Thanks for braving the snow flurries and coming out to meet me. I feel honored."

Chloe rolls her exotically dark eyes at me as she gives me her best *duh* face. "Molly, please, I know what today is. Of course, I'm here. Where else would I be?"

When I texted Chloe last night, asking her to meet me today for lunch, she didn't hesitate to say yes. Yeah, she knows what today is.

A young woman buzzes by our table just long enough to leave two glasses of ice water and two straws. "I'll be right back to get your orders," she says, hurrying off.

Chloe raises her glass in a toast. "Happy anniversary! How does it feel to be divorced for a whole year?"

I touch my glass to hers. "It feels pretty good actually."

Has it really been a year? It sure doesn't feel like it. Exactly one year ago, my divorce from my husband of ten years became final. It's been a rough year, to say the least. Learning to be on my own for the first time in my life, running my own business, learning how to deal with Todd post-divorce... yeah, it's been rough. Rougher than I ever imagined it would be. Not the living on my own part – that part I actually enjoy. It's the dealing with my ex that's the problem. My ex, who seems to have lost his mind.

Our server returns to take our orders. "Sorry, we're short-handed today. What can I get you?"

"I'll have the Power Greens Salad with Strawberries and Walnuts," Chloe says. "Baked sweet potato fries, coffee, because it's cold as hell outside, and a brownie. But wrap up the brownie to go, please."

"That sounds good," I say. "I'll have the same salad and the fries, but Mango Green Tea to drink. And skip the brownie."

Chloe scowls at me as our server walks away. "Party pooper." She shakes her head. "I'm not going to feel bad about eating a brownie, so don't even try to guilt me."

I laugh. "I'm not. You go right ahead and enjoy your brownie."

Chloe can eat like a horse and still retain her willowy figure. Me, on the other hand... if I even look at sweets, five pounds magically appear on my hips. Life is so unfair.

"Oooh, look at these!" she says, pulling back the sleeve of her bulky, knitted sweater. A trail of dainty little paw prints meanders the length of her forearm, from inside her elbow to her wrist, then turns to travel up the back of her hand. The skin surrounding the tattoos is still pink, so I know the tats must be new.

"Cute. What kind of prints are those?"

She wrinkles her nose. "Wolf. I'm going with wolf. Do you like them?"

I smile. "Yes. Very nice."

I happen to know she's got tattoos on various places on her body. She has a sunflower tramp stamp, a tiny heart tattoo behind her left ear, and a little tattoo of a butterfly just above her mons – which you can only see if she waxes. *Yes, I've seen it*. Chloe's not shy. Right above the butterfly tattoo is a naval piercing featuring a pink butterfly charm.

I met Chloe right after I moved to Wicker Park a year ago. In fact, we met right here in this café. We were both waiting for a table one afternoon and got to chatting, and we ended up eating together. We've been friends ever since. I honestly don't know where I'd be without Chloe's unwavering support. These days, it feels like she's my *only* friend.

I lost half of my friends after the divorce. To be honest, they were Todd's friends first, and when we split up, they went with him. I guess that's only natural. Todd's pretty charismatic on the surface, at least he used to be. His friends probably thought I was crazy for divorcing him. Too bad they don't know him like I do. In the past couple years, he's changed. He's no longer the considerate, carefree guy I first met. Now he's angry and aggressive all the time, borderline paranoid, and very narcissistic.

I did have a few college friends of my own before coming into the marriage, but I've intentionally distanced myself from them, for their own good. Being around me, and subsequently finding yourself on Todd's radar screen, is a risky prospect these days. He's irrationally jealous of everyone I spend time with – even Chloe.

Chloe Montoya is the only one who knows what's really going on – well, Chloe, my attorney, and the judge who issued a restraining order against Todd six months ago. The only reason Chloe's still hanging around is because she's fearless and has absolutely no sense of self-preservation. She refuses to abandon me, even for her own sake.

No one else knows what Todd's been doing lately. I certainly can't burden my parents with this. It would only distress them, and their health can't take it. Telling them I'd filed for divorce was hard enough on them. They don't need to know their ex-son-in-law, whom they'd adored, has turned into a violent stalker.

After our server brings our beverages, Chloe tears open two packets of organic cane sugar and slowly pours the fine crystals into her coffee and stirs. "Has the douchebag reared his ugly head today?"

"No." Thank God for small favors. And then, out of sheer habit, I surreptitiously scan the café just to be sure.

"Maybe he forgot what today is." Chloe opens a little package of creamer and pours it into her coffee, stirs, then blows on the steaming mug.

I shake my head. "Todd doesn't forget anything." *Except for the wedding vows he made to me ten years ago, and then proceeded to break.* He didn't just break our wedding vows; he pulverized them in glorious, full-frontal nudity with his pretty college intern on our living room sofa. If I hadn't come home unexpectedly for lunch that day and interrupted their nooner mid-progress, I might never have known my husband was having an affair.

Chloe shakes her head in disgust. "Men are such pigs." She takes a tentative sip of her coffee, frowns, then adds one more packet of sugar and stirs briskly. "I think lesbians have it right. Women are so much easier to deal with."

I laugh. "I don't know. I've known some pretty difficult women in my life."

Our server arrives with our orders, and the two of us eat in companionable silence as Chloe responds to a minor emergency text message from the tattoo parlor.

Despite how hungry I was earlier, I find myself picking at my food. It's not the food that's the problem, though. It's me. My mood isn't the best. My marriage may be over, but the nightmare continues.

When Todd was carrying on with his assistant, Mindy, he really didn't pay much attention to what I was doing. I filed for a dissolution and got through the process relatively unchallenged because Todd was focused on screwing his new girlfriend. But once their liaison soured and she broke up with him, he suddenly refocused his attention on me. Lucky me.

Right after the divorce was finalized, Todd started showing up everywhere I was, at my new apartment, at my art studio, at restaurants and bars where I happened to be hanging out with the few friends I had left. He told me repeatedly that the divorce had been a mistake and that he wanted me back.

"I fucked up, Molly," he'd said. "In a moment of weakness, I made the worst mistake of my life."

Later, I found out that his "moment of weakness" had been going on right under my nose for six months. His infidelity wasn't a mistake; it was a lifestyle.

Of course, he didn't see it that way. When I refused to even discuss reconciliation, he'd grown angry and defensive. "You have no one to blame but yourself, Molly. All of this is your fault!"

It's so ironic. Todd's the one who had the affair, and yet he blamed *me* for our marriage falling apart. Maybe he's right, I don't know.

He put the blame for his affair squarely on me. Yet another irony because in the beginning he supported my decision to have the surgery. If he'd balked at my choice of treatment in the beginning, I might have considered other options, but he hadn't. He told me he was behind me all the way. It wasn't until later – when reality hit him – when the consequences of my choice were staring him in the face that he changed his tune.

When he eventually realized I had no intention of coming back to him, he became increasingly erratic and aggressive. Before long,

I found myself filing a restraining order in an effort to keep him away.

Every time the café door opens, I automatically glance over to see who's coming in. It's become a habit now, second nature. I feel like I'm always watching my back and peering into dark corners, just waiting for the boogie man to jump out at me. This time, when the little bell over the door jingles, I look up to see a familiar face walk into the restaurant... my new neighbor. This is the first time I've seen him since he moved in. He's got a gorgeous young blonde on his arm and a dog with him, a Yellow Lab.

I nudge Chloe's foot with mine. "Don't look now, but the guy who just walked in – the one with the cute blonde – that's my new neighbor."

It's the first time since my divorce that I've given a guy a second look. And this one – he inspires all kinds of feels and reminds me what I'm missing out on. He's beautiful – tall, with broad shoulders and a lean waist; beautiful, thick chestnut-colored hair and a trim beard and mustache. His dark aviator sunglasses – the kind worn by movie stars and FBI agents – make him look sexy and mysterious.

He plays the role of the gallant gentleman as he helps his blonde lunch companion take off her coat and drapes it over the back of her chair. Then he pulls her chair out for her to sit. His lunch date, who is considerably younger than he is, reminds me of an elfin princess with her long, pale blonde hair and lovely, oval face. Wearing a pale blue dress with a white lacey sweater, she's elegant and graceful... everything I'm not. I'm about the same height as she – five-eight – but I'm more of the solid and sturdy type, with good child-bearing hips, as my ex-mother-in-law liked to say.

When the blonde happens to look in my direction, I glance

down at my fingernails and busy myself chipping off a bit of blue acrylic paint. I'll bet she doesn't have splatters of paint on her hands and clothes.

I hate her already.

I'd told Chloe all about my new neighbor. That day had brought a pure overload of attractive men into my building. Between my new neighbor and his buddy, I didn't think our little apartment building could handle so much testosterone. Poor old Mrs. Powell on the first floor might have had a heart attack if she'd seen the two of them coming into the building.

After waiting a respectable five seconds, Chloe casually turns her head toward the front of the restaurant to sneak a peek. Her eyes widen. "Damn. He's fine." She sticks a sweet potato fry in her mouth and chews. "That girl he's with, though... she looks barely legal, and he's got to be at least thirty, maybe thirty-five."

I shrug. "Hey, when you look as good as he does, you can have your pick of beautiful women."

Chloe rolls her eyes, looking disgusted, which is kind of funny considering Chloe is drop-dead gorgeous in her own right. With her perfect café-au-lait complexion, sinfully pouty lips, and gorgeous waterfall of dark, lustrous hair, she turns heads wherever she goes.

I give the couple seated by the window one last glance. When the blonde laughs at something he said, my chest constricts painfully. Yeah, I'm starting to realize what I'm missing in my life.

3

Molly

After we finish our meals, Chloe and I part ways outside the café. She heads back to the tattoo parlor and I head to my favorite little neighborhood grocery store to pick up a few things. I could take the bus or a cab two miles to a big-box grocery store that takes up half a city block, but I prefer the little mom-and-pop shop in my neighborhood. They have a surprisingly large selection of fresh, organic produce, which now makes up the bulk of my diet these days. A cancer diagnosis will do that to you.

The kid who works in the produce department hands me a pint-sized carton of fresh blueberries imported from warmer climates. "I saved these for you, Molly," he says. "We just got a shipment in this morning, and they're going like crazy."

I tuck the blueberries into my shopping basket. "Thanks, Stephan."

I fill up two bags with enough fresh food to last me the rest of the week, then head to my apartment. The nice thing about living and working in a small city neighborhood is how conveniently located everything is. I can go to the grocery store, run home to put everything away, and be back at my art studio in less than an hour.

As I'm approaching my building, I catch sight of my new neighbor and his lunch date standing at the curb, talking. As a sleek, vintage silver Jaguar pulls up to the curb, the blonde gives Jamie an enthusiastic hug and kisses his cheek.

The Jag's driver door opens and out steps a guy in a sharp, dark gray suit, white shirt, and dark glasses. He whips off his sunglasses and smiles at the couple on the sidewalk, saying something I can't quite hear. If I'm not mistaken, this is the same guy who was with Jamie the day he moved into my building.

The blonde lit up the moment the Jaguar arrived, and when the driver reaches her side, he pulls her into his arms and kisses the daylights out of her. Good grief, what is it with this girl? She's a guy magnet.

The guy in the suit opens the vehicle's front passenger door and helps the blonde into the car. After helping her buckle her seat belt, he closes her door and turns back to say something to Jamie. The two men shake hands, and it occurs to me that they might be related. There's a strong physical resemblance between them, and they have that comfortable way with each other that screams familiarity.

As the Jaguar pulls away from the curb, I hasten up the stone steps to the door to my apartment building and punch in the entry code. Some lights flash and there's a beep, and then the door unlocks. It's all very high-tech.

Just a couple of weeks ago, the landlord sold the building unexpectedly, and shortly thereafter a fancy new security and surveillance system was installed in the building. It seemed overkill to me at first – after all, it's just an old apartment building. It's not like this is the Metropolitan Art Museum. But hey, I'm not complaining about the enhanced security. Given the issues with my stalker-ex, it was a bit of good luck for me. I've been sleeping a little easier since the upgraded security system was installed.

Just as I'm walking up the stairs, the door opens behind me and in walks my new neighbor with his dog.

He follows me up the stairs. "Hi. Molly, right?" he says.

His voice is deep and resonant, and it makes my nerve endings tingle. It fits his appearance – male, rugged, too handsome for his own good. He's still wearing those dark glasses, though, and I can't see the color of his eyes, darn it.

"Hi," I stammer, wondering if he saw me gawking at him outside the building just now.

I'm about halfway up the stairs when the heel of my boot catches on one of the risers, and I lurch forward. As I reach out to brace myself, my big slouchy purse slides off my shoulder and down my arm, crashing into the groceries I'm carrying. I'm about to lose everything. "Crap!"

A long, muscular arm snakes around my waist, catching me midfall, and hauls me back against a hard male body. I can feel the warmth of his body even through the fabric of my jacket, and he smells divine.

He steadies me. "Are you okay?"

My heart's pounding, and I'm short of breath. "Yes. Thank you."

He deftly relieves me of my groceries. "Here, I'll take these."

It takes me a moment to catch my breath. After regaining my balance and my composure, I turn to face him. We're practically eye-to-eye, even though he's standing one step below me. With his dark glasses, I can't even see his eyes, though. Very bad ass of him.

"I'm fine, thanks," I say. "My boot caught on the step." I reach for my groceries. "I can carry those."

"It's okay. I'll carry them up for you."

I'm at a loss for words. Not only is this guy absolutely gorgeous, but he's also really nice. "Thank you."

He smiles, displaying perfect white teeth and the hint of dimples beneath his trim beard. "No problem."

I turn to face forward and make my way to the top of the stairs, trying to ignore the pounding of my heart. Once I reach the landing, I turn right and head down the short hallway to my apartment. There are just two apartments up here – his and mine. We're next door neighbors. Our apartments share a common wall.

As far as neighbors go, he's been pretty quiet so far. No loud noises; no wild parties. Since he moved in, I've rarely heard a peep from him. Occasionally I can hear his TV, but it's so quiet I can't make out what he's watching. It's mostly white noise, which I don't mind. As far as I can tell, he lives alone, which I find astonishing. Surely this guy has a girlfriend.

When I reach my apartment, my gaze zeroes in on the bright yellow sticky note affixed to my door. I grab the note, immediately recognizing Todd's scratchy handwriting before I wad it up and shove it into the front pocket of my jeans.

How in the hell did he get in the building this time? I had hoped the new security system would keep him out, but no such luck. It looks like I'll need to have another talk with Mrs. Powell about letting unauthorized people into the building. The poor woman can't say no to anyone. She also can't remember the rules.

I fish my keys out of my bag and unlock my door, wondering what I'll find on the other side. As I push it open, I half expect to see Todd standing there waiting for me, but the living room is empty except for Charlie, who rushes to greet me, entwining his furry orange body around my ankles and purring loudly in greeting.

"Hey, you've got a cat," Jamie says.

Charlie cautiously sniffs Jamie, and then, apparently approving, he starts rubbing against Jamie's leg too.

"That's Charlie," I say, relieving Jamie of my groceries. "I hope you're not allergic."

"I'm not. I grew up in a house full of pets."

Jamie scoops Charlie into his arms and scratches his ears. "Hey, little guy."

Charlie rolls over onto his back and lets Jamie scratch his belly.

"Wow. It looks like you have a fan," I say, as I head to the kitchen to set down my groceries. Feeling paranoid, I open the door to the laundry-room-slash-pantry to make sure I don't have any surprise visitors lurking behind the door.

When I turn, Jamie's standing just inside my apartment door, smiling as Charlie rubs his head against Jamie's jaw, practically assaulting him with affection. I can hear the purrs from halfway across the apartment.

"Sorry." I walk over and extract Charlie from his new perch and set him on the floor. As much as I'm enjoying having Jamie in my apartment, I really need for him to leave so I can do a thorough search of the place. It wouldn't be the first time Todd picked the lock and let himself into my apartment. "Thanks for the help."

"Anytime." Jamie steps back through my open doorway, out

into the hallway, then pauses. "Is everything okay?"

For a moment, I'm stunned speechless. How can he tell I'm on edge? Is it that obvious? "I'm fine. Why do you ask?"

"You seemed a little upset a few moments ago, when you reached your door."

"Everything's fine. But thank you for asking."

"Sure." He nods toward his apartment door. "I'm right down the hall if you need something. Just holler, okay?"

"Okay. I will."

4

Molly

Once Jamie is gone, I lock the door, including the dead bolt and the chain, and begin a systematic search of my apartment. I hate to think I'm becoming paranoid, but he's gotten in before. Once, I came home from a late night in the studio to find Charlie locked in the bathroom and Todd naked in my bed, waiting for me. I honestly don't think he's here this time, though. If he was, Charlie wouldn't be following me around the apartment so calmly. He'd be hiding. He and Todd hate each other.

The first time Todd came to my apartment – before I obtained a restraining order – Charlie made it abundantly clear that he didn't like my ex-husband. Charlie arched his back, his hair rising on end, and hissed at Todd like a tiny, four-legged avenger. Charlie's my little protector. I'm surprised he took so readily to Jamie. Charlie's usually a bit cautious when it comes to meeting new people, but he took to Jamie like the man was a giant kitty treat on two legs. Animals are supposedly good judges of character. I sure hope that's true.

I have a system for searching my apartment. First, I check the small coat closet in the living room. Then I make a quick search of both bedrooms, including the closets and under the beds, then the bathroom, sweeping aside the shower curtain to peer behind it. I shudder at the thought of someone hiding in my shower – that's just way too *Psycho* for me.

Once I'm assured that I have no unwanted visitors, I return to the kitchen to put away my groceries. Charlie hops up onto the kitchen counter and bawls at me in the hope I'll give him a kitty treat. He's such a pig.

"All right, just one," I tell him, reaching into the cupboard for the packet of soft cat treats. "But get off the counter first." I hold the treat near the floor and he jumps down to claim his prize. Then I pat him on the head and scratch behind his ears. "Be a good boy while I go back to work. I'll see you at dinner time."

On my way out, I stop to pay a visit to my elderly downstairs neighbor. I knock, and she opens her door dressed in a floral housecoat and pink slippers.

"Hi, Mrs. Powell."

She smiles at me. "Oh! Hello, dear. How are you?"

"I'm fine, thank you."

Mrs. Powell qualifies as a sweet little old lady. The problem is, she's too sweet, and far too trusting. She'd give a stranger the shirt off her back, or the last dime in her pocket, and she'll let anyone into the building who asks nicely.

"Mrs. Powell, did you let someone into the building this morning? Someone who doesn't live here?"

She purses her soft, wrinkled lips for a moment, looking a bit confused. Then she smiles. "Oh, yes, that nice young man of yours. Your husband. I let him in. He buzzed my apartment, said he forgot his key."

Inwardly, I roll my eyes. But I really can't blame Mrs. Powell. Todd is a master manipulator. "He's my *ex*-husband, Mrs. Powell, not my husband. And he's not supposed to be in this building. I have a restraining order against him. He's not allowed to be here, okay? If he asks again, please don't let him in. All right?"

She smiles at me, a multitude of tiny crow's feet crinkling the corners of her eyes. "Why would you want to divorce him, honey? He's quite the looker." She chuckles. "If you don't want him, I'll take him."

Trust me, you don't want him. "Please, Mrs. Powell, promise me you won't let him in the building anymore."

"All right," she agrees. "But it's a shame, if you ask me. A nice young lady like yourself needs a husband."

* * *

I pass the tattoo parlor where Chloe works and wave at her through the storefront windows filled with drawings of some of the tattoos they offer. She waves back as she rings up a customer.

It's just another block to my studio. As I pass an alleyway between two blocks, I glance down the long, narrow corridor out of habit. Todd's definitely making me paranoid. I was never like this before. I never felt the need to peer into dark corners or watch my back.

When I reach my studio, I unlock the door and step inside, flipping the "Out to lunch" sign over so it says "Open!"

The front half of the shop smells faintly like acrylic paint, varnish, and lilacs, thanks to the numerous glass vases of freshly cut lilacs decorating the front room. Lilacs are my favorite flower, and I love how the pale purple flowers look against the stark white walls of my gallery.

The front room is my showroom, where I display completed paintings for sale, postcards, maps, and posters. The wood floors are original to the building and burnished a deep, warm whiskey color from years of use. The wall to the right is exposed red brick, and the two other walls are painted white. The front is all glass, which lets in lots of natural light. The high ceilings make the space feel larger than it really is, and the pipes and ductwork that run along the ceiling are painted a matte black, giving the place an urban, industrial feel.

Paintings of all sizes, from tiny postcard size up to large wall paintings, are displayed throughout the gallery, hanging on the walls, and propped up on shelves and display counters and little tables. I paint abstract landscapes, so there are lots of blues and teals suggesting bodies of water, the greens of foliage and grasses, and lots of browns and ochre and creams depicting rock formations and sandy beaches. My inspiration comes from Lake Michigan, and nearly all of my paintings depict some aspect of the lake. During the warm months, I spend hours combing the shoreline, collecting bits of sea glass and staring out across the vast expanse of water.

I head through a curtained doorway to the rear half of the shop, which is where I paint. While the front half is kept neat and tidy for the benefit of customers, the back half is my private workspace, and it's anything but neat. Table after table is filled with various canvases propped up on easels, big and small, all in various stages of production, from initial pencil sketches to partially-painted canvases to varnished paintings that are ready to go. There are glass jars filled with brushes of all sorts and sizes, jars of water for cleaning, and lots of wooden palettes for mixing paints. Large wooden tripods lining the walls hold the larger canvases.

I have a mini fridge back here, a microwave, a well-worn brown sofa that doubles as a comfy bed on the nights I stay too late to walk home, and a tiny, bare-bones bathroom with a shower. All the comforts of home.

I check on the commissioned painting that's going home soon to its new owner's dentistry office. He's scheduled to stop by any minute for a final inspection and to pay the balance of his bill. I grab a cold drink from the fridge and sit down to wait.

At just a few minutes before two, the jingle of the little bell hanging over the front door announces the arrival of a visitor. I head to the front of the studio to greet my client.

As I pass through the curtained doorway, I halt mid-step to stare at the man standing just inside the shop. "You're not supposed to be in here," I say, swallowing hard. My heart starts pounding, but I take a deep breath and force myself to remain calm.

"It's a free country, Molly," Todd says, a snide smile on his face as he ambles into the gallery.

"Not for you, it isn't. In case you've forgotten, I have this little thing called a restraining order. If I call the police, you'll be arrested." I sigh, tired of this game of cat-and-mouse he insists on playing. "Just go, Todd, please. I'm expecting a client any minute. I don't have time for this."

He saunters toward me. Dressed in a tailor-made, navy suit,

white shirt, and cobalt blue tie, with his blond hair brushed back, he looks perfectly respectable, but I know firsthand that looks can be deceiving. He didn't look quite so respectable when he was shoving his cock into his assistant's vagina on my living room sofa. I still can't get the image of his pale white butt bobbing up and down out of my head.

I'd put up with a lot from Todd over the last couple of years we were married, but I drew the line at infidelity.

"Molly," he says, his voice low and deceptively smooth. He's using his courtroom voice on me, as if I'm a member of a jury he's trying to convince of something. He reaches out to tuck my wayward brown hair behind my ear. It used to be an affectionate gesture on his part, but now it just feels threatening.

I flinch and step out of his reach. "Todd, just go. Please."

He gives me his winning courtroom smile. "Molly, baby, please don't be like that. I just want to see you."

I hate when he calls me *baby.* It's so passive-aggressive coming from *him*. I shake my head. "Well, I don't want to see you, so go." I have to bite my tongue to keep from adding "please." I'm tired of playing nice with him.

His smile fades. "Look, you know Mindy and I are through. She's out of the picture, gone for good. I admit I made a mistake. Now I just want you to come home. Let's put all the unpleasantness behind us and pick up where we left off."

I shake my head in disbelief. "Where we left off was with you having sex with someone else in our home. No, I don't want to pick up where we left off. We're divorced, and I have no intention of coming back. I have a new life now, and I'm happy. So just go, please."

His expression darkens and a muscle in his jaw starts twitching.

I can see his Mr. Nice Guy persona slipping. "You can't blame me for what happened, Molly. Any man would have done the same in my situation."

"That's bullshit! Not all men respond to a wife's illness and loss by screwing their co-workers. You told me you were okay with my treatment decision. I might have reconsidered if you'd been against it, but you said you supported me. It wasn't until after the fact that you decided you couldn't live with the consequences."

Todd's gaze drops to my chest, and he scowls. I have to fight not to cross my arms defensively over my chest. From the outside, my body appears the way it always has. But he and I both know my outward appearance is just an illusion. I'm wearing a bra fitted with two prosthetic breast forms. My real chest is flat, with scars that are still healing.

I hate him for making me feel self-conscious, for acting like I'm defective now, less of a woman. I hate him for it, and I hate myself even more for letting him get to me. I have to force myself to keep my arms firmly at my sides, refusing to give in to my insecurities, and I lift my chin. I'm not ashamed of my choices or the way my body looks beneath my clothes. *This is me now! And I'm okay with that.*

He looks away. "I thought you would have reconstruction." He makes a vague motion toward my chest. "You know. I just assumed – plastic surgeons can do amazing things with reconstruction, Molly. They look just like the real thing."

I shake my head. "I never said I was having breast reconstruction surgery. I prefer to go *au naturale*. I told you that. This is my body now. Like it or not, this is *me*."

He shrugs off my statement. "I thought surely you'd reconsider once you saw what you looked like."

My face burns with humiliation. "What do I look like, Todd?" I say, anger getting the best of me. I can feel my blood pressure skyrocketing. "You tell me, what do I look like?"

Without warning, Todd grabs my arms and hauls me against his chest. I'm disgusted by the feel of his erection digging into my belly.

"Enough of this, Molly," he growls, gritting his teeth. "Stop being ridiculous! You're coming back home with me, and that's that. You'll have the surgery, and everything will be fine again."

He leans forward to kiss me, and I struggle to put some space between us.

"Let me go," I hiss, turning my face away from his. I'll die before I let this man kiss me again.

The door opens, and in walks my client. I close my eyes in relief as Todd lets go of me and steps back.

"Is this a bad time?" Dr. Hewett says, eyeing Todd and me warily.

I smile at the man. "No, it's a perfect time. Come, let me show you your painting."

Ignoring Todd completely, I walk my client to the back room to show him the painting. He's seen sketches and photos of various stages of the painting in progress, but this is the first time he's seen the final result in person. I lift the sheet off the four-foot high canvas, trying to hide the fact that my hands are shaking. I can only hope that Todd has left.

"Oh, wow," the young man breathes as his gaze eats up the painting depicting his favorite Lake Michigan landmark – a spot where the lake washes up against a high cliff wall formed from layers of sedimentary rocks built up over millennia. "This is so much better than I dreamed it would be. Thank you, Molly."

Absently, he hands me an envelope containing a check for the balance due.

"You're very welcome," I say. "I'll have it delivered and hung in your office by the end of the week."

He nods, his head bobbing up and down eagerly. "Thank you." Staring contemplatively at the painting, he presses his hands together as if in prayer. "I was thinking if the painting turned out well, I'd have you do two smaller companion pieces to hang with it." He looks at me. "That would look nice, wouldn't it? Can you do that?"

I nod. "Sure. I'd be happy to. It might be a few weeks before I can start on them, though. I'm rather booked up at the moment."

"That's all right," he says, staring at the painting. "I'll wait."

After my customer takes his leave, I use my phone to deposit his check into my bank account. Gazing at the updated account balance, I smile. I'm not only making enough to pay the bills, but I have a nice safety net accumulating in my bank account. Finally, after a year on my own, I can breathe a little easier.

5

Molly

The rest of my afternoon passes quietly, with no sign of Todd. I finish up a few smaller pieces earmarked to go into the gallery – the smaller paintings are popular with tourists who want to take home a visual reminder of the lake. The UPS truck drops off a shipment of postcard-sized prints of my paintings, also good sellers for price-conscious customers looking for unique and meaningful souvenirs of their time in Chicago.

At six o'clock, I lock up the shop and head for home. When I reach my building, I come across my new neighbor out front with his dog, a large Yellow Labrador Retriever wearing what I now realize is a service-dog harness. The dog is clearly little more than a big puppy.

At the sight of Jamie, my heart starts racing and I feel the fluttering of tiny butterflies in my belly. No man has the right to look that good.

I debate whether to stop to speak to him or just head inside the building. I hardly know the man, and yet he is my neighbor. There'd be nothing wrong with me stopping a moment to chat with him. Just being a friendly neighbor, right?

I take a deep breath and remind myself I'm a grown-up now, not a high school wallflower. "Hi, Jamie."

"Molly, hi." Jamie tugs gently on the dog's harness, and the dog sits, gazing up at me hopefully with his big soulful eyes. "This is Gus."

"Can I pet him?"

"Sure. Technically, you're not supposed to pet a service dog, but Gus isn't officially in service. He flunked out of his training program because he's afraid of water. But I'd already fallen in love with him, so I arranged to adopt him as a pet. I've been working on furthering his training myself."

"A Lab afraid of water?" I say. "I thought they love water."

Jamie nods. "Yeah. It's hard to believe, I know."

I offer Gus the back of my hand to sniff, and he licks it, then nudges my hand with his nose. Taking that as a good sign, I scratch beneath his chin, then reach up to gently stroke a velvety soft ear. He groans in delight and rolls his head, leaning into my touch. For a crazy second, I imagine his owner doing the same thing. "He's very laid back."

Jamie laughs. "He is, as long as it's not raining. Then I have to fend for myself."

"We can't all be perfect," I say, thinking of my interaction with Todd earlier that afternoon and his blatant disapproval of my body. And if Jamie needs a service dog, then he's got issues of his own too.

"No, we can't," Jamie says. "I guess that's why I had such a soft spot for him. I could relate. I've got my own imperfections."

Jamie McIntyre is a temptingly handsome man, physically certainly, but I'm starting to realize that his personality is just as attractive as the outward package. I already know he's kind and empathetic. And despite being so darn attractive, he doesn't seem to have a big ego – and that makes me like him even more.

I think back to how naïve and inexperienced I was when I started dating Todd in college. He was my first, and only, serious boyfriend, and he swept me off my feet easily. That sun-kissed blond hair and those baby blue eyes dazzled my naïve, twenty-year-old self. Before I'd even graduated with an art degree from University of Chicago, I'd found myself married.

Todd was a little self-absorbed even in the beginning, but he was a nice guy, and he'd treated me well. It wasn't until the past couple of years that I began to see troubling aspects in his personality.

"Well, I'm heading inside," I say, taking my leave.

I head inside the building, stopping in the foyer to grab my mail. As I'm pulling the collection of junk mail flyers and the few bills out of my box, I see that one of them is addressed to *Mr. James McIntyre*, Apt. 2A. As I'm Molly Ferguson in 2B, it's clearly not intended for me.

The door opens and in walks James McIntyre. He heads straight toward me. As it appears he's headed my way – or, rather toward the mailboxes – I take a quiet step back to get out of his way.

He pauses and cocks his head just the slightest bit. "Molly?"

His voice is deep and resonant, and it makes my nerve endings tingle. It fits his appearance – male, rugged, too handsome for his own good. He's wearing those dark glasses, though, and I still can't see the color of his eyes.

"Yes," I stammer, embarrassed at being caught gawking at him. I close the door to my mail cubby and turn the little brass key to lock it. "Sorry, I'll get out of your way."

"Take your time. Has the mail come?"

I wave my little stack of white envelopes in the air. "Yes." And then I remember he's new to the building and probably doesn't know the routine. "Our mail carrier's always here by noon – you could set your clock by her."

I take another step back as he heads in my direction, fishing a key out of the front pocket of his jeans. Then he lays his hand on the wall, sliding it over to feel his way to his assigned mailbox. I wonder if he has impaired vision – is that why he has a service dog? His fingers glide over to locate the lock, and he inserts his key. Damn it, even his hands are sexy, with those long fingers with trim, blunt nails. He's got quite a lot of mail jammed into that little box – mostly real mail, not the junk fliers I usually receive.

I glance down at my own mail and see his envelope on the top, and it reminds me. "This was put in my mailbox by mistake." I hold the envelope in question out to him, but he doesn't take it. The moment drags out into two, and I feel awkward.

"Here, this is yours," I say, slipping the envelope into his hand.

His broad shoulders lift as he sighs. "I'm sorry," he says. "I didn't realize you were handing me something. I'm blind."

Blind? As in completely blind? "I'm so sorry. I didn't realize."

The corner of his mouth lifts with a small smile. "There's no need to apologize."

I find myself staring at him, barely following what he's saying. He's – well, he's really nice to look at. Up close, I can see how broad his chest is, and inside his open black leather jacket, I can just make out a lean waist. He has a straight blade of a nose and wide, beautifully-shaped lips. His cheeks and jaw are covered with a neatly trimmed beard.

"Well, I'm right next door," I say. "If you ever need anything, just let me know."

"I will. Thanks, Molly." Jamie reaches down to pat Gus on the head. "Gus and I are headed down the street to pick up some Chinese carryout. Would you like to join us?"

His invitation takes me by surprise. He hardly knows me. Why would he ask me to join him? "Um, sure. I'd love to." I'd planned to heat up some leftovers for dinner, nothing special. But the truth is, I'd jump at the chance to spend time with him. I can have a self-indulgent, secret crush on the guy, and he'll never know. I can simply sit back and enjoy his company.

He steps forward and holds out his arm to me. "Do you mind?"

It takes me a moment to catch on. Oh! I guess it's my turn to act as his eyes. He's asking me to guide him. I smile, relieved he can't see my pleased reaction, and secretly thrilled at the opportunity to touch him. I link my arm with his. "I don't mind."

The three of us stroll down the sidewalk, with me on one side of Jamie and Gus on the other. The warm weight of his arm linked with mine is both comforting and scintillating. Even through the sleeves of our coats, I can feel how firm his muscles are.

Acting as his tour guide, I tell him a little bit about the neighborhood – at least the little bit I know as I've only lived here a year myself. I'm still learning about the place. I give him a description of each shop we pass and make recommendations for the best places to frequent. The pedestrian traffic flows easily around us, as most folks give us a wide berth. A couple of times I have to caution him about obstacles in our path, such as an oversized trash container in one spot and a sidewalk sign advertising ice cream in another.

It dawns on me that it would be hard for him to find a specific business without assistance if he wasn't already familiar with the landmarks. He can't just tell Gus, "Take me to Dragon City," can he? Can a service dog learn the names of places? I wonder if the reason Jamie asked me to join him was simply so he could borrow my eyes.

"How do you find new places?" I ask him, my curiosity winning out. "How would you find the take-out place if I weren't with you?"

His hands are full – holding Gus's harness with one hand and my arm with the other, so he simply tips his chin toward his jacket pocket. "GPS. I don't know how I'd survive without my phone."

"Oh, right." GPS, of course.

He tightens his hold on my arm. "But having you along for company is far more enjoyable than using GPS."

I feel my cheeks heat up, and I'm pretty sure I'm blushing. If I didn't know better, I'd think he was flirting with me. But that's impossible. He hardly knows me, and he can't even see me. He has absolutely no idea what I look like. I could have four eyes and two horns for all he knows.

"Here we are," I tell him, stopping outside our destination. There's a steady stream of people in and out of the small carryout, and the aromas wafting out the open door are mouth-watering. Suddenly I'm starving.

Jamie releases my arm and holds the door for me. "After you," he says.

I step inside the carryout, sure my face is still flushed. If anyone asks, I'll blame it on the cold. Jamie and Gus follow me inside, and we place an order for two entrees, steamed rice, and a half dozen egg rolls.

When the cashier rings up our total, Jamie reaches into his back pocket and pulls out his wallet. Before I can say a word, he withdraws a credit card and hands it to the cashier, who swipes it in the machine.

"Wait! I'll pay for my own."

"It's all right," he says, putting his wallet away. "I've got it."

"I should pay for my half of the meal," I say, once we've stepped out of the way and are waiting on our order.

"Let me buy your meal. It's the least I can do as a thank-you for accompanying me."

For a moment, I'm at a loss for words. I'm not accustomed to men paying for me. Todd and I split every single expense right down the middle, including restaurant meals and date nights. Frankly, I'm a little out of my element here. Does it mean something that he's paying for my meal? Does that make this a date?

When the cashier calls out our ticket number, Jamie and Gus step forward to collect our food. It's my turn to hold the door, as Jamie has his hands full. Once we're back out on the sidewalk, I'm not sure if he needs my arm or not to guide him back. Gus seems to be doing a pretty competent job of it. I don't think Jamie needs my help. My question is answered, though, when Jamie offers me his arm. Secretly, I'm pleased as I slip my arm into the crook of his elbow.

6

Molly

"Why don't you come back with us to my apartment?" Jamie says when we reach our building. "We can eat together."

I hesitate for a moment. Surely he's not thinking this is a date. The idea makes me uncomfortable. Yes, I enjoy looking at him, and I'd love to be friends with him, but I'm not interested in dating *anyone*. Not even Jamie. That just can't happen.

"If you have things to do, that's fine," he says.

I think he's detecting my hesitation and giving me an easy out, which makes me like him even more.

I know I'm just being silly. Of course he's not thinking of this as a date. He just doesn't know anyone in the neighborhood, and he's probably a bit lonely and would appreciate some company. *Get a grip,* I tell myself. *It's just dinner. Don't make it into something more.* "No, that's fine. I'd love to."

I punch in the security code to unlock the door as Jamie holds Gus's harness and our carryout sacks. Once we reach the top of the stairs, I follow Jamie to his apartment. He lets us in and hands me the food so he can remove the dog's harness and hang it up on a hook next to a high-tech, fancy-looking cane. Relieved of duty, Gus runs off to tackle a bright green tennis ball lying on the floor in the center of the living room.

"What can I get you to drink?" Jamie says, heading for the kitchen. "I have soft drinks, beer, water. Some nice red wine, if you'd like."

I set the take-out sacks down on the dining table situated between the kitchen and the living room. "Water for me, please."

"Cold or room temperature?"

"Cold, thank you."

I glance around the apartment, which is very sparsely, yet tastefully, furnished in masculine shades of browns and blues. His apartment is a carbon copy of my own, and it feels a little surreal being here. I half expect to see Charlie come walking down the hallway to greet me.

Jamie brings a chilled bottle of spring water and a bottle of cold beer to the table, along with two plates, napkins, and silverware. "Help yourself," he says as he sets everything down.

I grab a plate and fork and dish some of the rice onto my plate. Then I locate the carton of Veggie Delight.

"It's nice to have some company," he says, dishing his broccoli and beef onto his plate. "I'm still getting used to living alone. Sometimes it's a little too quiet. I'm used to having people around.

Noise, activity. Gus makes plenty of noise, trust me, but it's not quite the same."

"I know what you mean. When I moved here a year ago, it took me some adjusting too." I take a bite of my steamed rice and sautéed veggies and moan when the sweet and sour sauce hits my taste buds. "Oh, God, this is so good. I should do this more often."

He laughs. "You're easy to please."

As we enjoy our meals, I'm tempted to ask him about the blonde I've seen him with, but I'm not sure I want to know. I can pretend he's single and available, and I can enjoy having him to myself for these few minutes.

There are so many things I want to ask him... like how he lost his sight. And what he does for a living. Does he work, or is he on disability? But I don't see how I can ask him those things without coming across as too nosy.

"So, Molly, what do you do?"

I have to smile. Obviously, we're both thinking along the same lines. "I'm an artist. I have a small gallery and studio down the street."

He seems surprised. "What kind of art?"

"I paint abstract landscapes."

"Acrylic or oil? Or watercolor?"

I'm impressed that he's actually paying attention. "Acrylic, because it cures faster. But my paintings are very textured, so they often look like oils."

"I guess we have something in common, then. I'm an artist of sorts. I'm a writer."

"You're a writer?"

He laughs at my blatant incredulity.

If he's blind, how can he write? "But how do you..." Again with the nosy questions. "I'm sorry, never mind."

He laughs. "Don't be sorry, Molly. You can ask me anything. So, how can a blind man write books? It's not that hard, really. I write using dictation software, and then I use software to transcribe the audio. The manuscript then goes to my editor, and eventually to my proofreader. It's definitely a team effort. I couldn't do it alone."

"What do you write?"

"Fiction, specifically military thrillers. I was in the military for quite a few years."

"Oh. Is that when you lost your sight? In the military?"

He nods, and his lips flatten. "I was too close to an explosion."

"I'm so sorry."

He shakes his head. "Don't be. I was the lucky one – I survived. My two best friends weren't so lucky."

Oh, God. I'm so sorry. My words seem far too inadequate, so I hold my tongue, not wanting to dredge up painful memories for him. I'm sure whatever happened was horrific. I guess he is lucky he wasn't hurt worse, or even killed.

As we eat our meals, I watch him, taking advantage of the fact that he can't see me studying him. I can't help noticing how the fabric of his T-shirt stretches and strains over his chest and arms, hugging his torso, which looks like it's cut from stone. He may no longer be in the military, but he's still incredibly fit.

I glance up at his dark glasses. They're so dark I can't see anything behind them. I wonder, are his eyes scarred? The rest of his handsome face is unmarred. I know what it's like to be scarred. Like him, I hide those wounds from the rest of the world.

When we're done, I carry the dirty dishes to the kitchen. He follows me and starts rinsing them off.

"Don't take this the wrong way," I say, leaning against the kitchen counter, watching him as he puts the dirty dishes into the dishwasher with methodical precision. "For a blind person, you seem to do everything so effortlessly. If I couldn't see, I'd be stumbling all over myself."

He smiles. "Before I moved here, I lived in my brother's house in Kenilworth, and there was someone there to do everything for me. I was waited on hand-and-foot by the housekeeper. I felt... suffocated. And whenever I went out to walk in the woods or swim in the pond, I was shadowed every step of the way by the groundskeeper. They both meant well, and I understood that, but I wanted to be self-sufficient. I *needed* to be self-sufficient. I wanted to prove that I could take care of myself, so I moved out."

"You seem to be doing a good job of it. You live alone, you manage a career."

"Thanks. It takes practice, and a lot of memorization. There are eight steps between the kitchen sink and the door to my apartment. It's twelve steps from my apartment door to the stairs. There are ten steps down to the ground floor, and another six steps down to the sidewalk."

"Wow, that's very precise," I say, biting my tongue to keep from laughing.

"I have to be precise," he says. "That's how I function, how I navigate. I know exactly where everything is, how many steps to take, when to turn. I know where every piece of furniture is in this apartment."

After we finish cleaning up the kitchen, I thank him for the impromptu dinner invitation and wish him a good evening.

Jamie walks me to the door. "Molly?"

"Yes?"

"Don't take this the wrong way, but do you mind if I touch your face?"

His unorthodox request takes me by surprise. "Why do you want to touch my face?"

"So I can see you. I'd just like to get a sense of what you look like. Tall or short? Long hair or short hair? Straight or curly? The shape of your eyes, your nose, your lips. Do you wear glasses? I can get a much better sense of you if I can touch your face. Do you mind?"

I swallow, thinking this has to be the strangest request a man has ever made of me. If he'd tried to cop a feel, I might have been less surprised. "No, I don't mind. Go ahead."

He raises both of his hands toward my face and hesitates, as if waiting for permission. I reach for his hands and guide them to my face. His fingers are warm and slightly rough, and very methodical as he systematically maps my head, starting at the crown and making his way down.

He touches my hair, measuring its length and texture, and then he brushes his thumbs across my forehead and traces the shape of my eyebrows. With the tips of his fingers, he skims the contours of my face, learning the shape of my eyes, the length of my nose, the width of my lips.

I stand perfectly still as I'm mesmerized by his inquisitive touch, which is both clinical and personal. There's absolutely nothing sexual in his exploration, and yet I feel intimately connected to him. For a self-indulgent moment, I imagine what it would be like if his fingers traced the scars that run across my chest, one on each side of my sternum. I can easily picture him as a mindful, patient lover. Just the thought of him touching me like *that* sends a rush of liquid heat straight to my core, and I shiver.

His nostrils flare, and for a crazy moment, I'm sure he can smell my heated reaction to his touch.

"I smell vanilla and peppermint," he says, sounding curious.

I laugh nervously. "The vanilla is my lotion, and the peppermint is actually tea tree oil – my shampoo."

"It's nice."

For a moment, I lose myself in him. He's so observant, figuratively speaking. He pays attention to the smallest little detail. I think he'd make some lucky woman an amazing partner, not just in bed but out of it too. Shaking myself from that pointless reverie, I step back putting an end to his exploration.

He drops his hands to his sides. "Sorry."

"No! It's fine. You have nothing to apologize for. It's just... I'm not used to being touched. I've been alone for a while."

"You've never mentioned a husband, or a significant other. Are you single?"

"Yes. Well, I'm divorced."

He frowns. "I'm sorry if I made you feel uncomfortable."

"It's fine, really. I'm just not used to it. Did you get what you were looking for?"

He smiles. "Yes. What color is your hair, though? I can tell it's just past your shoulders and wavy, but I can't tell the color by touching."

I laugh, feeling self-conscious at his scrutiny. "Mud brown."

He grins. "And your eyes?"

"Also brown. What about you? What color are your eyes? I can't see them behind those dark glasses."

"Brown," he says. "They were brown."

Were? Oh, my God. I steel myself to ask. "Were?"

He nods. "The damage was extensive. My doctors couldn't save them. I have prosthetic eyes."

"I'm so sorry." My normal reaction would be to reach out and touch his arm to offer sympathy for what he's been through, but I immediately squelch the impulse. There's no point in muddying the waters by initiating more physical contact between us. Instead, I reach for the door knob.

"Wait," he says. "I'll walk you to your door. I wouldn't be much of a gentleman if I didn't see you safely home."

Inwardly, I chuckle. The man's blind. I don't think he'd be much help in an emergency, but I appreciate the gesture. "Thank you. That's very chivalrous of you."

Jamie removes the dog's harness off its hook, and the dog comes bounding over to him, obviously excited to be going out again. After quickly harnessing the dog, he opens the door for us.

"Go to Molly's door," Jamie tells Gus, as he directs the dog toward my apartment.

"Surely he doesn't know where I live," I say, shutting the door behind me and following them down the hall.

"Not yet, but he'll learn. This is all part of his training – to learn a new destination."

Once we reach my apartment, Jamie pats my door and says "Molly's door" several times to Gus, who listens intently, cocking his head as he watches Jamie's hand.

I fish my key out of my purse and unlock the door. "Thanks for dinner," I tell him.

"You're welcome. I hope we can do it again sometime."

"Sure. I'd like that."

"How about tomorrow? Can I take you out for dinner?"

My breath hitches in my chest as I'm taken aback by his invitation. Is he asking me out on a date? It sure sounds like a date. I suppose I should just come right out and ask him. My heart races at the thought he'd ask me out, but then reality rears its ugly head at the thought of my ex-husband. I can't involve Jamie in my problems. Todd can be mean and vindictive, and I wouldn't want him to set his sights on Jamie, who can't defend himself. "I'm sorry, I can't. I already have plans tomorrow."

I'm afraid he'll suggest another time, but fortunately he doesn't, sparing me having to come up with another excuse. Instead, he nods graciously and smiles. "Maybe another time."

My heart sinks a little as he wishes me a good evening.

"All right, Gus, take us home," Jamie says, and the dog leads him back down the hall.

As I watch Jamie walk away, I can't help wondering what it might have been like if I'd met him at a different time in my life, without the specter of Todd hanging over my head like a black cloud. Things might have been very different then.

7

Jamie

It's close to midnight when I take Gus outside one last time before we call it a night. It's downright frigid tonight, and I'm freezing my balls off. I don't think Gus wants to be out here any more than I do, and thankfully he takes care of business quickly. There's a tree planted right outside our apartment building, and it makes a convenient spot for a quick doggy pee break.

Once that's taken care of, we head back up the steps to the apartment door. As I'm about to punch in the security access code, I hear a faint sound behind me... a quiet scuff of a shoe on the smooth stone steps. My senses instantly go on high alert because whoever's behind me is making an effort to be stealthy, and in my experience, stealthy never bodes well for anyone.

I lower my hand from the security panel. "Can I help you?"

"Oh, hey, pal, sorry," a man says in a friendly voice, as he pats me on the shoulder. "I didn't mean to sneak up on you."

The hairs on the back of my neck start tingling. I learned years ago in the military to trust my gut instincts, and they've served me well for many years. This guy is raising all kinds of red flags. He has no business trying to get into our building at this time of night.

Besides me and Molly, the only other residents are an elderly woman who lives alone and a young married couple. I've met all of them, and this guy isn't one of them. Molly didn't mention that she was seeing anyone. She only mentioned an ex-husband.

I have a hard time believing this guy has a legitimate reason for coming into our building. "How can I help you?" I say.

"You can let me into the building," he says, chuckling in a buddy-buddy kind of way that confirms my suspicions. "I'm on my way up to see Molly. She's expecting me."

No, she's not. "There's the intercom. You can buzz her apartment yourself, and she can let you in."

"Well, it's late, and I don't want to disturb her. Since you're already out here, I'll just go in with you if that's all right."

The guy crowds me from behind, and I'm sure it's an attempt to slip inside the building the minute I unlock the door. Or, he's attempting to intimidate me. Either way, it's not happening.

"I think you'd better buzz her yourself," I say. "Go ahead. I'll wait."

He exhales impatiently. "Come on, buddy, give a guy a break. It's freezing out here!"

I'm tempted to grab this guy by the throat and smack him up against the building. Losing my patience, I give him an ultimatum. "Either buzz her yourself, or take a hike. I'm not letting you in."

"You know what?" he growls. "Fuck you!" Then I hear his footfalls as he jogs down the steps and walks away.

I wait a couple of minutes to ensure he's really gone. Then I punch in the access code and let myself and Gus into the building, securing the door behind us.

"Upstairs," I tell Gus, and we head up. "Go to Molly's door." And I direct him to the right as I reinforce his training. I have a feeling – or maybe it's just wishful thinking on my part – that Molly's apartment will become a frequent destination for us.

It's late, and I'm afraid she might already be asleep. If she is, I don't want to disturb her. But if she's still up, we need to have a little chat. I stand outside her door and listen for a moment. Nothing. I hear absolutely nothing. Just as I'm about to turn away and head to my own apartment, I hear Charlie's plaintive meow, and then I hear Molly's quiet voice as she responds. *She's awake.*

I knock quietly on her door. "Molly? It's Jamie."

A moment later, I hear her unlocking the deadbolt and pulling the slide chain. The door opens.

"Jamie," she says, sounding a bit wary and a whole lot sleepy.

"I'm sorry to bother you this late, but I was just on my way back inside after walking Gus when I was intercepted by a guy trying to get into the building. He said he was here to see you, and he asked me to let him in. He said you were expecting him. I suggested that he buzz your apartment, but he said he didn't want to disturb you this late. When I refused to let him in, he left in a huff. It seemed suspicious, so I thought you should know."

Molly takes a shaky breath and lets out a heavy sigh. "That must have been my ex-husband, Todd. I have a restraining order against him, but it hasn't stopped him from attempting to get into the building. He's managed to get in several times in the past few weeks to leave notes on my door."

Now I wish I had slammed the guy into the building. "How the hell is he getting into the building?"

She laughs. "Usually it's Mrs. Powell who lets him in. She's just trying to be nice. I've asked her repeatedly not to do it, but she's very easily confused. And Todd can be very persuasive. And the young couple downstairs might have let him in once. They didn't mean any harm."

My chest tightens at the idea of someone encroaching on Molly's private space. "Have you called the police?"

"Yes, but he's long gone before they get here. And I have no proof… I only have the notes he leaves on my door."

I hear a slight tremor in her voice. "You're afraid of him."

For a moment, she hesitates, and I think she may refuse to acknowledge my statement. But eventually, she sighs. "Yes. I am. I filed for divorce about a year ago when I discovered my husband was having an affair. Once their affair ended, he started pressuring me into coming back to him."

"I take it you don't want to go back."

She laughs bitterly. "Not in this lifetime."

"If he gets into the building again, let me know. I'll deal with him."

I hear the swift intake of her breath.

"Jamie, no! I don't want you getting involved in my problems. Todd can be… difficult. I wouldn't put it past him to threaten you. Please stay out of it. I don't want you getting hurt."

I smile. Her concern for my welfare is touching, but misplaced. In a one-on-one confrontation, I can handle myself just fine. But Molly doesn't know that. "Don't worry about me, Molly. I can take care of myself."

"Jamie...." She sounds frustrated. "Don't underestimate Todd. Promise me you'll steer clear of him. Please, promise me."

"Don't worry, Molly." That's the best I can do, because there's no way in hell I'm going to make that promise.

* * *

I wait until Molly locks up before I tell Gus to take us home. She's obviously afraid of her ex. The fact that this prick's trying to intimidate her pisses me off. I hate bullies and predators. I'm half tempted to go back outside just to see if the guy shows up again. I'd like to put the fear of God into him, do a little bit of intimidating myself. I'll be damned if I'll let this guy hurt Molly.

Back in my apartment, I release Gus from duty, and he immediately goes off in search of his tennis ball. Not just any tennis ball, but his personal favorite. I grab a bottle of water from the kitchen and head to the bathroom to get ready for bed.

As I get undressed, my brain keeps replaying my interaction with Molly's ex. She said he'd been getting into the building lately. I can only imagine that the residents in the downstairs apartments have been letting him in, probably buying his story about being Molly's friend. I'll have a talk with them first thing tomorrow, and make sure they know they're not to let any unauthorized individuals into the building.

Gus follows me into the bedroom and plops down on his stuffed dog bed which lies on the floor at the foot of my bed. I crawl into bed with my phone to listen to an audiobook for a while. As I lay there, paying absolutely no attention to my book, my mind keeps wandering back to Molly, who is presumably lying in her own bed just a few dozen feet away.

Before long, Gus is snoring quietly. I stop the audiobook as it's a lost cause now. I can't stop thinking about Molly. She's afraid of this guy. I could hear it in her voice. I hate the idea of her alone in her bed, possibly wondering if her ex is going to get into the building again.

I wonder if she'd be okay with me putting some surveillance cameras in the upstairs hallway. At least I'd be alerted if someone comes upstairs.

God, I wish I could *see* Molly. I have a generic picture of her in my mind, but it's not the same thing as seeing her myself. But I'm a practical man, and I don't waste time or energy lamenting what can never be. I'll never see again. I've accepted that. And usually I'm okay with it. But this time... God, I think I'd give anything to see her face, just once.

As I lie here, I relive the memory of running my hands over Molly's hair, feeling the length and the texture of it. I remember the shape of her face, the arch of her eyebrow. It's been a long time since any woman has held my interest like this, certainly the first time since I was blinded.

When I was in the SEAL teams, I was too busy to think much about women. We were deployed so often there was hardly any time for dating. Then the explosion happened, and everything changed for me after that. My focus became relearning how to do everything without sight. Then it became learning how to be independent again. Now that I've gotten that far, for the most part anyway – I still have plenty of limitations – my mind and body are starting to want more. And now, when I hear Molly's voice, that *more* becomes painfully obvious to me.

I never seriously considered dating after the accident. One, I had so much to relearn, I just didn't have the time or energy to even think about it. And two – the real reason – I didn't want to saddle any woman with a defective partner. Even though I've learned how to do a lot, I can't do everything. There are some things I'll never be able to do again. But thanks to technology, I can compensate for my blindness in many regards.

Molly's the first woman I've met since my accident who makes me realize what's missing in my life.

And why Molly? What is it about Molly that makes me think about romance and sex?

It's not her appearance. Because I'll never be able to see her myself, her appearance is pretty irrelevant to me.

I replay our conversation from dinner tonight. There's something about listening to her talk that soothes me. The sound of her voice, her quiet gentleness, her compassion. I like being with her. She makes me feel good... like I've finally come home.

For the first time since my accident, I seriously ponder whether or not I have enough to offer a woman. I know women like my looks – I know because I've heard that all of my life. I have a good income – my books sell well and I've already got enough money socked away in the bank to retire if I wanted to. Beth tells me I'm a good listener and that women like that. She tells me I'm kind, caring, and empathetic – also that women like that. She's been trying for months now to get me to think about dating again. She's deliriously in love with my brother and thinks everyone else should be in love too.

As I finally doze off, I remember skimming my fingertips over Molly's face earlier this evening, learning the shape of her nose and her lips. I remember how soft her skin felt. How good she smelled... not just the vanilla and the peppermint, but the underlying scent of her as a woman. I remember how still she stood as I touched her face and hair, like a startled doe caught in the headlights.

I like her. I like being with her. I like how she makes me feel when I'm with her. Even assuming she could possibly be interested in me – and that's one hell of an assumption – I still have to wonder if she'd be willing to settle for a blind boyfriend.

8

Molly

The next morning, as I leave my apartment to head to the studio, I run into Jamie and Gus in front of our building. My heart rate kicks into high gear and I feel almost giddy with excitement at seeing Jamie again. Gus is watering the lamp post like a good boy.

"Good morning," I say, stopping.

"Good morning." Jamie turns to face me, seeming almost bashful this morning. "We're just taking care of morning business."

"I see that." I reach down to scratch Gus's head, and he pushes his wet nose into the palm of my hand. "Hey, boy."

"Off to work?" Jamie says.

"Yes. I have a meeting with a big client this morning to discuss a series of paintings for the Children's Hospital."

His brow rises. "Impressive. Do you mind if Gus and I walk with you to your shop? We were just heading out for some exercise."

I grin like a fool, and I'm relieved he can't see my stupid reaction. I'm sure I'm blushing like an idiot – something I seem to do a lot around him. "I don't mind. I'd love the company."

He offers me his arm, and I link my elbow with his. I suspect he doesn't need me to guide him, as he has Gus, so why the close contact? Is he just being gallant? Whatever his reason, I'm thrilled for a chance to walk arm-in-arm with him.

The sidewalks are pretty crowded this time of morning as folks head to work or out for breakfast. Fortunately, the crowd makes way for Jamie, most people giving him and Gus a wide berth. I'm not surprised, though, to see quite a few women checking him out with furtive glances.

As we walk side-by-side, I can't help sneaking peeks at him myself. He's sexy as hell in faded blue jeans and a pair of well-worn hiking boots. The fit of his leather jacket emphasizes the breadth of his shoulders. The morning sun brings out hints of red in his auburn hair.

I picture him as one of the cool kids I remember from high school. He's like one of those drool-worthy boys who roamed the school hallways completely unaware of their own appeal, as legions of besotted girls mooned over them in secret agony.

"So, tell me about your ex-husband," Jamie says, taking me by surprise.

"My ex?" His question seems an odd one. "Why do you want to know about him?"

He shrugs. "I'm just curious."

I don't believe that for a second. "What do you want to know?"

"Does he have any military experience? Any martial arts training? Or weapons training? Does he own a firearm?"

These aren't random questions. He's assessing how much of a threat Todd is. And that makes me wonder just what Jamie's background is. I mean, I know he's former military, but I'm not sure how much he knows about weapons and martial arts.

"No, to all of those questions," I finally say. "Well, I think he does have his grandfather's old hunting rifle in his closet, but I don't think it's functional. He's never shot it, at least to my knowledge. Why are you asking?"

"So I'll know what I'm dealing with when he shows up again."

He says *when,* not *if.* My heart stutters painfully. "Jamie, you can't confront Todd. Please, promise me you won't."

He gives me a half smile, his lips curving just slightly, but says nothing.

"I'm serious!" I say.

Again, that half-smile, as if he's trying to placate me, but has no intention of making any such promise.

He squeezes my arm. "Don't worry."

My heart kicks painfully in my chest. The thought of Todd setting his sights on Jamie scares me to death. Jamie's such a nice guy, and with his disability, he wouldn't stand a chance against Todd. I don't want to be responsible for Jamie getting bullied, or even worse.

Jamie and Gus navigate the crowded sidewalk confidently, weaving through a steady stream of people and circumventing a few sidewalk obstacles. Gus stays close to Jamie, walking right beside him and just a bit ahead. As the dog changes course to avoid trash containers and benches in their way, Jamie keeps in step with him. They've obviously been practicing for a while.

As we pass the tattoo parlor where Chloe works, I glance through the front windows and catch sight of her standing behind the sales counter, talking to a customer. I wave, and she waves back eagerly. When she sees Jamie, her eyes widen and she mouths something at me that I can't quite make out. When I shrug, she gives me a *call me!* sign with her fingers.

My shop's not far. When I turn my attention forward, I'm caught completely off guard by the sight of Todd waiting outside my studio door. He's leaning against the building with his arms crossed over his chest in a seemingly casual pose. But his hard gaze is locked on Jamie. *Oh, shit.*

It's time for some damage control. I release Jamie's arm. "Well, this is me. Thanks for the escort. I'll see you later, okay?"

Jamie signals for Gus to stop. "We're at your shop?"

"Yes. Enjoy the rest of your walk. I'll see you later." I can only hope he takes the hint and keeps on walking.

I head toward the door of my shop, hoping to distract Todd. But Todd has his own agenda. He brushes right past me, almost knocking me over as he stalks over to Jamie.

"Todd, don't!" I say, chasing after him. But I might as well be talking to a brick wall.

"Hey, buddy, remember me?" Todd says, in a deceptively friendly tone. He stops in front of Jamie, his hands propped onto his hips as he glares at Jamie.

When Gus starts growling at Todd, Jamie lays his hand on the dog's head and gives him a reassuring pat. "Hush, boy." Then, to Todd, he says, "Of course I do."

"You're the asshole who wouldn't let me in the building to see Molly last night."

"Why didn't you buzz her apartment? She could have let you in if she'd wanted to."

Todd scowls at Jamie. "Look, prick, Molly and I are none of your fucking business."

I grab hold of Todd's coat sleeve. "Todd, that's enough. Leave him alone."

My heart's pounding, and I'm desperate to get Todd away from Jamie.

Jamie takes a step forward, literally going toe-to-toe with Todd. He's an intimidating sight as he towers a few inches over Todd. "Molly's my friend, and that makes it my business."

At that moment, Chloe joins us on the sidewalk, her keen gaze bouncing from one of us to the other, until if finally lights on me. "Hi, Molly," she says, breathless and shivering from the cold. "Is everything okay?"

Todd frowns at Chloe, then at me. Then he shakes his head and walks away.

I watch as Todd jogs across the busy street and gets into his car and drives off. "He's gone," I tell Jamie, releasing a pent-up breath. "I'm so sorry about that."

Jamie turns to me, surprised. "Molly, I can handle Todd."

"Don't underestimate him, Jamie. He's used to getting his own way. He doesn't take kindly to being thwarted."

"Don't underestimate *me*, Molly," Jamie says, his expression tightening. "You have no idea what I'm capable of. Don't let my blindness fool you."

9

Molly

As Jamie and Gus resume their walk, Chloe follows me into my shop. I flip on the overhead lights and turn up the heat to ward off the overnight chill.

"What in the fresh hell was that all about?" she says, shrugging out of her coat and hanging it on a wall hook behind the sales counter.

I laugh as I turn on the cash register. I can always count on Chloe to make me smile, no matter how stressed I am. "What fresh hell are you referring to, specifically? Jamie or Todd?"

She hops up on the sales counter and swings her legs. "Both! Dish, girlfriend! I was afraid those two were going to start throwing down any second."

"I've told you, Todd is very territorial."

"I know *that*. But what about Jamie? He got right in Todd's face. What's with that? And why was he walking you to work in the first place? And was that a service dog with him?"

I sigh. "Okay. One, Jamie's just watching out for me. I guess he doesn't like Todd – but then, who does? Two, I saw Jamie this morning as I was leaving the building and he asked if he could walk me to my shop. And three, yes, Gus is his service dog."

"Why does he need a service dog?"

"Jamie's blind."

Chloe's eyes widen. "He's blind? Like, partially blind or totally blind?"

"Totally blind."

"You're shitting me! He didn't seem blind yesterday when we saw him in the café with that hot blonde."

"I think he hides it well."

"Did you find out what kind of friend she is? Are we talking girlfriend? Friend with benefits? Or, just one of his harem? Because, let's face it, this guy is hot. I'm sure he has lots of women panting after him."

"I saw them later in the afternoon, standing outside our apartment building. A guy in a Jaguar came to pick her up, and he kissed the daylights out of her, so I think she's with him, and not with Jamie. I haven't had the nerve to ask him if he has a girlfriend."

Chloe hops down from the counter. "I can't stay. I just wanted to get the dish on Mr. Hottie. You should find out if he has a girlfriend. Who knows, maybe he's available."

I shake my head. "It wouldn't matter if he is. I can't get involved with anyone."

Chloe rolls her eyes. "Why? Because of Todd the Douchebag?"

"Partly. Todd's a menace to anyone who's associated with me... including *you*. You need to be careful around him, Chloe. And Jamie – his blindness puts him at a significant disadvantage. But it's more than that."

She gives me a knowing look. "Don't be ridiculous. You're a great catch, Molly. Any guy would be lucky to be with you, even with your *unfortunate deformities*."

I shake my head, fighting a grin at Chloe's euphemism for my lack of breasts. Now it's my turn to give Chloe a look. "In case you haven't noticed, men are obsessed with breasts, and I no longer have any. That makes me 'incomplete as a woman' – at least that's what Todd said to justify his infidelity. I'm not going to enter into a relationship that's doomed from the start."

Chloe shakes her head as she slips on her coat and heads for the door. "You don't know it's doomed from the start. I think you're wrong. You're talented and smart. You're kind and caring. Who cares if you don't have boobs?" She shrugs, giving me a parting grin as she reaches for the door handle. "I'd do you in a heartbeat, if I swung that way."

* * *

That evening, as I sit on my sofa eating a baby kale and spinach salad and watching CNN, I hear heavy footsteps and male voices coming up the stairs. Lots of them, as in a small stampede. Curious, I get up and peer through the peep hole in my door just in time to see three guys come up the stairs and turn toward Jamie's apartment. One of them I recognize as the guy who was driving the Jaguar yesterday – the one who kissed the blonde. One of them looks just like the lead singer of the pop band Locke, but that can't be right. What in the world would he be doing in my apartment building? The third one, an older guy with short salt-and-pepper hair and a chiseled upper torso, is carrying a case of beer.

I can no longer see them, but I hear when they knock on Jamie's door. It looks like Jamie's having a party. A few minutes later, there are more boots coming up the stairs and heading to Jamie's door.

I'm happy for him. I'm glad he's got friends.

I, on the other hand, am alone for the evening. After watching a chick flick and eating popcorn and M&Ms, I read a little bit, then think about getting ready for bed. As I'm carrying my empty dishes to the kitchen, I hear voices out in the hallway. Female voices this time. I can't resist peeking out the peep hole just as the blonde from yesterday comes up the stairs, followed by a petite blonde girl and a redhead with a manbun.

The blonde looks upset. As she glances toward Jamie's apartment, her expression lights up when she sees someone. I can't see who she's looking at, but I imagine it's Jamie.

As I turn away from my door, I tell myself it's for the best. I don't need to waste time mooning over someone I can't have.

* * *

The walls in this building aren't very thick, and as I'm lying in bed in the dark, I can hear the faint rumble of male laughter coming from Jamie's apartment. It's not loud enough to be annoying – it's more like white noise, rising and falling in quiet waves, and lulling me to sleep. I'm glad he's got a lot of friends.

I feel a sharp twinge in my chest as a frayed neuron misfires and slip my hand beneath my oversized nightshirt to rub the spot. Occasionally those severed nerves act up, like now, zapping me unexpectedly with a painful tingle. This time it's beneath the scar that crosses the left side of my chest, where my left breast once was. That was the breast where my cancer was found. You have an aggressive form of cancer, my doctor had said, stage zero. "You're very lucky, Molly."

It was detected in a routine mammogram. After a quick surgical procedure, the cancer was gone, along with approximately ninety-seven percent of my breast tissue. They can't ever get it all. There's always a risk of recurrence. But I made a choice. I could have had a lumpectomy, but I chose to remove my breasts. Both of them. Still, that's not a guarantee.

My chest is still mostly numb, making it feel weird to the touch, but I can tell the nerves are slowly growing back. I have a little more sensation these days than I did a year ago, when I had the surgery.

Once I received the cancer diagnosis, my life changed so dramatically, seemingly overnight. A biopsy, then scheduling the surgery. It all happened so quickly.

After reviewing my options, I opted for a double mastectomy. I'd watched my maternal grandmother deal with breast cancer for the last two decades of her life, first in one breast, then in the other. I didn't want to go through that.

At first Todd had been supportive. The breakdown occurred after the surgery, when he got a good look at my newly disfigured chest. In hindsight, it was a failure of communication on both of our parts. He'd assumed I'd have reconstructive surgery and come out of the treatment with a pair of perfect, plump breasts. Instead, I'd opted to go *au naturale*, which meant having no breasts at all. Just two irregular, shiny scars meandering across my now flat chest, constant reminders of what I'd lost.

I guess it's not fair to blame him for his reaction. He hadn't signed on for this when we got married. But still, his disappointment was no justification for violating our marriage vows and screwing his assistant on our living room sofa. If he'd wanted out of our marriage, he should have told me himself. He should have done it the right way, instead of being a coward and sneaking around behind my back, irrevocably destroying my trust in him.

I turn onto my side and wrap my arms around the spare pillow, savoring the comfort it provides. The last thing I remember is hearing a muted cheer next door. At least someone is having a good time tonight.

* * *

Sunday afternoon, I'm in the back of my shop applying glazes to a set of newly finished paintings when my phone chimes with an incoming text. I glance at the screen to see Chloe's brief message: *Open the damn door. I have pizza.*

I put my brushes down and go unlock the front door. Chloe follows me through the beaded curtain. "I come bearing lunch... fresh out of the oven, thin crust with veggies and light cheese, just how you like it."

She sets the pizza box down on one of the worktables and heads for my little kitchenette to collect paper plates and napkins.

"That sounds really good," I tell her, dropping my brushes into a jar of cleaning solution. "I skipped breakfast this morning, and I'm starved."

While I'm washing up and grabbing water bottles for the both of us, she loads two slices of pizza onto a paper plate and hops up on the table.

"Are you working today?" I ask her, as I help myself to a slice of pizza.

"I filled in for Mitch for half a day today, but I'm off now. I thought I'd come by to visit for a while."

I take a bite of pizza and moan in appreciation. "God, thank you, this is just what I needed."

"You're welcome."

"So, how was your hot date last night?" I remember Chloe telling me she was going out with a guy she met on an Internet dating site.

She rolls her eyes. "It was a total disaster. The guy couldn't get off his phone for more than five minutes at a time – when he should have been looking at *all this*." Chloe gestures to her own rocking body. "I got tired of sitting there staring at the top of his head, holding one-sided conversations. What's wrong with people these days? It's too bad, too, because he was hot. Still, he's an idiot."

I smile. "I'm sorry it didn't work out. Do you think you'll see him again?"

She shakes her head as she opens a chilled bottle of water. "Nope. Not interested. One strike, he's out. I don't waste time on losers."

I laugh. Chloe's had one disastrous blind date after another lately. As beautiful as she is, she has no trouble getting dates. It's just that most of them turn out to be duds.

"Don't you dare laugh," she says. "At least I'm going out. When was the last time you went out with *anyone* besides that loser ex-husband of yours?"

I scrunch up my nose, thinking back. Way back. "Um, eleven years ago?"

"Ha! Then don't make fun of my lame dates. At least I'm getting out there."

The doorbell chimes, and as I start to remove my paint-splattered smock, Chloe hops off the table. "Relax and eat your pizza. I'll handle it."

A moment later, she pops her head back through the beaded curtain with a mischievous grin on her face. "Someone's here to see you," she says, in a sing-songy voice, giving me a pointed look.

Well, I know it's not Todd, because if it were, Chloe would be glaring daggers, not grinning at me like an idiot. When I head to the front of the store to see for myself who's here, I'm pleasantly surprised to find Jamie and Gus standing in my shop. "Jamie. This is a nice surprise."

"That's my cue," Chloe says, winking at me. "Time for me to get going." She grabs her coat from the backroom and heads for the door. "You kids have fun. Don't do anything I wouldn't do."

I watch as Chloe darts out the door and down the sidewalk. "Just ignore her," I say to Jamie.

He grins at me, and my pulse starts racing as I'm struck anew by how handsome he is. His dark aviator glasses make him look like a bad-ass hottie. I wish my body would stop reacting this way every time he shows up. It's embarrassing.

"I hope I'm not interrupting anything," he says.

"No, not at all. Chloe and I were just grabbing a bite to eat. I'm glad you stopped by. I noticed you had some friends over last night. A party?"

"My brothers and a couple friends came over for a poker game. I hope we weren't too loud."

"Oh, no, you weren't." I reach down to pet Gus. "I used to play poker with some dormmates in college. I wasn't half bad. I won my share of big pots. Wait – you play cards?"

"Sure." He grins, as if he's amused by my question. "We play with Braille cards."

"Oh, right."

"Hey, the reason I stopped by was because I wanted to invite you over for dinner tonight. If you're free. I make a pretty decent lasagna. Fresh garlic bread, a little red wine. What do you say?"

For a moment, I allow myself to marvel that this handsome, amazing man is offering to cook me dinner. Todd never once cooked a meal for me. I'm so tempted to say yes. There's nothing I'd like better than to spend some quality alone time with him, get to know him better, and find out if he's really all he appears to be.

I so desperately want to say yes, but that way lies madness. I'd be putting Jamie at great risk where Todd is concerned, and I just can't do that to him. Besides, I'm still not sure about the nature of his relationship with the pretty blonde. If they are a couple, or even just dating, I don't need to get my hopes up in vain. And, if I'm going to be completely honest with myself, I'd risk getting my heart crushed when he discovers I'm missing a couple of key body parts. Body parts that men tend to be particularly fond of.

My stomach sinks with the realization that I can't possibly say yes. "Thanks for the offer – I really mean that – but I'm afraid I can't."

His expression falls just the slightest bit, his brow furrowing with what looks like frustration, and he's quiet for a moment. I feel like a complete ass for turning him down.

"How about another night?" he says. "I'd love to have you over. And I promise you, I'm a pretty decent cook."

"Jamie, it's not that. I'm really busy this time of year, with the holidays coming up." My excuse sounds lame even to my own ears.

Despite his dark glasses, I can see he's frowning. "Of course. No problem."

He's clearly disappointed, and I feel like crap. I swallow around a painful lump in my throat, wishing things could be different. Wishing Todd wasn't in the picture, wishing I could say yes, and that Jamie would cook me dinner. I would love that.

10

Molly

Monday passes with no sign of Jamie. Well, I do hear him taking Gus outside for a potty break early in the morning, while I'm sipping my coffee, but I can hardly run out dressed in my PJs just to catch a glimpse. I try not to feel disappointed, but it's difficult. The last thing I need right now is to develop a school-girl crush on someone I can't have.

Tuesday, I head home during lunch to grab a quick bite and pick up some packages I need to mail. Just as I'm coming out of my apartment, I encounter Jamie and Gus coming up the stairs. And they're not alone. Jamie has the pretty blonde with him, as well as the hunky redhead I saw a few nights ago.

"Jamie, hi," I say, as I lock my apartment door.

Jamie looks so handsome in his black leather jacket and dark glasses that it makes my chest hurt. I notice that the blonde's eyes are wet with tears. When she sees me, she wipes her cheeks with the sleeve of her sweater and smiles hesitantly.

Jamie smiles too. "Hi, Molly. Going out?"

"Just running to the post office," I say. "I have some small paintings to mail."

I try not to look at the blonde, who seems a little upset at the moment. She really is stunning, with her hair pulled back in a ponytail and a lovely face dominated by beautiful blue-green eyes. Although we're about the same height, she's willowy thin and I'm not. Jamie has his arm around her, and he's rubbing her arm.

"Molly, this is Beth Jamison, my brother Shane's fiancée. Beth, this is Molly Ferguson, my neighbor. She's a very talented artist."

"Shane's fiancée? *Oh.*" Well, that certainly clears up the mystery of who the blonde is. I can feel some pent-up tension seeping out of me. *She's not his girlfriend.* Still, that doesn't mean he's unattached. Besides, even if he was free, I have no business getting involved with him.

"It's nice to meet you, Beth," I say, giving her what I hope is a genuinely warm and friendly smile. I feel ashamed for having been jealous of her. I glance once more at Jamie, drinking in the sight of him. "Well, I'd better get going. I'll see you later, Jamie."

He smiles at me. "I'm looking forward to it."

I head downstairs and out of the building before I pause to take a deep breath. *She's his brother's fiancée.* Not his girlfriend then. I shouldn't feel so relieved, because her relationship to Jamie is none of my business, but I can't help noticing there's an extra bounce in my step as I go about my business.

* * *

After work, I hop a train out to Naperville to visit my parents. They're both retired and living quite happily in a condo community for seniors in the suburb. They're both faring well in retirement, considering my mom is eighty and my dad is eighty-four. I was a bit of a late-in-life surprise. They'd long given up on the idea of conceiving a child, until one day, surprise! They found themselves expecting me.

They have the typical ailments of adults their age, but overall they're doing fine. I make it a point to visit weekly, to check on them and see if they need anything.

"Hi, honey!" my mom cries, as she greets me at the door.

"Hi, Mom." I give her a hug. She smells like cinnamon, so I know she's been baking, which is not a surprise. "What smells so good?"

"I made Snickerdoodles," she says. "And a pot roast for supper tonight. I hope you're hungry."

"You bet I am." My mother's a wonderful cook, and as we all know, "food is love." She tries to fatten me up every time I visit. I appreciate the gesture, but I don't need any more extra pounds. "Thanks, Mom. It smells delicious."

"Hey, there's my Molly-Moo," my dad says, as he joins us in the foyer, towering over my mom's petite form. He wraps me in his long arms and gives me a tight squeeze. "How's it going, kiddo?"

"Fine, Dad." I may be thirty-two years old, but I'll always be a kid to my parents. My mom still calls me on rainy mornings to remind me to take an umbrella with me if I go out. "How about you?"

"Fine, fine. I got eighteen holes in yesterday before the snow started, so that's good."

My dad took up golf after he retired from his career as a pediatrician. My mom, also a former pediatrician, took up baking and bird watching. Both of their hobbies keep them physically active, which is good.

We sit down to a delicious dinner, followed by my favorite cookies for dessert. As we're eating cookies and drinking coffee, they grill me on my business. They were both terrified that I'd go broke after I divorced Todd and had to support myself on my fledgling art business. But I'm happy to inform them that I'm not in danger of missing a rent payment or starving anytime soon.

After our meal, we sit in the sunroom, surrounded by my mother's jungle of plants, and listen to the chirps and tweets coming from her little aviary of finches. Mom's little black cat, Yuki, curls up in my lap and purrs as I scratch behind her ears.

We talk about everything and nothing until the hour grows late and my dad nods off in his favorite recliner chair. I say goodnight and call for an Uber to take me back to the train station, as it's too cold and dark for me to walk.

On the train, I make a valiant attempt to occupy myself with reading, but my mind keeps straying to thoughts of Jamie. I think about the dinner he might have made for me if I'd had the guts to say yes. My excuse was that I was keeping him safe from Todd, but I'm not sure that's the whole truth. I think I'm afraid to get close to someone again. Afraid to face more rejection.

I recall how Jamie comforted Beth in the hallway earlier today, rubbing her arm and holding her close. She's obviously going through a rough patch right now. I think Jamie would be a dream partner for any woman, even with his blindness. I just wish I could be a dream girlfriend. But I'm not. I'm defective, and I'm only just now beginning to realize the ramifications of my choices.

11

Molly

The next day, I take a break in the afternoon to pop in at the tattoo parlor to see Chloe. I find her sitting on a tall stool behind the sales counter sketching an intricately detailed picture of a rose on a sheet of drawing paper. Her long, dark hair is braided into pigtails, and she's wearing a loose-fitting bohemian-style dress. She reminds me of an exotic gypsy princess.

"That's really pretty," I tell her, watching as she eyes her sketch critically.

She scowls. "I can't get the perspective right. I have a customer who wants a rose on her breast." She eyes me critically. "If it's going on her boob, it's got to be absolutely perfect, right?"

She tears the page out of her sketchbook and wads it up, then tosses it in the trashcan. Then her expression brightens as she lays her pencil down and gives me her full attention. "Good afternoon, cupcake." She smiles brightly. "What's new with you?"

"Not much. I just wanted to stop in and say hi."

She gives me a knowing grin. "I saw your hottie walk by a few minutes ago with his dog."

Reflexively, I glance out the front windows, but of course he's not there. "He's not *my* hottie."

Chloe looks at me, a skeptical expression on her pretty face. Her big eyes are so dark and expressive, and so diabolically cynical. "So, anything going on there?"

"What do you mean?"

"I mean with the hot neighbor. Is anything going on?"

"No. We're just friends."

Chloe shrugs. "I'm just wondering if you have dibs on him."

I laugh, hoping to mask the swift surge of panic I feel. "Dibs? Of course I don't have dibs on him."

"So, you don't mind if I ask him out then?"

Yes, I mind! "No. Not at all."

"You are such a liar, Molly!" Chloe picks up her pencil and starts sketching the outline of a rose on the pristine white sheet of paper. "So, when are you going to let me ink you?" she says.

I frown. "I'm not really the tattoo type."

"Oh, come on! Just a tiny one. How about a tramp stamp, just above your ass? No one will ever see it – well, except for your hottie. No, scratch that – he wouldn't be able to see it anyway."

"Chloe!" I say, shocked. "That's an awful thing to say."

"Oh, come on, it was funny. So, why not get a tattoo?"

"Because – they hurt."

She laughs. "So? The pain is only temporary, but the artwork lasts for a lifetime."

I shake my head, smiling apologetically. "I don't think so."

"How about a piercing then? Perhaps a belly button ring, since nipple rings are clearly out."

"Chloe!" I cry, nearly choking on my laughter. Chloe's irreverent humor is exactly what I need sometimes to keep from taking myself too seriously.

She rips the sheet of paper containing her latest attempt off her sketchpad, balls it up, and throws it at me.

* * *

When I return to my shop, I'm greeted by a trio of tourists peeking through the front windows. I unlock the door and invite them in. While they're browsing, especially interested in my collection of Chicago postcards based on photographs I took, the bell over the door rings. I glance up, and my heart skips a beat when I see Jamie and Gus coming inside.

"Go to Molly," Jamie says, and Gus leads him right to me.

My gaze eats Jamie up as I reach down to pet Gus. "Hey, guys!"

"Hi, yourself," Jamie says. He cocks his head, as if listening to the chatter of the three tourists. "You have company?"

"Just a few customers browsing."

He nods. "I came to talk to you about doing a commission."

"You want to commission a painting?"

"Yes."

I feel a warm rush of pleasure knowing that he's not holding a grudge because I said no to dinner. "What do you want me to paint?"

"The beach view outside my brother's estate in Kenilworth. I'd like to commission you to paint it for their wedding gift. The lake view from the back of the house is spectacular, and I know they'd be thrilled to have a painting of it."

I'm totally bowled over by his request. "I'd love to do it," I tell him, giddy with relief and excitement. Painting a commission for Jamie means I'll get to spend time with him. A lot of time. "I'll need to see the view, of course," I say, trying to sound nonchalant. "I'll need to take some photographs for reference. Can I visit the property?"

"Of course. I'll take you out there myself, and you can look around all you want."

My pulse starts racing at the thought of having a legitimate excuse to spend time with Jamie... just the two of us on a road trip, going out of town. Well, not far, but it's at least a forty minute drive from Wicker Park. "When are they getting married?"

"In a couple weeks. But you don't have to have the painting done by then. I realize this is rather short notice, and I know you're booked up with other commissions. I've been wracking my brain for an idea for a wedding gift, and this occurred to me last night. I know they'd love it."

"Jamie, I'm flattered. Yes, I'd love to go see the property."

"Great. I'll take care of the arrangements. My brother Jake has offered to drive us."

"My goodness, how many brothers do you have?"

"Three. And three sisters. I wouldn't be standing here today – I probably wouldn't still be alive – if it weren't for them."

My heart contracts painfully at his admission. The explosion that cost him his eyesight must have been a nightmare. Maybe someday he'll feel comfortable telling me about it.

12

Molly

We make plans to drive north to Shane's estate in Kenilworth. At ten o'clock Saturday morning, Jamie, Gus, and I are waiting on the front steps of our building as a black SUV with darkly tinted windows pulls up to the curb. The driver's door opens, and out steps someone who could easily pass as a hitman. He's dark and dangerous – closely-cropped black hair, black jeans and a black leather jacket, dark sunglasses, and muscles that just won't quit. As he walks up the steps, I'm reminded of a sleek black panther on the prowl. The guy just radiates tension.

This is Jake? Holy cow. I'd hate to run into him in a dark alley.

I glance down at Gus, who's fairly quivering with excitement at

Jake's arrival. I guess if Gus likes this guy, he must be okay.

When Jake reaches us, I can't help noticing what a big guy he is. Not just tall, but muscular as well. I think it would be fair to characterize him as brawny, like a heavyweight champion would be. The numerous small scars on his face only add to his fighter persona, and it looks like his nose has been broken a time or two.

Jake claps his brother on his right shoulder and squeezes. "Hey, bro." Then his hand slides down Jamie's arm and the two men shake.

Jake takes off his sunglasses, hooks them on the collar of his dark T-shirt beneath his jacket, and turns to me expectantly. "Good morning."

"Jake, this is my friend Molly Ferguson," Jamie says. "Molly, this is Jake."

Jake extends his big hand to me, and we shake as well. His hand is huge, and it engulfs mine. His hand is warm, and he holds my hand carefully, as if he's tempering his strength.

"Nice to meet you, Molly," he says. His voice fits him – deep and a little rough. "You guys ready to hit the road?" He reaches for Gus's harness. "I'll take this guy and load him into the back." Then Jake looks at me. "You've got Jamie?"

I nod, linking my arm with Jamie's, as we've done on so many occasions before. As Jamie and I head down the steps to the SUV, Jake helps Gus into the rear of the vehicle. Jamie opens the front passenger door for me and offers to let me sit in the front, but I opt for the back seat and encourage Jamie to sit up front with his brother.

I settle myself in the back seat, with my camera bag beside me, and buckle my seatbelt. From my vantage point in the back, seated directly behind Jamie, I have a perfect view of two very handsome, albeit very different men. I eavesdrop on their conversation as they catch up, discussing their brother Shane's upcoming wedding... something about switching gears from a large church wedding to a small event with just family and friends. Apparently, Beth is rather shy, and the original wedding plans got to be a little too much.

As we head north away from the city, I relax into my seat and let my mind wander. While my gaze is fixed on the scenery out the window, part of my brain picks up bits and pieces of the conversation in the front seat.

Traffic heading north is pretty light this time of morning, so we make good time getting to our destination. I already knew Kenilworth was a lovely suburb full of grand houses and large properties, but nothing could have prepared me for our destination. Shane has a huge estate right on Lake Michigan. When Jake pulls off the main road and drives down a paved lane that meanders through the woods, I can't help but be impressed.

As we stop at a wrought iron gate, Jake rolls down his window and speaks to a disembodied voice coming out of the intercom. The gate swings open for us, and we proceed. After passing a second gated checkpoint, I start to feel like I'm entering Fort Knox.

"This place is pretty secure," I murmur to Jamie, leaning forward.

He nods. "A lot of dignitaries - politicians and celebrities - stay here when they're in Chicago. The security's very tight."

We pass a huge pond on the left. A couple of rowboats are moored to the wooden dock, and several canoes lie upside down on the grassy bank.

The right side of the road is lined with gently rolling pastures, and I see a small herd of horses - four adults and one foal - grazing on the crest of a gentle hill. Their tails flick languidly as they bask in the sun.

I lean closer to the window to get a better view. "Your brother has horses," I say, stating the obvious and unable to hide my surprise.

Jamie turns back to me. "Yes. Well, they're Elly's horses. Elly's our housekeeper, and those horses are her babies."

We pass a tall, sturdy older man with closely-cropped gray hair riding a lawn mower along the edge of the lane. He waves at us as we pass, and Jake waves back.

"That's Elly's husband, George," Jake says. "He's the groundskeeper."

Gus wakes from his impromptu nap in the back of the vehicle and starts pacing eagerly, whining softly. It's obvious he knows where we are, and he's clearly excited.

We pull into a circular drive in front of a huge house. Jake parks the SUV near the front steps and cuts off the engine.

Before I can even unbuckle my seat belt, Jamie's out of the SUV and opening my door. He offers me his hand and helps me climb down from the vehicle. I'm perfectly capable of getting out myself, but I can't pass up the opportunity to hold his hand, even if just for a moment.

The front double doors open, and out steps a tall, slender woman looking very much at home in a pair of well-worn jeans, riding boots, and a denim jacket with beaded fringe. Her long silver hair hangs in a thick braid halfway down her back.

The woman's face lights up when she sees Jamie, and she makes a beeline for him, wrapping her arms around his waist. She squeezes him tightly. "Oh, my God, I've missed you, honey," she whispers, and then she goes up on her toes to kiss his cheek just above the top edge of his beard.

Jamie hugs her back and kisses the top of her head. "I've missed you, too."

Jake opens the tailgate, and Gus leaps out of the vehicle and runs straight to Elly, rubbing against her legs and whining with excitement.

Elly reaches down to pet Gus, but her eyes are glued to Jamie.

Jamie lays his hand on Gus's head, and the dog immediately settles down at his side. "Molly, this is Elly Peterson. Elly, this is Molly Ferguson."

Elly wipes her hands on her jeans and reaches out to shake my hand, giving me a quick, welcoming smile. "Sorry, Molly, where are my manners? It's just that I'm so happy to see Jamie. It's just not the same around here without him."

Jake gives Elly a hug, too. "I'm going to take off now," he says to Jamie, clapping his brother on the back. "I'm going to make a quick run up to Harbor Springs to check on the cabin. I'll be back by dark."

Elly waves to Jake as he drives away, then turns to us. "Well, you two make yourselves at home. Let me know when you get hungry. I'll have a nice, hot meal ready for you."

* * *

Elly goes back to doing whatever it was she was doing before we arrived, leaving Jamie to take me on a tour of the house. With Gus leading the way, Jamie leads me inside, into a spacious two-story foyer filled with natural light. There's a wide, curved staircase that leads up to the second floor.

"The family bedrooms are up there," Jamie says. "All private suites. The recreation facilities are located downstairs – there's an indoor pool, a fitness center, a theatre, an arcade. The south wing houses security personnel, who are on site twenty-four seven, as well as private suites for the occasional client who requires secure accommodations. Elly and her husband live here full time. Come, I'll show you the lake view out the back of the house. That's the view I'd like you to paint."

I follow Jamie and Gus down a hallway to the rear of the house, passing a library on the left and a huge, formal dining room on the right.

"Is that an elevator?" I say, when we pass a wooden panel embedded in the wall.

"Yes."

The hallway leads to an impressive great room at the rear of the house. I walk to the center of the room, trying to take it all in. The space is huge, yet visually organized into several distinct areas, which makes the space feel cozy in spite of its size.

There are several seating areas arranged beneath soaring ceilings. There's a full-sized bar in one corner of the room. And the focal point is a massive stone hearth that extends all the way up to the exposed wooden rafters overhead. But my eye is drawn to the back wall, which is floor-to-ceiling glass providing a sweeping view of the Lake Michigan shoreline and the vast body of water that extends as far as the eye can see.

I walk up to the glass and peer outside at the wooden terrace that wraps around the back of the house, with several bistro style tables arranged for entertaining. Wooden steps lead down to a beautifully tended lawn that slopes gently toward the shoreline. I can see docks off to the south where quite a few boats are moored beneath metal canopies. I can make out at least two speed boats, a pontoon, a sailboat, and a catamaran, all bobbing gently with the ebb and flow of the water. In the distance a number of yachts glide effortlessly over the surface of the water.

My heart rate picks up. "What a magnificent view."

Jamie laughs. "So I've been told."

I'm such an idiot! "You've never seen it?"

He shakes his head. "I was still active in the military when Shane built this place. I was stationed either at Coronado, in California, or overseas in Afghanistan or Iraq. I never had a chance to visit before my accident. After I left the military, Shane brought me here to recuperate, and I lived here for several years until I moved to Wicker Park."

He leans close and bumps my shoulder with his. "Describe it for me."

"I'm sure someone's described it to you before now."

"Yes, but I want to hear it from your perspective. You're the artist. I'm sure your interpretation is different than anything I've ever heard."

I do my best to ignore the thrill that flashes through me at his compliment. He has no idea how validating his words are – and how much I need that kind of validation. Todd humored my career choice, but he never took it seriously. In college, where we met, he saw my art major as cute and quirky. He indulged me only because he could afford to. As soon as he finished his law degree and started working for his father's law firm, he'd be raking in a six-figure income right off the bat. He could afford to support a wife who had a frivolous career, as he viewed it.

"Well?" Jamie says, leaning into me.

"You really want me to?"

"I wouldn't have asked if I didn't."

I glance at him, taking advantage of the fact that I can secretly admire his profile. Then I look back at the view and describe it to him as a painter would see it. I describe the shape of the land, the movement of color and form as the view transitions from lawn to wild grasses to the sandy shore. I describe the trees surrounding the beach, as well as the outcroppings of rocks in the water. I describe the waves of water cresting against the rocks, splashing and spraying before they flow back out into the lake. I describe the colors I see, the multitudes of blues and greens, the creams, ochres, and browns, even the complex layers of blue and gray and white filling the skies. It looks like rain is headed our way.

"It's beautiful," I say wistfully, already mentally sketching out my plan for capturing the view.

He lays his arm across my shoulders and pulls me close. "That's the best description I've ever heard. You win, hands down."

13

Molly

Jamie's arm feels solid and comforting across my shoulders, sending waves of warm pleasure down my spine. I glance at his face, which is turned toward the window, and study his profile. I love how his beard frames his lips. The contrast between the short, neat hairs of his beard and the dusky pink flesh of his lips makes my pulse race.

I've kissed more than a few guys in my life. I dated several guys in high school and college before I met Todd. But I've never paid such acute attention to the nuances of a man's body.

Even now, the heat radiating from his big body warms me, making me want to lean into him. I breathe in, drawing in the subtle fragrances of laundry soap and a man's expensive cologne, and something else, something far less tangible, the natural scent of him, of his skin, his maleness. He smells so good.

I'm overwhelmed by a sudden desire to melt into him, to turn to him and feel those long arms wrap around me and hold me close. I want to press my nose against his shirt and breathe him in.

I swallow hard, shaking myself out of my fantasy, and attempt to focus on the reason we're here. "The view really is lovely," I say, desperate to change the subject. "It'll be a pleasure to paint."

He chuckles. "So, how will you paint it?"

"Since I paint abstracts, it's not my goal to realistically recreate the view. Instead, I latch on to the *themes* of the view, to the shapes and the lines and the color palette. My goal is to capture the *feel* of the place and recreate that in color and texture. It'll be recognizable to those who are familiar with this view, but it won't be a photographic representation by any means."

He's facing forward again, as if looking out the window, and smiling. I look outside again and put my artist's hat on, trying to focus on the landscape and not on the man standing beside me.

"I love the color palette of Lake Michigan," I say. "The greens of the foliage, the neutrals of the sandy and rocky shoreline, and the grays and blues of the water. I love the way the light and shadows interact with each other on the water's surface. Looks like there's a storm rolling in, I see lots of ominous storm clouds bringing shadows and depth as they swallow the light."

He nods. "The juxtaposition of calm versus the storm."

I smile, thrilled that he gets what I see. "The moment before all hell breaks loose."

Jamie nods in approval. "Shane and Beth have faced some pretty significant challenges in their relationship. I think they can weather the threat of an oncoming storm. Besides, stormy seas are much more exciting to sail than calm ones."

I wonder if he's still talking about his brother and Beth, or if he's talking about himself now, because God knows, he's had his own stormy seas to navigate.

Jamie skims his hand across the glass until he locates the latch on the sliding door. "Let's walk down to the shore," he says.

As he slides open the door, cool air wafts inside, bringing with it the scent of water and foliage and earth. I shiver as I zip up my jacket.

Gus jumps to his feet, eager to join us outside, but Jamie tells him to lie down. "You'd better stay inside, buddy," he tells the dog. "We're walking down to the water, and you won't like that." Then he offers me his arm. "Do you mind being my guide?"

I slip my arm around his, smiling. "I'd be happy to."

* * *

I grab my camera bag, and we step through the open door out onto the wooden terrace.

I pause at the edge of the terrace to get out my camera. "Before we go down to the shore, I want to take some reference shots from here." I get some panoramic shots of the landscape and the vista, trying to set the stage for the painting. Once I have enough shots, we start down the terrace steps.

Jamie lays his hand on my shoulder and follows right behind me down the steps and along the well-worn path leading to the beach.

He squeezes my shoulder and laughs. "You don't have to go slowly on my account. I can keep up."

We walk down to the shoreline, which is mostly sand. There

are some outcroppings of rocks and tall grasses along the edge of the private beach. I take pictures of everything from every possible angle… the rocks, the sandy beach, the water as it laps against the shore. I take pictures of the boats docked to the south.

Jamie is patient and silent as I concentrate on surveying the area. I jot down notes in my little fieldbook and make some rough sketches.

I glance out across the water, watching sailboats zip across the horizon. "If I lived here, I'd never want to leave."

As soon as I say that, we hear a chorus of horses whinnying off in the distance.

"Elly's probably giving them hay," Jamie says. "Would you like to see the horses and the barn?"

"I'd love to." I glance up at the darkening skies, thinking our opportunity for exploring will be coming to an end soon. "We'd better hurry. The rain isn't far off."

Jamie points me toward the sound of the horses. "There's a path that cuts through the woods and leads right up to the barn. Do you see it?"

There's an opening in the trees and a shady path through the woods. "I see it."

He lays his hand my shoulder and follows me, matching his steps with mine. I'm amazed by how confidently he moves through space, following my lead. If I were in his shoes, I don't think I would be nearly as confident.

When we come into view of the barn, I see Elly in the corral with the horses, who are all busy munching on hay. Two of the adults are a lovely chestnut color, reddish brown with darker manes and tales. The third adult is a lovely silvery gray. The fourth – the foal's mother – is a pale cream color with even paler mane and tail. The foal looks like a perfect miniature version of the mother.

"I know absolutely nothing about horses," I say.

"Take us to the gate," he says. "It's near the barn. They're all American Quarter horses, three geldings and one mare."

"How old is the baby?" I ask.

"He's about four months old."

Just as thunder rumbles in the distance, Elly disappears inside the barn. She returns a moment later carrying a halter with an attached lead. "Would you two mind bringing Giselle and Casper in for me? I don't want the colt out in this storm, and I need to go inside to start on your supper."

As Jamie holds the gate open for Elly, she hands him the lead and gives me a warm smile and a wink.

Jamie latches the gate behind us. "Would you lead me to the mare?"

Just as before, I walk Jamie to the mare and her foal. Once I get him there, he takes over, clearly in his element.

Talking in a low, soothing voice, he reaches for the mare's head and gently strokes her face, running the tips of his fingers from her forehead to her muzzle. He leans closer, brushing his nose against hers, blowing air out of his nostrils. She returns the gesture, nickering at him in greeting. It's obvious they're old friends. Giselle moves closer to him, brushing her head against Jamie's shoulder as he settles the halter over her head and buckles it in place.

Just as we hear thunder rumbling in the distance, a light rain begins to fall. The colt prances nervously around his mother, never straying far from her side.

"Would you walk us to the barn doors?" Jamie says, laying his hand on my shoulder.

I lead Jamie to the barn, and he leads the mare. The foal follows his mother.

The inside of the barn is warm and smells like freshly-cut hay, leather, and grain. There are several horse stalls on each side of the wide central corridor, and in the loft above the stalls there are countless stacks of hay and straw bales.

The mare pushes eagerly forward, heading straight for an open stall.

"They go in the third stall on the right," Jamie says, controlling the mare's eager progress.

I lead him to the designated stall, and Jamie guides the mare right inside, the foal following her in. Once they are both safely inside, he latches the stall door, then removes the mare's halter as she hangs her head over the door. The foal nuzzles its mother and begins to nurse.

The other three horses stroll single file into the barn and head for their respective stalls. Jamie walks up and down the corridor, latching the stall doors and securing the horses. Then he throws a bit of hay into each occupied stall.

"Just in time," I say, because I can hear the rain hitting the roof. I move to stand by the open barn doors to look out at the approaching storm and watch the rain, which is now coming down pretty hard. Lightning streaks across the darkened skies, followed quickly by deafening cracks of thunder.

It looks like we're stuck in the barn unless we don't mind getting drenched. I, for one, am content to wait here for the rain to pass.

I set my camera bag down on a stack of straw bales, safely out of the way of the raining blowing in through the open barn doors.

"Molly?"

"I'm over here," I say.

Jamie follows the sound of my voice, using a rough-hewn walking stick as a guide. When he reaches me, he props the stick against the barn wall and stands beside me. Outside, it's chilly, but inside the barn it's rather cozy.

"That was pretty impressive," I say. "You haltering the horse and leading her in."

He laughs. "Elly did that on purpose. I can take care of these horses with my hands tied behind my back. I can groom them, muck out their stalls, feed them, saddle them, even ride. I used to spend hours each day out here working with the horses. There's something very comforting about manual labor and carrying for animals. I think Elly sees it as a form of therapy."

"Elly sounds like a pretty smart woman."

He nods. "Yeah. She is."

We stand there for a few moments, listening to the storm. The cool, damp air blowing into the barn feels good on my face.

I shiver when I feel Jamie tug on a strand of my hair. Then his hand slips beneath my hair and cups the back of my neck, giving it a gentle squeeze.

He runs his fingers down a strand of my hair, measuring its length. His fingers complete their trek just shy of my bra strap, making me nervous. I pull away.

"I'm sorry," he says, releasing my hair.

"No, it's fine." I laugh nervously to cover up the awkward moment. His touch felt good. Too good, in fact. That's the problem. "It's fine, really. I'm just not accustomed to being touched."

He's pensive for a moment. "Have you dated anyone since your divorce?"

"No."

"Do you still love him?"

"Who, Todd? God no."

"How can you be so sure?"

"Because, he's not the same man he was when I met him. He's changed. Or, maybe he let down his guard and is showing his true colors now. No, I don't love him. The day he betrayed our marriage vows, he became someone I could *never* love."

"Do you think about dating again?"

His question takes me by surprise. "Not really." *I've had enough rejection to last a lifetime.* I can't tell him that, though, so I tell him the other part of it – which is also true. "Frankly, I'm enjoying being on my own for the first time in my life. I've never lived alone before now, and I'm finding I like it. I'm finally figuring out who *I* am."

He nods. "I know what you mean. I'm living on my own for the first time too. I went from my parent's home to a college dorm to the military, where I shared a house with two other guys. Then, after my accident, I came to live here. Now, I've got my own place, and I'm enjoying it."

Lightning fills the sky to the south, followed by a deafening crack of thunder that sounds like it's awfully close. I jump, taking a step back from the open door and coming up against Jamie. He lays his hands on my shoulders to steady me.

"Sorry," I say.

"That's all right."

The wind changes direction and begins blowing rain through the open barn doors, spraying us with a fine, icy mist. Jamie draws me away from the opening.

"It looks like we're stuck here for a while," I say.

"I'm okay with that. I'm in good company."

I laugh nervously. *Oh, my God, is he flirting with me? Surely not.* "What about you? Are you dating someone? Is there a girlfriend in the picture? For a while, I thought Beth might be your girlfriend. You two seem close."

"We are close, yes. She lived here for a couple of months over the summer, and we got to know each other well. She was having a rough time of it, recuperating from some injuries. She needed a friend. I think we both did. She's one of my best friends now."

"She seems nice."

"She is. She's one of the kindest, most caring people I've ever met. Shane's very lucky. And to answer your question, no. I'm not seeing anyone."

His hand slides down my arm until it reaches my hand, and he links our fingers together. His big hand practically swallows mine, and his grasp is warm and comforting. His touch makes me go weak in the knees.

He squeezes my hand gently. "Molly? Would you consider going out with me?"

My heartbeat quickens. "You mean, on a date?"

The corners of his mouth quirk up in a half smile, betraying his amusement. "Yes, on a date."

Of course, he meant on a date! But I don't know what to say. God, I want to, yes. But I can't. "Jamie, I – " My response comes to a stuttering end as my desires go to war with my common sense.

"I know you think you're not ready to be with someone again. I realize your ex-husband hurt you, and maybe you're not over that yet. I know you're afraid that he'll target me if I get too close to you. I get all that, and I understand. But I also think we'd be really good together, and we're worth taking a chance on. I'm hoping you agree."

I forget my train of thought when he brings his hands up to cradle my face, moving carefully, deliberately, as if gentling a skittish animal. His thumbs brush against my cheeks, and I stand there frozen. I look up into his face, into a pair of dark glasses that mask his emotions. I wish he'd take the glasses off, so I could see his face and read him better.

He swallows hard and parts his lips on a shaky inhalation.

Oh, my God, he's going to kiss me.

14

Molly

I realize his intentions just a heartbeat before he lowers his mouth to mine. His warm hands feel good on my chilled face as he tips my face up to meet his. My eyelids drift shut as I savor the feel of his lips as they gently brush against mine, soft and coaxing, sending a spark of pleasure coursing through me.

It's been so long since anyone has kissed me I've almost forgotten what it feels like. The relationship with Todd had been strained long before I caught him in bed with another woman, so it's truly been a while for me. I'm not sure I'm ready for this.

His lips graze mine, gently at first, tentatively, as if asking for permission. The fact that he's not demanding or assuming anything makes me like him that much more. Desire starts coiling low in my belly, warming me, giving me a tantalizing taste of what it would be like to surrender to my body's desires.

I feel shaken, completely unbalanced. In a desperate effort to find something solid to hang onto, I reach out and grasp his arms. His biceps are hard as rocks. And when I touch them, they flex and tense, as if he's just as affected by the contact.

I'm convinced I have to put a stop to this when his lips settle more firmly on mine, creating pull and suction as he seals our kiss. My brain short-circuits, and I lose all coherent thought. His lips coax mine open, and I selfishly give in to the pleasure. *Just for a moment.*

I indulge myself, letting his lips mold themselves to mine. When I suck in a shaky breath, he takes advantage of the opportunity to slip his tongue in and explore the inside of my mouth. When his tongue strokes mine, I feel a direct connection low in my belly, where desire is throbbing inside me. All I can do is hold onto his arms for dear life.

Jamie groans low in his throat as he cups the back of my head with one hand, cushioning me as he presses me against the barn wall. He looms over me, deepening our kiss with a hunger that matches my own.

Through the haze of my arousal, I remind myself to maintain some distance between us. I grab hold of the front halves of his jacket, both of my hands fisting the material to prevent him from pressing his chest fully against mine and coming into contact with my prosthetic breast forms. I don't know if he'd be able to tell they're prosthetics or not, and frankly, I don't want to find out. I can't afford to let him get too close. I never realized how self-conscious I am about my body until now. But then, no one's ever come so close before, other than Todd.

Jamie abruptly breaks away and steps back, releasing me to run his fingers through his hair. His chest is heaving as he sucks in air. I should be grateful he put a stop to the kiss, but in all honesty, I feel sadly bereft.

A second later, I realize why he pulled back. We're not alone.

Elly is standing just inside the barn, her blue eyes wide as she gawks at us. She was clearly caught by surprise, but I'm not sure if it's a good surprise or a bad one.

She's wearing an oversized raincoat and galoshes and holding an umbrella. Tucked under her other arm is another umbrella. "Oh, my God, I'm so sorry," she gasps, her free hand pressed to her lips. "I had no idea."

That makes two of us. I smile at her, despite the awkwardness of the situation.

"It was raining so hard," she says, "I figured you'd need an umbrella to make it back to the house. And since supper is nearly ready..." Her voice trails off as she looks from Jamie to me and back to Jamie. When her gaze settles on me once more, she smiles warmly.

I hold my hand out for the umbrella. "Thanks, Elly."

She hands it to me. "I'll just head back to the kitchen to finish getting supper ready. You two take your time. There's no rush. I'll keep your food warm."

When she dashes back out into the rain, gone as quickly as she arrived, Jamie and I both dissolve into quiet laughter.

"I think she got an eye full," I say.

Jamie seems amused. "I'd say she did."

I open the umbrella, eager to take the cowardly way out. If I pretend it never happened, maybe he'll follow my lead. "We'd better head to the house."

He catches my arm. "Molly, wait."

My heart climbs up into my throat. "What?"

"You never answered me."

Oh, crap. After that kiss, how can he possibly expect me to remember what we were discussing? "I'm sorry. What was the question?"

"Molly, I want to see you. Will you have dinner with me tomorrow?"

My ears are ringing, and my face is flushed. Our kiss may have been short – and prematurely interrupted – but I'd wanted more. I'd wanted it to go on and on and on. It had felt *so* good.

Every time he touches me, it feels good. But my disastrous marriage comes to mind, and I immediately nix the idea of letting this go any further. I was wrong to think that losing my breasts wouldn't come with serious repercussions. Obviously, it did. I don't want to experience that kind of rejection again, especially from Jamie.

I close my eyes, the pain of regret knifing through me before I even open my mouth. "Jamie, I'm sorry. I really like you, a lot, but I'm just not looking to date anyone right now. It's nothing personal. I'm not sure I'll ever be ready to do that again."

Even as I say the words, I hate myself. I hate myself for being a coward, because every damn word I said was a lie. I hate myself for hurting him – surely it took a lot of courage on his part to even ask me. I'm sure he has his own insecurities and misgivings given his blindness.

Jamie nods, although he's frowning. "Sure, I understand."

He holds his hand out to me, and it takes me a moment to realize he wants the umbrella. I hand it to him, and he holds it high above our heads.

"Do you mind?" he says, laying his other hand on my shoulder.

I hate that he even needs to ask if I'll be his eyes. "Of course, I don't mind. You don't need to ask."

We head out into the rain, Jamie holding the big umbrella over both of us, shielding us from the worst of the rain. Neither one of us says a word on the way to the house, and I'm afraid my rejection has put a damper on our new-found friendship.

I was so focused on myself and my reaction to his kiss that I never truly considered how my answer to his question might affect him. The last thing I want to do is hurt him.

"Head for the side door with an awning over it," Jamie says, as we near the house. "That door leads right into the mud room off the kitchen. We can dry off there."

When we reach the side entrance, Jamie reaches around me to open the door and hold it for me. I step inside the warm mud room, and Jamie shakes the excess rain from the umbrella and follows me inside.

We hang up our coats, then head into the kitchen. My stomach growls when I smell the savory aroma of a roasting chicken. Elly's standing at the island counter tossing a salad.

She glances up at us. "Perfect timing. Your supper's ready. I'm sorry the weather's not cooperating with your visit today."

"It's all right," I say. "I was able to see the view of the lake from the house well before the rain started. I got what I needed."

There's a small table in the kitchen, situated in front of a brick hearth with a blazing log fire, and it's already set for two.

"I thought it would be cozier for the two of you to eat in here," she says, carrying the salad bowl to the table. "The fire will help warm your bones."

"Thank you, Elly," I say, truly touched by her thoughtfulness.

"This is lovely."

At the sound of my voice, Gus comes running into the kitchen. Jamie greets the dog, then pulls out a chair for me. He seems subdued, and there's a tightness in his expression that tells me he's trying to hide his disappointment.

"Thank you," I say.

"No problem."

Even when he's unhappy, he's still unfailingly polite.

Gus lies down on a rug in front of the hearth as Jamie takes the seat opposite mine.

"This looks wonderful, Elly, thank you," I tell her when she serves us a very delicious meal – roasted chicken breasts and potatoes, steamed asparagus, salad and warm rolls. I wish she hadn't gone to such trouble.

Her pensive gaze gravitates to Jamie's stoic expression. Finally, she gives me a hopeful smile. "I'll just leave you two to enjoy your meal. There's warm apple cobbler on the stove and vanilla ice cream in the freezer. Please help yourselves."

Elly departs, leaving us alone again, which I'm sure was her goal. We eat in silence, the only sounds coming from the dog snoring on the hearth rug and the crackling pops and steaming hisses made by the burning logs in the fireplace.

Jamie has barely said a word to me since the barn. I feel like I owe him an apology. "Jamie – "

"It's fine, Molly," he says, his voice calm, yet curt. "You don't have to explain yourself."

I watch Jamie's long fingers as he deftly cuts his chicken and eats his meal. I remember very clearly how those fingers felt on my face. And, of course, that leads to reliving the feel of his lips on mine. I still can't believe he kissed me.

I try once more to explain myself. "I value your friendship very much," I tell him, cringing as I know how condescending that sounds, how cliché. It's the oldest excuse in the book, but in this case, it's true. "I wouldn't want to jeopardize that."

"Our friendship means a lot to me, too." He wipes his mouth on a napkin and sighs. "I apologize if I was out of line earlier. Back in the barn. I shouldn't have kissed you. I'm sorry."

The suggestion that he regrets kissing me hurts.

Elly pops her head through the open kitchen door. "Jake's back. He just pulled up," she says. "I just thought I'd let you know."

After we finish our meal, we head to the great room to sit and relax a bit before the fire in the big hearth. The warm, cheery fire in the great room is a welcome sight, as the day has turned decidedly cold and bleak, and not just because of the weather. Jamie joins his brother and Elly's husband, George, at the bar for drinks. Gus comes to lie down on the rug in front of the sofa, laying his head at my feet.

"Nothing for me, thanks," I say, when Jake offers to make me a drink. "I'm just going to sit here and watch the storm." Outside the wall of windows, the storm rages on. Lightning streaks across the dark sky, followed by the distant crack of thunder.

"Quite a storm we're having this evening," Elly says, taking a seat beside me on the sofa. She's holding a cup of hot tea.

I smile at her. "Yes, it is."

"Can I get you a cup?"

"No, thanks. I'm still full from that delicious meal."

Elly's gaze drifts over to the bar, where the three men are conversing. Jake's standing behind the bar, acting as the bartender. Jamie and George are seated on adjacent barstools facing him. I can't quite make out what they're saying, but at least they're laughing.

"He's doing all right by himself, isn't he?" Elly says, watching Jamie wistfully.

I know exactly who she's referring to. "Yes, he is. He has incredible coping skills. I've seen him do things I'd never thought a blind person capable of."

Elly nods, and I can tell from the set of her lips that she's suppressing strong emotions.

"He's like a son to me," she says. "I didn't want him to leave this house. In fact, I begged him not to, but he said it was something he had to do. Now, I can see he was right. There's something different about him. He seems more settled, happier."

"He seems happy to me, but then I don't really know him that well. I do know that he has lots of visitors coming to his apartment."

She smiles. "His brothers, I'm sure. And friends." She looks at me out of the corner of her eye, a sly smile on her face. "Are you, by chance, one of those visitors?"

I'm not sure how to answer that. "I'm his neighbor, so yes. We run into each other frequently."

She frowns. "Pardon me for being blunt, but what I saw you two doing in the barn was more than just being neighborly."

My face heats with embarrassment as I think about what she walked in on. She'd never believe me, though, if I told her that was the only time we'd kissed.

"I'm sorry," she says, eyeing my discomfort. "I didn't mean to pry."

My gaze drifts over to the bar, to Jamie in particular. He's laughing at something his brother said. Elly's husband claps Jamie on the back good naturedly, and it's clear that whatever Jake said, it was at Jamie's expense.

Elly sighs. "It's good to see him like that, laughing, just being one of the guys. When he first came here, he was sullen and kept to himself. It was so painful to watch him just trying to get through each day. It's taken him a long time to reclaim his life." She looks at me, a hopeful smile on her softly-wrinkled face. "He's a good man, Molly. He would make a wonderful husband."

* * *

It's almost six o'clock when Jamie asks me if I'm ready to head home.

"Sure," I say, hating that we have to leave. I've enjoyed chatting with Elly and watching Jamie interact with his brother and Elly's husband. But I guess all good things must come to an end, including our little road trip.

Packing up my camera gear and fieldbook, I follow Elly and the guys to the front door. The rain has stopped, but it's unusually dark this evening because of the heavy cloud cover. When Jamie relies on Gus to lead him down the front steps to the waiting SUV, regret stabs me. I feel like I lost something today, something precious and fragile that I'm just now realizing meant something to me.

After Jamie climbs into the front passenger seat, Jake puts Gus in the back of the vehicle. Then he opens the rear passenger door for me. I settle into the back seat and buckle my seat belt.

Jake climbs into the driver's seat. "Got everything?" he says, eyeing me in the rearview mirror as he starts the engine.

"Yes."

As Jake pulls away from the house, my heart is heavy, and there's a painful lump in my throat. Jamie hasn't said a word to me since dinner. I'm sure he regrets kissing me, and I really can't blame him. He went out on a limb for me – probably the first time he's done so since his accident – and I shot him down.

* * *

I'm lulled into a state of half-wakefulness on the drive home. The vehicle is toasty warm inside, and my belly is full from a wonderful dinner. The guys speak quietly, their baritone voices a soothing backdrop to the sounds of the vehicle driving on wet pavement.

I'm startled into wakefulness when Jake pulls up in front of our apartment building. The light from the lamp post blinds me as I gather my things.

Jake walks us up the steps to our building, and we say goodnight, thanking him for the ride and his company. He pats Jamie on the back, then gives my arm a gentle squeeze. "Goodnight, guys."

Jamie enters the security code and opens the door for me. We both stop in the foyer to collect our mail, then head up to our respective apartments. We may live just yards from each other, but right now it feels like we're miles apart. I just want to get inside my apartment before I start bawling like a baby.

The moment I close my apartment door behind me, I feel my throat tighten up as hot tears sting my eyes. What happened today? Somehow, we went from a budding friendship that meant the world to me to a total crash-and-burn. It happened so fast. Somewhere between an impromptu kiss and a rejected offer of a date, everything went wrong.

I jump when I hear a light knock on my door. After wiping my damp eyes, I glance out the peephole. It's Jamie, along with Gus.

My heart thuds painfully as I open the door partway. "Jamie," I say, hoping he won't hear the tears in my voice.

His hair is a tousled mess, as if he's been running his fingers through it. He braces one arm against the door frame and sighs. "May we come in? Just for a minute."

"Sure." I step back to give them room to enter. "Come on in."

Jamie takes a few hesitant steps into my apartment, then stops just a couple of feet from me. "Molly, I owe you an apology."

His heartfelt apology takes me completely by surprise. "For what?"

"For being an ass. I didn't handle this afternoon well. I hope you'll forgive me. I don't want to lose your friendship."

The pain in his voice magnifies my own. "There's nothing to forgive, Jamie. And I don't want to lose your friendship either."

He reaches for my hand, and I offer it to him. He squeezes it gently. "Good. I'm glad."

He looks relieved.

After one more light squeeze, he releases my hand and backs toward the door, reaching behind himself to feel for the door jamb. "Sleep well. I'll see you soon."

And then he's gone, closing my apartment door behind him.

I lock the door and head to the bathroom to get ready for bed. It's not that late, but I feel too out of sorts to do anything this evening. I just want to climb into bed and read for a while, anything to get my mind off Jamie and how much I want to call him and tell him I've changed my mind about that offer of a date.

15

Jamie

Discouraged and bereft, I head back to my apartment wondering what the hell happened today. It's all my fault. Just as we were growing closer, I jumped the gun and kissed her. I shouldn't have done that. Now she's running in the opposite direction.

When I get back to my own apartment, I remove Gus's harness and hang it on its designated hook by the door. Gus shakes, then runs off to do God knows what. I grab a bottle of beer from the fridge and crash on the living room sofa, propping my boots up on the coffee table. I grab my voice-activated remote control. "TV on. Play ESPN."

There's some kind of sports commentary show on, but I don't

really care which one. I turned it on mostly to have some background noise to help offset the noise in my head. One thing about being blind - you tend to spend a lot of time living inside your own head. It gets noisy in there sometimes, like right now when I'm reliving that kiss over and over.

What is it about Molly that draws me in? What do I know about her? I know the sound of her voice. I know the sound of her laughter. I know what she smells like. She's creative - she has to be, to be an artist. She's afraid of her ex-husband, who's an asshole. I'd like to go five minutes in the ring with him.

When I'm with her, my body vibrates with awareness, and my dick sits up and takes notice. I know that when I kissed her today in the barn I felt like I'd finally come home. I'd wanted to wrap her in my arms and roll her in the fresh hay. I'd wanted to unwrap her body and explore every inch of it. Taste every inch of it.

Instead, I fucked everything up. Damn it!

My phone rings, and I know it's Jake from the ringtone. I use a different ringtone for each family member and friend who's likely to call me. Jake's ringtone is "Born to Be Bad."

I answer the call. "Hey, what's up?"

"What the hell happened this afternoon? You and Molly didn't say a word to each other on the drive back from Kenilworth."

I take a swig of my beer and swallow. "I fucked up. That's what happened."

Jake laughs. "How so?"

"I kissed her in the barn."

"I see. And she took it badly?"

"Not exactly. I got the feeling she liked the kiss. I mean, she grabbed onto me and kissed me back. It was when I asked her out on a date that things went south. She put me squarely in the friend zone."

"Oh, man, that's rough."

"I stopped by her apartment a few minutes ago to apologize."

"What'd she say?"

"I told her I was sorry and that I didn't want to mess up our friendship. She agreed."

"Hey, man, don't give up, okay? I saw her watching you today. On the drive up and back, she hung on your every word. I don't think you should throw in the towel quite yet. Just take it slowly and be cool."

We say goodbye, and despite Jake's advice to not give up, I can't help thinking it's probably for the best that she doesn't want to go there with me. Molly's an amazing woman. Why would she saddle herself with a blind man? My goal is to be self-sufficient, and I am self-sufficient in most things. I have a secure job, and I make a decent income. But there will always be things I can't manage on my own. That's just a fact of life.

I mope on the couch for another couple of hours, mindlessly surfing the TV, listening to nothing worthwhile. Gus lies on the floor beside the couch. I wonder what Molly's doing. She's probably in bed by now. Maybe she's thinking about what happened in the barn too. Problem is, I don't know if her thoughts are good or bad.

"Come on, Gus," I say, getting off the couch. "Let's take you out so you can take a piss. And then we'll both hit the hay."

* * *

Early Sunday morning, Jake picks me up and we head to the gym to work out. There's a neighborhood fitness center we've started frequenting a few days a week. It's nothing fancy – it's hardcore fitness equipment, free weights, machines, ellipticals, treadmills, and an indoor running track. There are no giant TV screens or smoothie bars. No giftshop. It's just a bunch of fitness nuts working on strength and endurance.

Jake and I work out together, spotting each other with the free weights. I need his help with a few things, but I can manage a lot of it on my own.

"It's too bad you don't have room in your apartment for a weight machine or a treadmill," Jake says. "You could work out at home."

"Yeah, that would be nice."

"There are some storage rooms downstairs, beneath your apartment and Molly's. Maybe one of those could be renovated to make room for some equipment."

"I don't know if the new landlord would agree to that," I say. "It would increase his liability insurance."

Jake makes a scoffing sound. "You haven't figured out who your new landlord is yet? Seriously?"

"You're kidding."

"I'm not kidding. He bought the building as soon as Beth told him you'd signed a lease. I don't think you have to worry about getting the okay to add a workout room to the building."

16

Molly

After a quiet Sunday morning at home, just messing around the house, I decide to head out. My plan is to go to the studio to get a jump start on Jamie's commission. My shop is closed to the public on Sundays and Mondays, but I often go in anyway. I can get a lot of work done when it's just me there in the studio.

I love my studio. I love being surrounded by paintings in various stages of progress. Besides, I like to work. I like to keep busy. It's better than sitting alone in my apartment and contemplating my future. Right now I feel like I'm in limbo, still trying to completely separate Todd from my life and deciding where I want said future to lead.

As I exit my apartment, locking the deadbolt, I glance down the hallway toward Jamie's apartment. I'm tempted to knock on his door – just to say hi. I still feel unsettled about what happened yesterday at his brother's house – in the barn specifically. I can't believe he kissed me. My stomach is still doing somersaults just thinking about it. Even now, the thought of his lips on mine makes my heart race.

I feel horrible for turning down his offer of a date, but saying no was my only option. Todd would make Jamie's life hell if he thought we were dating, and I just can't expose him to that kind of jeopardy. Also, I'm just not ready to be intimate with someone.

Just this morning as I got out of the shower and dried off, I stared at my reflection in the foggy bathroom mirror. Even a year after the surgery, I still don't recognize my own body. The two scars are shiny, irregular lines, and even though it's been a year since the surgery, they're still pink. I'm afraid that if Jamie hugged me, he might be able to tell I have prosthetic breasts. I have to wonder if he'd still be interested in me if he knew I didn't have breasts.

As I'm heading out, I deviate slightly and find myself in front of Jamie's door. I stand there quietly, listening for signs that he's home, but I hear nothing. Part of me wants to knock, on the chance that he is home and I get to see his face and hear his voice. But another part of me thinks I shouldn't. I really do want to be friends with him – I'd rather have something of him in my life than nothing – but I don't want to lead him on.

The desire to see him, even if just for a few moments, wins out. Taking a deep breath to fortify myself, I knock on his door – three strong raps with my knuckles. I expect Gus to come running to the door, to bark, but there's nothing but silence on the other side. I wait a couple of minutes, giving him time to respond, then knock once more, louder this time. When there's no response, I head outside.

Tamping down my disappointment, I jog down the staircase and just as I reach for the door knob, the door opens, and there's Jamie with Gus. Jamie's dressed in jeans and sneakers, and his leather jacket. He's holding Gus's halter in one hand and a sack of groceries in the crook of his other arm.

"Jamie, hi!" My voice sounds breathless and flustered, and inwardly I cringe.

His thick hair is slightly tousled by the wind, making him look rakish, especially with those dark glasses. But it's the sudden smile lighting up his face that catches my attention. I was so afraid that my rejection yesterday would ruin our burgeoning friendship. Apparently not. He looks genuinely happy to see me.

He wedges the door open with a broad shoulder. "Hi, Molly. Where are you off to?"

I can't help the stupid, relieved smile on my face – the one he can't see. "I'm going to my studio to get a start on your brother's painting while the images are still fresh in my mind."

His smile broadens. "Do you mind if Gus and I stop by for a visit later?"

"I'd love it." My heart races at the thought of seeing him again. That, and I'm so relieved he's not angry at me. "The shop's closed today, but if you text me when you arrive, I can let you in."

I know there's a stupid grin on my face as I head toward my studio. I'm just happy that he's talking to me, and that I'm going to see him again this afternoon. I'm so glad what happened in his brother's barn didn't ruin our budding friendship. I don't want to lose the little bit of him that I'm allowed to have.

* * *

Despite being preoccupied with thoughts of Jamie, I'm actually able to get quite a bit of work done. I also prep the canvas for Jamie's commission. Even though I have a number of projects ahead of his in the queue, I'm anxious to start on his. So, in between laying down several layers of paint on a couple of other projects, I prime his canvas, then lay down a couple subtle washes of color and sketch out the general shape of the composition in pencil.

I know exactly how I want to paint the view out of Shane and Beth's home. I can picture it all – the gently sloping lawn, the sandy beach, the foamy surf, and finally the water, all of which will be overshadowed by a storm in full force. And yet, behind the churning storm clouds are skies of clear blue. Sort of the opposite of what happened yesterday. In my painting, the storm is on its way out, to be replaced with clear weather. My painting will represent the aftermath of the storm – symbolically, the promise of better times coming on the heels of adversity. Hopefully, this will be a good omen for Shane and Beth's upcoming wedding.

I'm just finishing up the final glaze on a pair of commissioned paintings when Jamie's text comes in. He's out front. I glance at the clock on the wall and am surprised to see it's almost five. The afternoon has flown.

I grab a hand towel and wipe my hands as I head to the front of the shop. There, standing outside my door, are Jamie and Gus. As I approach the door, I realize Jamie's holding a bouquet of lilacs and baby's breath wrapped in white tissue paper and tied off with a bow.

He brought me flowers.

My breath catches in my throat, and I find it difficult to breathe.

After all the times I've turned him down, he still brings me flowers? *Oh, my God, I don't deserve this.* My heart feels shredded, and I don't know how much longer I can make up excuses to avoid doing the one thing I want more than anything in the world.

I unlock the door and step aside as he and Gus come in, bringing in a gust of frigid air.

"A little birdy told me your favorite flowers are lilacs." He hands me the dainty bouquet. "It's not easy to find lilacs at this time of year, I'll have you know. I had to call three florists to find them."

A little birdy? I can guess who that is. I bring the bouquet to my nose and inhale its exquisite fragrance. "They're beautiful, Jamie." I suddenly find myself choking up as tears clog my throat. "Thank you."

"Hey." He drops Gus's harness and lays his hands on my shoulders, gripping me gently. "What's wrong?"

I sniff. "It's nothing. I just really love lilacs."

He chuckles. "Wow, you're easy to please. If I'd known you'd react like this, I would have been bringing you lilacs every day since I met you."

I laugh shakily. "I have an empty vase in the backroom. Let's go put them in some water."

Jamie and Gus follow me into the backroom, and I dig an empty vase out from the cupboard beneath the sink, fill it partway with water, and add the flowers along with the packet of plant food I find tucked inside the tissue paper.

I wipe my damp eyes and collect myself. "Can I get you something to drink?"

Jamie removes his jacket and drapes it over the back of a chair. He's wearing a gray Henley T-shirt that hugs his torso, emphasizing his strong shoulders and well-defined biceps. I can't help staring as his arm muscles bunch and flex when he moves.

The top two buttons of his shirt are undone, and my gaze lights on the bit of brown chest hair peeking out of the opening. I wonder what those hairs would feel like against my cheek. Todd has no hair on his chest, so I can only imagine. I'm struck with an urge to press my nose against his throat, to nuzzle him and breathe him in.

Jamie takes a seat at my little round table. "What have you got?"

"I have soft drinks, water, and a few bottles of Goose Island. Would you like a beer?"

"Water's fine," he says, surprising me. I thought for sure he'd go for the beer.

I grab two bottles of chilled spring water and bring them to the table, where I sit down in the chair opposite his.

"How's the work coming along?" he says, opening his bottle.

"Fine. The canvas for your painting is prepped. Once it's dry, I'll start on the composition, hopefully tomorrow."

"Tomorrow? Don't you ever take a break? You can't work seven days a week, Molly. You'll wear yourself out."

"I love what I do, so it's really not work." I open my bottle of water and take a sip. "How about you? What's your work schedule like?"

He smiles guiltily. "I write every day."

"Um, how?"

"I dictate into a digital recorder, then I send the recordings to my editor, who converts them to manuscripts. After they're edited, they come back to me for revisions, and we repeat the process."

"How long does it take you to write a book?"

"About six months, with all the back and forth between me and my editor. I'm working on my sixth novel now, so we have the routine worked out pretty well."

"I'm glad you have a job that you enjoy and that you can do from home."

"Right after the accident, my biggest fear was that I wouldn't be able to support myself. When I came to live in Shane's house, I spent hours sitting alone, feeling lost. Elly introduced me to the world of audiobooks, and that got me reading again."

"I'd tell Elly stories about my experiences in the teams, and she suggested I start capturing them. She bought me a digital recorder, and then one thing led to another. I'd always loved to read, but I never dreamed I'd end up writing for a living."

I love listening to him talk. His smooth baritone voice is sexy and soothing, very fitting for his big frame.

"Elly cares about you," I say. "A lot. She misses you."

He nods. "She didn't want me to move out. Neither did Shane. But Beth got it. She understood why I needed to live on my own for a while. She helped me find my apartment."

I'm startled by a sharp knock at the back door.

Jamie's head snaps up. "Are you expecting someone?"

"No." My heart starts hammering because there's only one person who ever comes to the back door besides the delivery people, and that's Todd. I can't let Todd see Jamie here.

As I rise from my seat, Jamie stands too. I can't help wondering if he's picking up on my unease. There's a second knock, and that propels me to the door, so I can see out the peep hole. Sure enough, Todd's standing there, his face illuminated by the light coming from the lamp overhead. "It's Todd."

I glance back at Jamie, who's facing me, his hands fisted at his sides. I've never seen him look so tense, like he's on high alert. I guess you can take the man out of the military, but you can't take the military out of the man.

Even Gus is up on his feet as he goes to stand at Jamie's side, pressing up against Jamie's leg as if he senses a threat. I'm not sure if Gus is trying to protect Jamie, or if he's looking for protection himself.

I hesitate, not wanting to open the door. If Todd sees me with Jamie, it'll only bring unwanted attention in Jamie's direction.

Todd knocks again, this time harder, and I flinch.

"Open the door, Molly," Jamie says in a firm but even voice.

"He shouldn't be here. It's a violation of the restraining order."

"I know, but go ahead and open it. I'd like to have a talk with him."

"Jamie, no. That's not a good idea. Maybe you should leave – go out the front door."

Jamie ignores my suggestion as Todd pounds on the door with his fist.

"Open up, Molly!" Todd yells. "I know you're in there."

17

Molly

Taking a deep breath, I unlock the door and open it just a few inches. "You shouldn't be here," I hiss at Todd.

Todd grips the edge of the door and shoves it open before pushing past me to get inside. His eyes widen when he spots Jamie. "What the fuck is *he* doing here?"

Jamie picks up Gus's harness. "Go to Molly," he tells the dog in a curt, no-nonsense voice.

"He's blind?" Todd says, laughing. "Are you fucking kidding me? You're screwing a blind guy?"

I gasp, stunned by the crude vehemence in Todd's voice. I would have been less shocked if he'd hauled off and slapped me. "Get out of my studio, now!"

Jamie reaches my side, his expression tense. His jaw is clenched so tightly I can see the veins flexing beneath his bearded cheeks. "You heard her," he grates, stepping in front of me. "Get out."

Todd surges forward. Gus starts growling, and Jamie makes a hushing sound and releases the dog's harness, giving him a terse hand signal. Gus moves a few feet away and lies down.

Todd is a couple inches shorter than Jamie, but it doesn't prevent him from trying to get right in Jamie's face. "You get out. And take your fucking dog with you."

Jamie looms over Todd, not giving an inch. "I'm giving you one more chance to leave," Jamie says. "Then all bets are off."

Todd laughs. "Oooh, I'm so scared."

My stomach sinks as it's obvious neither man is going to back down. I blame myself for putting Jamie in this position in the first place. I shouldn't have let him come. I step around Jamie and grab Todd's arm, trying to pull him toward the door. "Todd, please, just go."

Todd throws me off without once taking his eyes off Jamie. "Shut up, Molly. This is between me and him."

Jamie strikes so fast I can't even track his movements. One second, Todd's glaring at Jamie, and the next, Jamie has Todd pressed face first into the door, one of his arms ratcheted up high behind his back. Todd grunts in pain, struggling helplessly against Jamie's iron-clad hold.

Jamie leans into Todd, pressing him harder against the door, putting pressure on his arm. Jamie's other hand has a white-knuckled grip on the back of Todd's neck.

Jamie's mouth hovers just above Todd's ear. "Leave Molly the fuck alone, or you'll have to deal with me."

Jamie releases Todd's neck and reaches around him to turn the door knob. Then he pulls open the door and shoves Todd out into the dark alleyway, locking the door behind him.

Immediately Todd starts pounding on the closed door with his fists, yelling muffled threats at Jamie.

"Oh, my God, I'm so sorry," I say, reaching out to grasp Jamie's arm. "Are you all right?"

Aside from breathing hard, Jamie seems fine. "You're not responsible for what that ass does."

Hearing Jamie call Todd an ass makes me laugh, but it's a humorless sound as none of this is funny. Even though the pounding has stopped, Todd might still be out there. Jamie just made an enemy of someone who's more than capable of retaliation. And Jamie's blindness puts him at such a disadvantage over Todd.

Guilt makes me feel ill. "I'm so sorry."

Jamie turns to me, his expression softening. "Hey, I told you, it's not your fault." When he reaches for me, I step into his embrace, knowing I shouldn't, but unable to help myself.

When his arms come around me, pulling me close, I instinctively lay my head against his chest. I can feel his strong heartbeat beneath my cheek. "Jamie, please don't underestimate Todd. Jealousy's making him crazy."

I feel the rumble of a quiet chuckle against my ear as he rubs my back. "Don't worry. I may be blind, but I'm not helpless."

His arms tighten around me, and I shiver when I feel Jamie's lips in my hair.

"What do you say we call it a night?" he says. "It's getting late. I'll take you home."

"All right."

I finish cleaning up my brushes and put away my tools. We exit from the front of the shop, and I lock up. There's still plenty of people out on the sidewalk, and that's reassuring.

Gus is on one side of Jamie, and I'm on the other. He holds out his arm to me, and I link mine with his. I realize he doesn't need my help, but it's nice to walk arm in arm with him.

"Don't you have a security system?" he says, as we head for home.

"No. I've never had any problems before now. I didn't think it was necessary."

"Well, you need one. Jake's an expert in electronic surveillance. I'll ask him to install a security system."

"That sounds expensive."

"I'll take care of it."

"I'll think about it," I say, hedging. I can't have Jamie paying for a security system for my business.

"Okay, but don't wait too long. You need something soon."

During the entire walk home, I'm hyperaware of our surroundings, scanning the sidewalk as I watch for any sign of Todd. I wouldn't put it past him to ambush us along the way. Jamie seems relaxed enough, but a couple of times I catch him cocking his head and listening intently. I'm relieved when we've made it back to our building without mishap.

I punch in the security code to open the door. And like the gentlemen I've come to expect, Jamie walks me to my apartment door and waits patiently as I dig out my key and unlock my door. He and Gus follow me inside my apartment, and I set my purse down on the dining table.

I smile, feeling the tension ease away. We got home unscathed. And despite his run-in with my ex, Jamie seems in a good mood. "Thank you for keeping me company and for dealing with Todd."

He nods. “My pleasure. You can call me anytime, day or night, and I’ll be there.” He pulls his phone from his back pocket and pushes a couple of buttons. I get a brief glimpse of his phone, and it doesn’t look like any phone I’ve ever seen. It must be specially designed for users with vision impairment.

“What’s your phone number?” he says.

I rattle off my number, and he keys it into his phone and sends me a brief text message.

“There,” he says. “Now you have my number. If you need me, use it.”

“I will. Thanks.”

I walk him to the door, and he hesitates before stepping out into the hallway.

“Will you be all right?” he says.

I think back to the way he came to my rescue in the studio. He didn’t hesitate for a second to go toe-to-toe with Todd.

As if he can read my mind, he chuckles. “Don’t you dare apologize again. I mean it.”

“But, Jamie – the things he said about you. I am sorry.”

He wraps his free arm around my shoulder and draws me close for a one-armed hug. “Don’t give it another thought. I’ve heard a lot worse.” Then he leans close and kisses my forehead.

“If Todd bothers you again, call me,” he says.

I watch Jamie and Gus head down the hallway toward the other apartment. They get about a dozen feet away when Jamie stops and comes back.

“Did you forget something?” I say.

“Yes.”

To my utter shock, he takes me in his arms and kisses me. “Molly, is there any chance in hell you might change your mind and agree to go out with me?"

I burst into laughter. I'm so high-strung this evening that it's either laugh or cry, and frankly I'm tired of tears. I want this guy – I want to be with him – and I can't bear turning him down again. "Yes."

"Did you say yes?"

His shocked expression makes me laugh all over again. "I said yes."

He tightens his embrace. "Will you have dinner with me? Tonight?"

"Sure. I'd love to."

He takes a deep breath. "Do you like Italian?"

"Yes."

"Good. I make a mean lasagna. How about seven-thirty?"

"It's a date."

18

Molly

After Jamie heads back to his apartment to get ready for our dinner date, I freshen up and change out of my jeans and into a comfortable skirt and blouse. At five minutes before the appointed time, I walk down the short hallway and knock on his door.

I hear a soft bark from inside, and then the door opens.

Holy crap, he dressed for the occasion. His white button-down shirt, open at the collar, reveals the strong column of his neck and provides a tantalizing peek at his chest. The crisp white shirt contrasts nicely with his tanned skin and rich, auburn hair and beard. His sleeves are unbuttoned and rolled up, exposing strong forearms. For the first time, I notice the light dusting of freckles on his arms. He looks amazing.

He traded his faded jeans for a pair of black trousers that sit deliciously at his lean hips, and instead of his scuffed hiking boots, he's wearing a pair of polished black loafers. His beard has been freshly trimmed, and I detect a faint whiff of expensive men's cologne. The scent alone makes my insides quiver. Even through his dark glasses, I can sense the intensity of his expression.

Oh, my God, this is for real. We're on a date. A guy doesn't shower and shave, dress up, and put on cologne unless his goal is to impress someone.

"Molly, come in." He moves back to make way for me.

"Hi." As I step inside, I'm immediately struck by the mouth-watering aromas of simmering tomatoes and Italian spices, warm yeasty bread, and garlic. On top of that, I detect something sweet and coffee-scented. Tiramisu, maybe? I can't believe he's gone to this much trouble for me. And I can't believe he put all this together so quickly.

They say the way to a man's heart is through his stomach. Now I have to wonder if that sentiment applies to women as well. Why wouldn't it? It's not so much about the food as it is about the fact that he's gone to so much effort to prepare a nice meal for me.

I glance around his apartment, which is surprisingly tidy. I guess I was expecting something a little more bachelor pad. The chocolate brown sofa looks very comfy, as does the matching recliner.

The table is already set for two with white china plates with gold trim and two tall wine glasses. There's a large salad bowl on the table, and a bottle of red wine on ice. There's even a candle centerpiece on the table. Good grief, how did he manage all this on his own, and so quickly?

The timer on the stove goes off, announcing dinner.

"Perfect timing," he says, as he closes the door behind me. "I hope you're hungry."

"I am. I'm starving." And as I take him in, I realize it's not just food I'm hungry for. I'm starved for this. For something that feels an awful lot like coming home.

"Have a seat and help yourself to the salad," he says. "There's a bottle of red wine chilling on the table. Why don't you pour us glasses while I get the lasagna out of the oven?"

* * *

The meal is perfect. Lasagna, fresh garlic bread, salad, and wine. And for dessert... Tiramisu. He couldn't have planned this any better. We enjoy a long, leisurely meal, and while we eat, we talk about everything from Shane and Beth's painting to the new book Jamie's working on to how Gus is progressing with his training.

"I'd love to read one of your books," I tell him. "Are they published under your name?"

"Yes."

"I'll download one tonight and start reading it."

He fights a grin, and I could swear he's blushing. "Please, don't feel like you have to. They're military thrillers – that may not be your thing. Don't force yourself to read them if you're not really interested."

"Are these stories autobiographical?"

He shrugs. "Bits and pieces of them are, yes. The overall plots are purely fictional, and the bad guys are made up. Even though I'm out of the service, I'm still bound to a certain level of confidentiality. I use what I can and make up the rest."

"So, by reading your books, I'll get an idea of what you did in the military?"

"Yes."

"Good. Then I'll definitely read one, because I want to know what it was like for you in the service." I take a bite of my delicious dessert, moaning with pleasure as the coffee-flavored cream melts on my tongue. "Jamie, this meal is amazing. You outdid yourself."

He sets his wine glass on the table and reaches for the bottle. "Thanks. I may not be able to do everything I want, but I can manage a lot with enough practice."

"I can see that. But you don't have anything to prove, you know. Not to me, certainly. Not to anyone."

He faces me directly as I talk, and if I didn't know better, I'd think he was looking right at me. But those dark glasses are a constant reminder of what he's lost... something so precious.

He deftly pours himself a second glass of wine and holds the bottle out to me. "Would you like another glass?"

"No, thanks." I chuckle. "One's my limit. I'm not much of a drinker."

* * *

After he finishes his wine, he invites me to sit on the sofa and relax while he cleans off the table. Of course, there's no way I'm going to sit and watch while he does all the work.

"I'd rather help you," I say.

I carry the dishes to the sink, and he rinses them off and puts them in the dishwasher. It's incredibly domestic.

My relationship with Todd was never anything like this. After dinner, he'd disappear to the living room to watch television while I cleaned up. He never once offered to help me in the kitchen.

The one and only time I asked him to help, early in our marriage, he'd done it so grudgingly that I never asked again. Going into it, I thought marriage was supposed to be a partnership, but that ideal got quickly squashed.

When we're done cleaning up after dinner, Jamie closes the dishwasher door and dries his hands on a hand towel.

He leans against the kitchen counter and faces me. "Thank you for helping."

I'm tempted to say something clever about how we make a good team, but I'm afraid to go there. That's a slippery slope that I'm not willing to risk. "Thank you for a wonderful meal. You do make a mean lasagna."

He laughs. "You're easy to please." He pushes away from the counter and heads toward me. "Would you like to sit down and relax?"

The thought of sitting with him on the sofa makes my heart race. There wouldn't be anything relaxing about it. I'd be a nervous wreck. I'm not sure I'm ready for this – for this kind of intimacy. For a new relationship. "It's getting late," I say, chickening out. "I'd probably better get going."

I regret the words as soon as I say them.

His smile falls, but he nods nonetheless. "Sure. I'll bet you're tired." He reaches for my hand. "Thank you for coming over this evening. I loved having you here. Just let me grab my cane, and I'll walk you home."

"How many steps is it from my apartment to yours?" I ask as we walk down the hallway.

He smiles. "Twenty-six."

When we reach my door, Jamie waits patiently while I locate my keys and unlock my door. Thankfully, there are no post-it notes stuck to my door this time. Maybe my pleas have finally gotten through to Mrs. Powell.

"Thanks again for dinner," I say, opening my door. I'm nervous all of a sudden, wondering if he'll kiss me again.

"Molly?" Jamie runs his hand down my arm until he reaches my hand. "I enjoyed this evening." And then he cups my face with both hands and brushes his thumbs across my cheeks. He frowns. "God, I wish I could see your face."

The wistful nature of his remark makes my chest hurt, because no matter how much I might want to, I can't give him that. "You're not missing much," I say, laughing to lighten the moment. "It's passable, as far as faces go."

He smiles. "I still wish I could see it." Slowly and deliberately, with his hands cradling my face, he leans down and touches his lips to mine. I wouldn't even call it a kiss – it's more just a quick meeting of our lips, something even friends might do. "Sleep well, Molly."

The next thing I know, I'm standing inside my apartment, closing the door and locking it, and Jamie is gone.

Charlie rubs eagerly against my ankles, meowing plaintively.

"Come on, buddy," I tell him, scooping him up into my arms. I carry him to the kitchen and open a can of cat food.

In a daze, I head to my bedroom to undress, my head swirling with emotion. What just happened tonight, and why do I feel like everything has changed?

* * *

That night, I dream about Jamie.

I leave my apartment in the middle of the night and walk down the hall toward his. When I try the door knob, it's unlocked, and I let my-self in. All the lights are off, and it's dark.

Dressed in nothing but an oversized T-shirt, I head down the hall-way to the last door on the left. Moonlight streams through the sheer curtains, illuminating the man sleeping on the bed. He's shirtless, lying with nothing but a sheet covering him from the waist down. His chest is a work of art, with well-defined muscles and dusted with a light sprinkling of dark hair.

Even in the dim lighting, I can make out the dusky discs of his flat nipples. His arms are muscular, too, his biceps and triceps well-defined even in sleep. I crawl into bed with him, and he stirs restlessly as I dis-turb the mattress. In his sleep he reaches for me, pulling me down to cuddle against him, wrapping his arm around me as I settle against his body.

"I'd give anything to see your face," he murmurs in his sleep.

I know it's just a dream, but his arms around me feel so good. The heat of his body and the male scent of him teases my senses. I can't help relaxing into his arms and nuzzling the skin stretched tautly over his bicep.

When I awake in the morning I hold the dream to me for as long as I can, until it starts to fade away, as all good dreams do. In its place is a comforting warmth that settles low in my belly.

19

Molly

On Monday, I spend the first part of the morning in my studio working on several paintings, including Jamie's. Then, as the shop is closed, I take advantage of my free time to catch an Uber ride downtown to do a little shopping. Christmas is just weeks away now, and I want to pick up some gifts for my parents, and for Chloe.

After browsing a few of my favorite shops, I find myself at the entrance to Clancy's Bookshop – one of my favorite downtown spots.

There's a strong security presence at the main entrance, which is something new. I don't remember ever seeing an armed security guard posted at the doors. But inside, the atmosphere is festive with all the colorful holiday displays and the seasonal music playing on the sound system.

I'm browsing a rack of calendars, looking for something for my dad, when I hear someone call my name.

"Molly?"

I turn, surprised to see a familiar face. The pretty blonde. "Oh, hi. You're Jamie's sister-in-law. Beth, right?"

"Right. Well, *almost* sister-in-law. Shane and I aren't getting married for a couple weeks yet, but the truth is, I already feel like his family is my family."

"That's nice." I smile at her. "I don't have much family, so I envy you. I know Jamie has a big family. I've seen his brothers and friends stopping by since he moved in. I think I've seen a sister, too. A petite blonde?"

Beth nods. "That's Lia. And there are two more sisters. So, what brings you in today? Is there anything I can help you find?"

"You work here?"

"Yes. Actually, I own this store."

That takes me completely by surprise. "You're kidding? It's a small world then. Clancy's my home-away-from home. I love this place."

Speak of the devil, Lia walks up behind Beth and bumps her hip, a big grin on her face. "Hey, princess."

Right behind Lia is an incredibly good-looking guy wearing a gray knit cap and dark sunglasses, dressed in a black leather jacket and distressed jeans.

Beth confers with the couple for a moment, discussing lunch plans. Then she introduces us. "Lia, this is Jamie's neighbor, Molly."

"Hey," Lia says, giving me the once over. "How's it going?"

"Great, thanks. I've seen you a couple of times in my apartment building. My apartment's on the second floor, next to Jamie's."

Her eyes light up. "Oh, you're *that* Molly – the one Jamie can't stop talking about." She offers me her hand. "Pleased to meet you. I'm Jamie's cool sister."

She says this with such a straight face, I can't help laughing. I like her already.

"And this is Jonah Locke, Lia's boyfriend," Beth says.

Jonah Locke? Holy cow! The name and the face register then, and I realize I'm talking to a real-life rock-and-roll celebrity. I can feel my face heating up. "Nice to meet you," I say, trying not to gush like a teenaged fan girl. "I have quite a few of your songs on my favorites playlist."

Jonah offers me his hand, and we shake. "Nice to meet you too."

"Why don't you join us for lunch?" Lia says. "Do you like Mexican food?"

"Absolutely! If you're sure you don't mind." I glance at Beth, trying to gauge her feelings on the matter. "I don't want to impose."

"Hey, the more, the merrier," Lia says. "Besides, any friend of Jamie's is a friend of ours."

A red-haired hunk who'd been lurking in the background comes forward. "Don't forget me!" He elbows Beth. "Let's go get your purse and coat. I'm starving."

"Don't mind him. That's Sam – Beth's bodyguard," Lia explains, as she catches me watching the redhead follow Beth up the staircase.

Beth has a bodyguard? Why does she need a bodyguard?

A few minutes later, Beth and Sam return, and the five of us head out. The restaurant's just ten minutes away, Lia explains, so we'll walk.

We hadn't gone more than a few blocks from the bookstore

when all hell breaks loose. Everything happens so quickly, I can't even make sense of it all. Just as we're crossing an intersection, a car comes barreling around the corner, and it's obvious it won't stop in time to miss the pedestrians in the street. Beth is directly in the path of the car, and I scream out a desperate warning. She would surely have been run down if Sam hadn't shoved her out of the way, sending her flying across the rough pavement. She lands on her hands and knees, rocking forward, and just barely avoids hitting her head on the road.

"Beth!" I scream. I run to her and drop down beside her to assess her injuries. Her palms and knees are covered in blood, abraded with tiny bits of gravel and broken glass. "Are you all right?"

She wavers unsteadily on her hands and knees, and I encourage her to sit before she topples over.

Sam's not so lucky. He must have been hit head on and thrown across the street directly into a lamppost. There's blood on the lamppost and Sam's lying like a lump of clay on the ground. Even from where I'm crouching beside Beth, I can see that Sam's left femur is at an unnatural angle. Clearly, his leg is broken. But what's far more worrisome is the bloody gash across his forehead. His face is coated with blood. He's not moving. *Oh, my God, is he...?* My stomach roils.

Beth catches sight of Sam and lets out a frantic scream.

"Beth, stay down," I tell her when she tries to get to her feet. I press my hands on her shoulders to coax her back down. "You're bleeding."

"Sam's hurt!" she cries, pointing in his direction.

My attention is momentarily diverted by the sound of angry shouts and gunfire. It looks like Lia shot out the back tires on the car that hit Sam.

"Get out of the fucking car!" Lia shouts, as she points a black handgun at the driver's window of the car that hit Sam. "Get out and put your hands up, now!"

Jonah's in the middle of the street trying to control traffic. "I called 911," he yells to Lia.

"Call Shane!" Lia yells back at him.

Crowds of curious gawkers gather on all corners of the intersection. It's utter chaos, with people milling about, and traffic at a dead stop. Angry motorists, many of whom probably don't realize that someone's been hit, start yelling and honking. Lia's holding the driver of the vehicle at gunpoint, threatening to shoot him right through the car window if he so much as moves a muscle.

I glance down at Beth, whose face is deathly pale. I think she's going into shock. "Beth?"

She glances up at me, her tearful eyes wide, but she says nothing. Then her gaze returns to Sam's lifeless body, and she cries out in agony before leaning over to retch. We both watch in horrified anticipation as a man leans down to press his fingers to Sam's throat as he searches for a pulse. His stoic expression tells us nothing. We honestly don't know if Sam's alive or not.

"Go to Sam," Beth gasps, her voice barely audible. "Please! I'm fine. Help Sam!"

I'm torn, loathe to leave Beth sitting alone out here in the middle of the street with all these cars. But Jonah's doing an effective job at blocking traffic. Lia has now dragged the driver out of his vehicle and has him pinned against the side of the car, his hands behind his back. I watch as she secures his wrists with a long plastic zip-tie.

Just as I honor Beth's request and go check on Sam, Beth passes out, slumping to the ground. Jonah runs to her and crouches on the ground beside her.

"Is she okay?" Lia yells to Jonah.

Jonah takes off his jacket and lays it beneath Beth's head, protecting her from the hard ground. "I think she passed out."

When I reach Sam's side, the stranger kneeling beside him is still checking Sam's pulse.

"Is he alive?" I ask, my voice quavering.

The air is rent with the sound of shrill sirens speeding to our location.

"He has a pulse," the man says, "but it's weak."

We both glance down at the spreading pool of blood beneath Sam's head.

"Head injuries bleed a lot, you know," the man says. "At least he's alive."

* * *

Three patrol cars arrive almost simultaneously, boxing in the chaotic scene in the intersection. One of the officers takes over directing traffic. Another takes custody of the driver from Lia.

A moment later, two emergency squads and a fire truck arrive. I stand back, my arms wrapped around my torso as I watch the EMTs tending to both Beth and Sam. One team of EMTs places Beth on a stretcher and loads her into an ambulance. Another team is carefully assessing Sam.

Lia climbs up into the ambulance with Beth. She looks right at me as the ambulance doors are shutting. "Call Jamie!"

It takes longer for the second team of EMTs to stabilize Sam and get him transferred to a stretcher and loaded into the remaining ambulance. Jonah climbs in with him.

I'm pulling out my phone even before the ambulances have pulled away. Jamie answers on the second ring, and it's difficult for me to hear him over the noise of the car horns and the sirens.

His voice is instantly sharp and to the point. "Molly? What's wrong?"

I finally lose my composure and give in to tears. "There's been an accident. Beth is hurt, but I don't think her injuries are life threatening. But Sam – he was hit by a car. He's alive, but he's hurt badly. He hit his head hard, and there's a lot of blood."

"Where are you?" he asks. He sounds a little breathless now, as if he's on the move.

"Downtown, a couple of blocks from Clancy's. I'll grab a cab and come get you. You'll need help navigating the hospital."

"I'll be waiting for you out front."

20

Molly

By the time I make my way back to N. Michigan Avenue, the traffic has cleared enough that I can finally flag down a cab. I give the driver my address and ask him to hurry.

I'm sitting in the back seat, shaking, my nerves completely frayed as I relive the past few minutes, over and over. Scenes from the accident loop through my mind like animated GIFs – Sam shoving Beth, Beth hitting the ground hard, Sam flying over the hood of a black sedan and lying in a pool of blood. It's all so unreal I have to keep asking myself if it really happened, or if my mind is playing tricks on me.

I'm barely aware of our location when the driver pulls up to the curb in front of my apartment building. Just as he promised, Jamie's waiting out on the sidewalk. He's got his cane, but no Gus.

I open the door and jump out of the cab. "Jamie! I'm here."

He zeroes in on the sound of my voice and meets me halfway. I grab his free hand and lead him to the cab. As soon as we're in the vehicle, I give the driver instructions.

As the car pulls into traffic, Jamie grabs my hand, holding it firmly. "Does Shane know?"

"Yes. Jonah called him."

"What about you?" He turns in his seat to face me and skims his hands up and down my arms. "Are you hurt?"

"No, I'm fine."

"Tell me what happened."

As I relay the events, moment by moment as best I can recollect, he squeezes my hand. When I'm done, he brings the back of my hand to his mouth and kisses it. "Thank you for calling me, and thanks for coming to meet me. It's times like this that my deficiencies really hit home."

I can't seem to stop shaking, and Jamie lays his arm across my shoulders and pulls me close. "Everything's going to be all right," he says. "Don't worry."

Feeling chilled to the bone, I lean into him, gravitating toward the comfort of his warm body. "It happened so fast. Everything was chaotic, and Beth was frantic about Sam. He looked terrible, Jamie. There was so much blood." I shudder at the memory, and Jamie tightens his hold.

"Sam pushed Beth out of the way of that car," I say, my throat tightening as reality hits me. Sam could die. "He may well have saved her life."

Lia's words from earlier come back to me. *Sam is Beth's bodyguard.* My God, did he risk his life for her? I'm simultaneously amazed and horrified. What if, God forbid, Sam dies? How will Beth ever get over that?

Our taxi pulls up at the main entrance to the Cook County Hospital Emergency Room. As we exit the vehicle, Jamie hands the driver cash to pay for our fare. There are a lot of people milling about outside the hospital's entrance, so I reach for Jamie's hand to guide him around the crowd and through the sliding doors and into the waiting room.

"Molly! Jamie! Over here!"

I turn to see Lia waving at us from across the room. "There's Lia and Jonah," I say, leading Jamie by the hand.

We take the two empty seats beside Lia, who fills us in. Now that I have a chance to sit down and decompress a little, I feel exhausted.

"Shane and Cooper are here," she says. "Shane's with Beth, and Cooper's with Sam."

Jamie keeps hold of my hand, resting our linked fingers on his thigh, and I take comfort in the physical connection. Even though he's caught up in conversation with his sister and her boyfriend, he never once lets go of my hand, and I'm glad. I definitely feel a little out of my element here, but his grip on my hand keeps me feeling connected to him.

It's not long before we're joined by other members of Jamie's family. His sister Sophie, a gorgeous brunette, arrives followed shortly by Jake. Another brother, Liam, arrives right on their heels, along with several people from Shane's company.

Amidst all the conversations going on around me, Jamie leans close and murmurs in my ear. "You didn't eat anything for lunch, so you've got to be hungry. Do you want to go downstairs and get something from the cafeteria?"

I feel shaky from low blood sugar, but the thought of food right now makes me queasy. "Thank you, but no. I can't eat anything right now."

"Molly, you have to eat. Let me go get you something."

"I can't, Jamie. Not right now. Maybe later."

Jake comes back from visiting the treatment area and gives us updates on both Beth and Sam. Beth is doing all right, but Sam is in critical condition. He's in surgery right now to stop the bleeding in his fractured skull.

Jamie and his sister Sophie go back to the treatment area to see Beth, and I wait with Jamie's family. I feel like an interloper, but everyone's very nice, and they make an effort to include me in their conversations.

The afternoon passes slowly, hour after hour, with the occasional updates. I'm exhausted, but when Jamie suggests I go home, I refuse. I'm staying, I don't care how long, until we know something about Beth and Sam. I'm staying until Jamie is ready to leave.

When I hear a gasp from someone seated near me, I glance up just as Beth walks into the waiting room. She's walking slowly, her arm in a sling, and she's cradling it protectively against her chest. Shane's got his arm around her, supporting her. I feel my eyes tearing up at the sight of her standing on her own two feet.

When she comes over to greet us, I shoot to my feet and hug her carefully. "Oh, thank God! I was so worried when I saw you fall. Is your arm broken?"

"No, it's just a sprain," she says, sounding exhausted. "Thank you for coming. But you didn't have to stay. I'm sure you're exhausted."

I am, but that's not important. "Your family told me you were okay, but I couldn't leave without seeing you with my own eyes. I'm so glad you're all right, Beth. And we've been told that Sam will be all right, too."

She nods as her eyes tear up. "Thank you for calling Jamie," she says.

"I knew he'd want to know."

She gives me a one-armed hug and smiles at Jamie. "You two should head home."

As Beth and Shane move on to talk to the rest of Shane's and Beth's families, Jamie holds out his hand to me.

"Come on, I'm taking you home," he says. "You haven't eaten anything all day, and you have to be exhausted."

The truth is, I am exhausted, but I didn't want to abandon Jamie during this crisis.

He pulls me to his feet as he says our goodbyes to his family and the others gathered here. In addition to all the family members, there are at least a dozen people in the waiting room who are here because of the accident, many of whom work for Shane's company.

As Jamie and I exit the hospital, we grab the nearest cab and head for home. I offer to pay the return fare, since he paid for our trip to the hospital, but Jamie insists on taking care of it himself.

21

Molly

On our way in, we stop to pick up our mail. The young couple in Apartment 1B comes in from an evening out, holding hands and stealing kisses as they fumble with trying to unlock their door. I think they might have had a little too much to drink. I can't help smiling, and Jamie just shakes his head at me as we head upstairs.

At the top of the stairs, Jamie takes my hand and says, "I need to take Gus out for a quick walk. Why don't you order us some take-out nearby, and I'll go pick it up?"

Us. He's already thinking of us as a couple. The thought fills me with pleasure, but it also scares the hell out of me. This feels so right between us, but if things continue there'll come a time when he'll want to be intimate, and then I'll have to face the music and risk rejection. I'll have to tell him about the cancer and my surgery. And if by some miracle that doesn't put him off, then I'll have to face getting naked with him. No, I can't deal with that right now. I'm worn out, and my ability to cope with anything beyond getting some food is nonexistent.

It's almost nine o'clock, and I hate the thought of Jamie wandering too far alone in the dark. "Jamie, it's dark out."

He laughs. "Honey, for me, it's always dark. Don't worry, I'll be fine."

"Why don't I come with you?"

He frowns. "Because you're exhausted."

True. But I don't want to be separated from him right now. "Look, why don't we both go? We can grab something from the sandwich shop down the street and bring it back. That's quick."

He sighs. "All right. If you're sure."

So, while Jamie's getting Gus, I take a quick bathroom break to freshen up, and the three of us head out.

On the sidewalk, Jamie holds my hand, and after stopping for Gus to take care of business, we walk the two blocks to the eatery and place an order for two sandwiches with fries.

We end up eating in my apartment, both of us seated on the sofa, with our food spread out on the coffee table. While we eat, Gus wanders around the apartment sniffing absolutely everything, and when Charlie makes an appearance, Gus gets excited and tries to initiate playtime.

As I'm carrying cold drinks back from the fridge – a beer for Jamie and flavored tea for me – Jake calls with further updates.

After he hangs up, Jamie fills me in. "Sam's regained consciousness. There's still some bleeding in his skull, and he's had a couple of seizures, but apparently that's to be expected. Sam will remain in the intensive care unit until he's out of danger."

I lean back in the sofa, my mind reeling. "I just happened to run into Beth in Clancy's this afternoon, and she invited me to eat lunch with them – with Lia and her boyfriend, and Sam. We were walking to the restaurant when the accident occurred."

"It wasn't an accident," Jamie says.

I can feel the blood drain from my face. "What?"

Jamie frowns. "Jake said the arresting officers found a photograph of Beth in the driver's wallet. It looks like it was a hired hit."

"Oh, my God, no! I can't believe that! Why in the world would anyone want to hurt Beth?"

"Hurt Shane is probably more like it."

My eyes widen. "Shane? Is that why she has a bodyguard? Because of Shane?"

"My brother's a very wealthy man, and he's made a few enemies over the years. He's been responsible for putting more than a few people behind bars – some of them pretty high profile."

"Do they know who's behind this hit-and-run?"

"Shane has his suspicions. The driver of the car is angling for a plea deal. He said he'd give up the name of the person who hired him for a lenient sentence."

"Poor Beth. And poor Sam. God, I hope he's going to be all right." I don't think I'll ever get the memory of seeing him lying in a pool of blood out of my head.

When I'm done eating, I observe Jamie as he finishes his meal. I notice he has no trouble locating everything... his sandwich, his fries, his bottle of beer. Every time he drinks from the bottle, he sets it back down in exactly the same spot.

Jamie leans back in the sofa and stretches his long legs with a groan. "God, what a day," he says, running his long fingers through his hair.

He rubs his hand on his thigh, and my gaze gravitates to it. His skin is tanned, and there are thick veins visible on the back of his hand. His fingers are long and masculine, his nails trimmed bluntly. He has sexy hands. And arms, too. Hell, everything about him is sexy.

As if he knows what's on my mind, he flexes his hand on his thigh, then rubs it the length of his leg, from his hip to his knee and back again. He seems almost... nervous.

And that makes me nervous.

"Molly?"

At the sound of my name, my stomach sinks like a stone. "Yes?"

He reaches for my left hand and lays it on his denim-covered thigh. Then his hand covers mine, and he links our fingers together. My heart starts tripping all over itself, and as I stare at our joined hands, I'm finding it hard to breathe.

He rubs my hand along his thigh and swallows hard. "I know we agreed not to complicate things - our friendship - with anything more... and I respect that. I do. It's just, my feelings haven't changed. In fact, they've grown."

He pivots on the sofa so that he's facing me. Our hands are still joined, and I can feel his thigh muscles tensing beneath my hand. With his free hand, he reaches for my face, his hand moving slowly, hovering just inches from my cheek, waiting, as if asking for permission to touch me. I can't resist reaching out and pulling his hand close, pressing it to my face.

He brushes his thumb along my bottom lip. "I keep thinking about our kiss in the barn, and I can't help wondering what might have happened if Elly hadn't walked in when she did."

Now it's my turn to swallow hard.

"I know you have your reasons," he says, his voice low and steady, "but I wish you'd give me a chance. I may not be ideal boyfriend material, but I'd work hard at being the person you need. I know you've been through a bad break-up, and you're still dealing with your ex, but maybe moving forward is the best way to let go of the past."

As I gaze into the darkened lenses of his glasses, I realize how desperately I wish I could see his eyes. I squeeze his hand. "Would you take off your glasses for me?"

He stills, and then his chest rises and falls with a heavy sigh. "I never take them off when I'm around people."

His statement doesn't come across as combative, or even a polite rejection. It almost sounds like a question. I think I caught him off guard.

"I want to know what you look like without them," I say, my voice not much more than a whisper.

His lips flatten, and I can tell my request has made him uncomfortable. I watch him as he struggles with a decision.

He sighs. "All right, I'll take them off. But you need to know that I rarely ever take them off for anyone."

I realize what a big deal this is for him. I feel honored that he trusts me enough to reveal this part of himself.

Jamie blows out a heavy breath, then reaches up to slowly remove his glasses and hook them on the neckline of his T-shirt. He turns to face forward, away from me, his eyelids closed. It's as if he has to steel himself to be so exposed.

I don't say a word. I just wait patiently for him to proceed at his own speed. Finally, he turns to me and opens his eyelids.

22

Molly

For a moment, I forget he's blind, because I'm looking into a pair of beautiful brown eyes, the color of fine whiskey and flecked with bits of green and gold. He looks right at me, then blinks a few times and looks away, as if embarrassed. I stare at his profile, fascinated at seeing him without the glasses. He looks so different – so normal. Just as handsome as I knew he would be.

I reach for his hand, squeezing it. "Jamie."

He squeezes back, then glances back at me. I'm astonished at how real his eyes look, how naturally they move.

When Charlie jumps up onto the sofa, landing between us, Jamie blinks as his eyes follow the cat's movement. It's uncanny. If

I didn't know he was blind, I'd never believe it.

"They're beautiful," I say, still holding onto his hand. "I honestly didn't know what to expect."

"They're a perfect replica of the eyes I was born with. The prosthetists painted them to match my eyes in my high school graduation picture. My mom says they got the color just right."

It takes me a moment before I notice the faint scars radiating outward from the edges of his eyes, undoubtedly remnants of the debris from the explosion that destroyed his sight.

I don't know what I was expecting, but I wasn't expecting this. He looks so... normal. I also realize, a little belatedly, how truly attractive he is. His whiskey-colored eyes are mesmerizing, and I could stare at them forever.

I go up on my knees to face him, gently tracing his eyebrows. I'm feeling choked up by the trust he's placing in me. He's obviously sensitive about his eyes, although I'm not sure why. They're beautiful. But still, they're prosthetic, just like my breast forms. They're placeholders for the real things, which we lost.

Holding my breath, I lean forward to gently kiss the skin around his eyes. As he lowers his lids and relaxes with an audible sigh, my heart breaks. One of his warm hands moves behind me and slips beneath my top to rub my back just above the waistband of my jeans.

All the skin-to-skin contact makes me ache for more.

I always thought he was attractive, even with his dark glasses, but now I'm getting the full impact and it's breathtaking. Why does he hide behind those glasses?

"You don't really need to wear the glasses, do you?" I say.

He shakes his head. "No."

"Why do you?"

"For two reasons. When strangers meet me without the glasses, they assume I can see, and that leads to all kinds of awkwardness. The glasses, along with the cane or Gus, make it more readily apparent that I can't see. Secondly, to be honest, I use them as a shield, to protect my privacy. I know my eyes *look* real – at least that's what my family tell me – but they make me feel self-conscious. I always wonder if people are staring at them. It's silly, I know, but there you go."

"It's not silly." I totally understand. Our prosthetics are outward signs that we're different. That we're somehow maimed. I often wear multiple layers of clothing just to shield my body from scrutiny.

Jamie visibly shudders when I trace his forehead with the tip of my index finger. His eyebrows are nicely shaped and a shade darker than his hair. I notice for the first time that the eyebrow over his right eye is bisected by a short, jagged scar.

He holds perfectly still as I run my finger down the side of his face, skimming the tip of it past the tiny, white scars bracketing his eyes, to the top edge of his beard. His nose is blade straight, and even beneath his beard, I can see that he has a strong jawline. I love how his beard and mustache frame his sensuous lips.

"Who trims your beard?" I ask him. He's always well groomed when I see him.

His lips quirk with a small smile. "I do." He intercepts my wandering finger and brings it close to his mouth, holding it hostage just an inch from his lips.

I stare at those beautiful lips, dying to taste them.

His lips part, and when I feel his warm breath on the tip of my finger, I shiver. His eyes shift naturally as they follow the flow of our conversation. And when he blinks periodically, just as a sighted person would, it's so easy to forget he can't see.

Jamie chuckles, the sound low and rough. His thigh muscles, which are pressed against my legs, tense. "You can't touch me like this and not expect me to want to kiss you. It's just not fair."

Oh, my God, he's aroused. We both are. I can feel heat building between my legs as desire pools low in my core, making me ache. "I – "

He releases my finger and slips his hand behind my nape, drawing me toward him until the tips of our noses barely touch. "What do you say?" he whispers. "Will you give us a chance? Will you give *me* a chance?"

When I pull back a few inches, my gaze goes to his lips again, and I unconsciously wet my own. I think he can hear that, as he barely manages to suppress a grin. How can he be so funny and so sexy at the same time?

"Maybe." I know I'm tempting fate by not adamantly saying no. I should put a stop to this right now, not lead him on. It's not fair to either of us. Even if I did let him kiss me, even if I *encouraged* him, where would it lead?

The idea of being intimate with someone again fills me with dread. The thought of him touching my chest, coming into direct contact with my body, feeling my scars and flat chest terrifies me. After Todd's reaction, my confidence is shaken to the core.

My God, I want to say yes, desperately. But I feel like I'm standing at the edge of a cliff, and he's asking me to blithely jump off. I'm petrified, frozen and afraid to move forward. "Jamie, I – " I choke on the words.

He frowns. "What are you afraid of, Molly? Surely you're not afraid of *me*. I would never do anything to hurt you."

"No. It's not that. It's not you." I may not have known Jamie for that long, but I trust him.

His fingers gently massage my nape, sending shivers down my spine. "Then what is it?"

"It's – " The words stick in my throat.

All I can think about are the words Todd threw in my face when I confronted him after catching him having sex with his assistant. "*How in the hell can you expect me to be happy about this, Molly? I assumed you'd have reconstruction! How in the hell do you expect me to be satisfied with a woman with no breasts?*"

"No!" I jump up from the sofa, bumping into the coffee table as I stumble back in a desperate attempt to put distance between us. "I can't do this! I'm sorry!"

Jamie shoots to his feet. "Molly, wait!" He holds his hands up in surrender, like he's trying to placate me. "I screwed up, and I'm sorry. I misread you. I thought – I thought I felt a connection between us. I thought you wanted – shit!" He scrubs his face with his hands, then runs his fingers through his hair. "Molly, I'm sorry I put you in an uncomfortable situation. I'll never do it again, I promise."

And now my face is burning with shame, because it's not his fault. He didn't misread the situation. He didn't misread *me*. I know full well I was giving him mixed signals. "It's not your fault, Jamie." *It's mine.*

He laughs with remorse. "I like to think my visual impairment doesn't hold me back, but obviously on occasion it does. Like now. I obviously misread you, and for that I'm sorry."

I close my eyes, dreading what I'm about to say. I can't in good conscience let him take the blame for this. I sigh. "Jamie, you didn't misread anything."

He goes still, and my confession hangs in the air between us.

He looks confused, a little bit hopeful, but also wary. "Say that again?"

"You heard me."

There's that little grin playing with the corners of his mouth again. He steps forward, slowly, reaching for my hands. When I give them to him, he pulls me against his chest and holds me tightly.

"Tell me what just happened," he says, his lips in my hair. The muscles in his arms are trembling. "Tell me what I'm missing here."

I have to crane my neck up to look into his face. He's still got his glasses off, and I love being able to see his eyes, prosthetic or not. I'm not used to seeing him like this… his face so totally open to me. It feels… intimate, like he's bared his soul.

He cradles my face with his hands. "Tell me what you're thinking, Molly. My ability to read body language is a bit limited, I'm afraid. Help a guy out here."

I laugh nervously.

"Is this about Todd?" he says, suddenly scowling. "Are you sure you're not still in love with him?"

"God, no! Absolutely not. Although he is dangerous – don't underestimate that."

"If it's not about Todd, then what is it?"

"Jamie, I – I don't want to talk about it."

His hands slip around my shoulders to my back, and I feel myself tensing in anticipation that he's going to embrace me again. I'm wearing my bra with prosthetic breasts forms, and I'm afraid he'll be able to tell. I hate that Todd's made me so self-conscious about my body.

I lay my hands against his chest and gently push back. He takes the hint and releases me, his hands falling to his sides.

"I won't push you," he says gently, taking a step back. "If you're not ready, I'll wait. As long as there's a chance, I'll wait."

"Thank you." But the truth is, part of me regrets not telling him. I'd give anything to feel his strong arms around me, holding me close to his body. Part of me is desperate to ask him to hold me.

I feel crushing disappointment when he slips on his glasses and starts picking up the trash from our meal and our empty bottles.

"You don't have to do that," I say. "I'll take care of it."

He smiles politely. "It's no problem. I want to."

I watch him as he makes his way to the kitchen, his hands full as he juggles both the trash and his cane. He walks right into one of my chairs and it topples over onto its side. He makes a rough sound of frustration and drops everything he's carrying on the table – a little too hard – and picks up the chair and rights it. Then he collects the trash again, and his cane, and continues to the kitchen, cursing incoherently beneath his breath.

I follow him into the kitchen, feeling a growing sense of dread. Have I pushed him too far? He must know I'm there, watching him – I'm not being stealthy – but he doesn't say anything. He just puts the trash in the can and the empty bottles in the recycling bin.

He turns to me, shoving his hands into his pockets. His expression – what I can see of it – is carefully schooled. "It's late, and you've had a stressful day. I'd better let you get to bed."

My throat tightens at the lack of emotion in his voice. He sounds so distant, and it's entirely my fault. "Thanks for helping me clean up."

He nods. "No problem. Thanks for going with me to the hospital."

It's like we're strangers all over again, politely thanking each other for things that people who care about each other shouldn't have to say thank-you for. "Jamie – "

"Molly, it's fine, really," he says, dismissively. He grabs his jacket off one of the kitchen chairs and slips it on. "Sleep well. I'll see you... later."

It feels like he's saying goodbye. Dread sinks in my belly like a stone, and I think I'm going to be sick. Part of me – the lonely, desperate part – is screaming at me not to let him leave, to take a chance and jump off that cliff.

"I'll let myself out," he says, gripping his cane and heading for the door.

I stand there in the kitchen, watching his back as he collects Gus and leaves, quietly shutting the door behind him.

I lock the deadbolt and the chain, just going through the motions, then turn out the lights and head for my bedroom. After stripping off my clothes, I head to the bathroom to get ready for bed. As I stand there brushing my teeth, I stare at the two scars that run in a drunken line across my chest. You'd think a surgeon could cut in a straight line. I think about what used to be there... a pair of C-cup breasts, soft and heavy, topped by a pair of pink nipples that used to pucker at the slightest stimulation. Nipples that might have nursed a baby one day, but now never will.

I assumed you would have reconstruction, Molly!

I chose not to. I didn't want more surgery, and I didn't want to deal with the complications of implants. If I had to do it all again tomorrow, I'd make the same choice. My body is what it is. I don't want to pretend it's something it's not. That's just not me. I can't put it into words – it's just who I am, for better or for worse.

I slip on a nightgown, then turn out the bathroom light and return to my bedroom to crawl under the sheet and blanket. Turning on my side, I wrap my arm around the spare pillow, cuddling the cool fabric.

I'd much rather be cuddling with Jamie right now. The realization that I could have had him here with me right now pains me. If I hadn't been such a coward.

I reach beneath my nightgown and run my fingertips along the path of the incisions, feeling flesh that's just now starting to regain sensation. I can trace the ribs that lie beneath my skin, and it amazes me to think that my heart sits just beneath their bony protection.

I wipe my wet cheeks on the spare pillow, ignoring the tears burning my face. "Enough with the self-pity already!"

Charlie jumps up onto the bed and rubs against my shoulder, purring loudly.

"You don't care if I'm defective, do you?"

He brushes against my shoulder, purring like a little motorboat. I fall asleep petting him.

23

Molly

The next couple of days pass uneventfully. I spend all of Tuesday holed up in my studio, working hard on my commissions, and other than the customers who stop in, I see no one.

On Wednesday, Chloe invites me out to lunch. We end up going to Big Star on Damon Avenue for their renowned taco sampler platters and margaritas. As we're heading back from the restaurant, we're greeted with the sight of Jamie and Gus waiting outside the front of my shop.

"Hey, handsome," Chloe says to Jamie when we reach my shop.

My heart is in my throat. I haven't seen Jamie since Monday

night... the night of Beth's and Sam's accident, the night he told me he wanted to kiss me... again. We ended that evening on a sour note, and I haven't seen him since. I've been afraid he was avoiding me.

"Chloe, hi," he says, coming away from the wall. He almost seems nervous. "Molly's door is locked. Do you know where she is?"

"I sure do," Chloe says, tossing me an evil grin.

"I'm right here, Jamie," I say before she can mess with him even more. "We're just coming back from lunch."

He turns to me and reaches for my hand. "Beth's coming over tomorrow for lunch. I was wondering if I could bring her by your studio afterward. She asked if she could see you."

Chloe gives me an *aw-shucks-isn't-he-cute* look, and I scowl at her. "Sure. I'd love to see her again. How's she doing?"

"She's fine. And Sam's out of danger. He's going to be okay."

Chloe lays her hand on my back and nudges me in Jamie's direction with all the subtly of a linebacker. "Well, if you two kids will excuse me, I have some skin to ink."

She gives me one last push for good measure, and I lose my balance and stumble forward.

Jamie catches me. "Whoa. You okay?"

"Later, Molls!" Chloe calls as she strolls away. "Later, James!"

"Later, Chloe," he says, shaking his head at me. "Can we come in?" he asks me, as I unlock my door.

"Sure."

He follows me into the shop. I flip the door sign back to OPEN.

"There's something I want to ask you," he says, following me over to the sales counter.

"Oh?"

"Shane and Beth's wedding is this Saturday afternoon, at their home in Kenilworth. It's a relatively small affair – just family and close friends. I was wondering... if you'd like to go with me. It's sort of a weekend house-party thing. We'd arrive Saturday morning, stay overnight, then come home Sunday afternoon."

He's inviting me to his brother's wedding? Wow. I'm not sure what to say.

"We'd just be going as friends," he adds, when I'm slow to answer.

I laugh. He reads me so well. "I'm honored that you would ask me."

"Don't be honored, just say yes. Please."

The idea of attending a wedding at that beautiful home is tempting. But even more so, I'm drawn to the idea of spending an entire day – no, an entire weekend – with Jamie. As long as he knows we're just going as friends... I guess it wouldn't hurt. "Yes, I'd love to go with you, Jamie. As your friend."

"Right," he says, not hesitating for a moment. "As friends."

24

Molly

The next day, I'm in the studio working on Jamie's painting when I hear the back door open behind me. I realize instantly that I must have forgotten to lock it this morning after I carried a bag of trash out to the dumpster in the alley. I make it a point to always keep the back door locked.

I turn to see who's there, but my response dies in my throat when I see Todd standing just inside the open door.

"You shouldn't be here, Todd," I say, trying to maintain a steady voice. My heart starts pounding. I don't think he'd hurt me, but he scares the hell out of me lately. When I look into his eyes, it's a stranger staring back at me.

"Who the hell is the guy, Molly?" he says, closing the door. "The blind guy. Who the fuck is he?"

"You need to leave," I say in a shaky voice. I point toward the back door, desperate for him to leave. Jamie and Beth are due to arrive any minute now, and I need to get Todd out of here before they do. "Just go right back out the way you came."

He reaches behind himself to turn the lock. "We need to talk."

"No, we don't. You need to leave. In case you've forgotten, I have a restraining order against you. That means you can't be here. If I call the police – "

He gives me a look of disappointment. "Molly, come on. Is that any way to talk to your husband?"

It scares me, how calmly he speaks, as if he's the rational one and I'm off my rocker. "You are not my husband!" I hiss. "I mean it, Todd. Leave now, or I'm calling the police."

We both glance at my cell phone, which is lying on a table across the room. He glances at my phone, then back at me, as if he's calculating how long it would take me to reach my phone and call for help.

He shakes his head. "Don't be so melodramatic. I just came to talk."

"We have nothing to talk about."

"Yes, we do. Like, how much longer are you going to continue punishing me? I told you, it's over with Mindy. You've made your point, and now it's time to come home."

Making a split-second decision, I make a move for my phone, fully intending to call 911, but Todd moves too, cutting me off. He spreads his arms, blocking my way, and then proceeds to drive me back until I'm pinned in the corner.

"Stop it, Todd!"

His expression hardens as I hit the wall. I'm trapped, and my heart's pounding so hard my chest feels like it's going to explode. I make another attempt to get around him, but he grabs me by the throat and slams me against the wall. The impact is so swift and sudden, I don't have time to brace myself, and my head rocks back and smacks against the bricks.

His long fingers tighten around my neck, cutting off my air. "Listen to me, and listen good," he says through gritted teeth. "I've had enough of this! You – "

The front bell chimes, alerting us to the arrival of company. The knowledge that it's probably Jamie and Beth makes me ill. I don't want either of them mixed up in my problems.

Todd watches the open doorway as Beth walks through. Her eyes widen at the sight of Todd clutching my throat, and she stops abruptly. Jamie's right behind Beth, and with little warning, he walks into her, nearly knocking her over.

Jamie grabs Beth's shoulders to steady her. "What's wrong?" he says.

A young man I've never seen before pushes past both of them and comes to stand directly in front of Beth. He's young, probably in his mid-twenties, with short black hair and obsidian eyes, his complexion a beautiful shade of café-au-lait. The instant his gaze lights on Todd's hand around my throat, he reaches inside his jacket and withdraws a black handgun.

He and Beth are both staring at Todd. All I can do is try to make eye contact with Beth, hoping she'll get my message. *Go back! Get out of here!*

"Molly?" Beth says in an even, measured voice. Her gaze darts back and forth between me and Todd. I know she's trying to play it cool, but I can see the fear in her eyes.

Todd releases my neck and exits through the back door, out into the alley. The dark-haired young man runs after him.

Jamie steps in front of Beth. "Molly? Is everything okay?"

"Yes," I say, trying to remain calm. "It is now."

"A man had Molly pinned to the wall, his hand around her throat," Beth says, her voice a little shaky now. "He ran out the back door, and Miguel went after him."

"Was it Todd?" Jamie says, facing my direction.

"Yes." I smile apologetically at Beth. "Todd's my ex-husband. He… shouldn't be in here. I have a restraining order against him."

"Are you all right?" Beth says, as she comes toward me. She reaches out and touches my arm hesitantly. "Did he hurt you?"

I shake my head, gently feeling my neck, and wincing when I come across a tender spot where this thumb had pressed hard enough to likely leave a bruise. "I'm all right. He just scared me." I glance at Jamie, who looks far from convinced. "I'm fine, really."

The back door opens and the dark-haired young man walks in. "He's gone. I lost him."

Using his cane to navigate around my work tables, Jamie heads my way, his other hand outstretched. I meet him halfway, reaching for his hand. He props his cane against a table and places his hands on my face, his thumbs brushing across my eyebrows, then down my cheeks to my lips. His fingers slip gently down my throat to my shoulders, as if feeling for injuries. "Are you sure he didn't hurt you?" he asks me.

"He startled me, that's all. I was back here painting when he came in through the rear door and caught me off guard. I must have forgotten to lock the door this morning."

Jamie frowns. "I'm having a security system installed here today. I'll take care of everything. It won't cost you a penny."

I shake my head. "Jamie, I can't let you do that."

"Yes, you can," he says, using a tone of voice I've never heard him use before. He takes hold of both my hands. "I'm not leaving you here without any kind of protection. End of story, so stop arguing with me."

I glance at Beth and roll my eyes. "Is he always this pushy?"

Beth laughs. "If you think this is pushy, you should meet his brother Shane."

"You're shaking," Jamie says to me. "Close up for the day, and come back to the apartment building with us."

I nod. "I think I've had enough excitement for one day."

While I turn off the lights and lock up, Jamie makes a quick phone call.

"I just spoke to my brother Jake," he tells me. "He said he can have a team over here this afternoon to install a state-of-the-art security and surveillance system. No more surprise visitors, okay?"

I share a look with Beth and resist rolling my eyes.

She presses her lips together to keep from smiling. "Welcome to my world. The McIntyre men don't mess around."

"I know you ladies are laughing at me," Jamie says. "But I don't care. Molly, your ex-husband violated a restraining order coming into your shop. You need to make a police report."

"Is he a threat?" Beth asks.

I nod. "He's grown more and more erratic over the past year, since our divorce."

"Why? What does he want?"

"He wants *me*, but I refuse to go back to him."

25

Molly

We head back to our apartment building. Jamie links his arm through mine, but I'm not sure which of us is supporting the other. Beth and her bodyguard take up the rear. After all the commotion, Beth introduced me to Miguel Rodriguez, who's filling in for Sam, who's still in the hospital and won't be returning to work any time soon. The handsome young Hispanic seems hyper-aware as he surveys the sidewalk. I imagine he's watching for Todd.

There's an Uber car waiting for Beth and Miguel near the curb in front of our apartment building.

Beth says her good-byes, hugging first Jamie and then me. "I'm so glad you're all right," she whispers in my ear. "If there's anything

I can help you with, just let me know, okay?"

After Miguel and Beth drive away, Jamie and I head inside and climb the stairs to our floor.

Jamie walks me to my door. "Can I come in?" he says. "We need to talk."

My pulse picks up. I'm still reeling from my run-in with Todd, and I'm not sure I can handle a serious conversation right now. "Okay."

I unlock my door with shaking hands and push it open. Fortunately, Charlie's there waiting for me, purring and rubbing against my leg. That's a good sign. It means I don't have any unwanted visitors in my apartment. Jamie follows me inside.

"Can I get you something to drink?" I ask him, mostly because I'm nervous and want to stall for time. I'm not sure what Jamie wants to discuss.

"No, thanks." He holds his free hand out toward me, palm up, and I lay my hand in his. Then he intertwines our fingers. "Are you sure you're all right?"

"I'm fine. He just scared me, that's all."

Jamie makes a scoffing sound. "Molly, he had his hand around your throat. I was serious about filing a police report. He violated your restraining order, and you need to report him. You have three witnesses to back you up."

I know he's right, but I dread getting the police involved. It's just going to make things worse. "All right."

He smiles, then leans down and kisses my forehead. "Call the police. I'll wait here with you."

The feel of his lips on my forehead sends a warm shiver down my spine. He has no idea of the effect he has on me. When I'm near him, my body comes alive. Dormant nerve endings awaken and beg for more contact.

I look up into his handsome face, at those sensuous lips. His glasses make him sexy and mysterious, but they're still a barrier between us. I feel like I can't see the real Jamie – all of him. "Take your glasses off," I whisper.

For a moment, he looks indecisive, almost vulnerable. Then he removes his glasses and hooks them on the neck of his shirt. He blinks and smiles. "Better?"

I return his smile, but of course he can't see that. So I have to communicate through words, as I can't rely on him reading my body language. I reach up and touch the side of his face. "When you wear your glasses, I feel like I can't see *you*. It feels like there's a barrier between us."

He closes his eyelids and I run the tip of my index finger gently across his right eyelid. "Your eyes are beautiful."

He chuckles. "They're artificial."

"Yes, but you told me they look just like the eyes you were born with, and they're beautiful. You don't need to hide them."

He opens his eyes and blinks. "How about a compromise? I'll take them off when it's just the two of us. Okay?"

"Okay." I'm touched that he's willing to do that much for me.

He pulls his phone out of his pocket and hands it to me. "It's time to call the police."

* * *

A half hour later, the intercom in my apartment buzzes, announcing the arrival of visitors downstairs. When I confirm their identity using the live video feed into my apartment – courtesy of the building's newly updated security system – I buzz them into the building. A few minutes later, there's a brisk knock on my apartment door. A quick glance through the peep hole reveals two uniformed officers, both young women, standing at the door.

"Thanks for coming," I say, after opening my door and inviting them in.

After introductions are made, I take a seat on the sofa beside Jamie. One of the officers sits in an armchair, and the other insists on standing. I notice Jamie had slipped on his glasses when I answered the door. When Officer O'Grady, a petite brunette, asks me what the problem is, I tell her. Jamie reaches for my hand, linking our fingers in silent support.

My voice shakes as I describe what happened today in the studio... how Todd came in through an unlocked back door, how he threatened me and cornered me, his fingers squeezing my throat and cutting off my air supply for a few seconds. I don't know what might have happened if Jamie and Beth and Miguel hadn't appeared when they did.

Officer Sherman, a tall woman with French-braided ash blonde hair, takes detailed notes as Officer O'Grady follows up with additional questions.

"There were witnesses?" she says.

"Yes," Jamie says. "There were three of us who walked in on Ferguson's assault on Molly. I was there, plus two others. I know the other two will be happy to provide statements."

Officer Sherman takes down contact information for Jamie, Beth, and Miguel.

"So, what happens next?" I ask when they say they have all the information they need.

"Mr. Ferguson will be arrested and charged with violating the restraining order," the officer says. "He'll likely face additional charges pertaining to assault, depending on what the D.A. finds."

The entire interview is over in less than an hour, and I get up to walk the two officers to the door.

"Thank you," I say, letting them out.

After locking up, I head back to the sofa and drop down beside Jamie.

He squeezes my hand. "You're shaking."

My nerves are overwrought, and I feel sick. "I'm worried about how Todd will react when they arrest him. He's going to be furious." He was furious when I got the restraining order – I can't even imagine how he'll react when he's arrested.

"Todd is responsible for his actions, Molly, not you. He should have considered the consequences before he put his hands on you today. Do you have an attorney?"

"Yes. I had to get one to obtain the restraining order."

"Shane has a really good attorney, Troy Spencer. I could talk to Troy about your situation, see what can be done."

"I would appreciate that." My gaze drops to Jamie's fingers, which are linked with mine. His fingers are much longer than mine. Like everything about him, they're so masculine. Mine are smaller and pale in comparison, my skin soft. Male and female, ying and yang.

My eye is drawn to the veins on the back of his hand, along with a few freckles. I swallow, imagining those hands on my body, touching me, exploring.

Sitting with him like this, I feel safe for the first time since Todd barged into my studio earlier. Right here, shut away from the rest of the world, nothing can touch me.

I stroke the back of Jamie's hand with mine, following the path of a vein as it meanders the length of his hand. The contrast between his body and mine fascinates me.

"Molly?" His voice is low and a little rough.

I try to speak, but I can't manage a coherent thought right now. "Hmm?"

He still has his glasses on, and I wish he'd take them off so I could see all of him. He must be reading my mind because he removes them abruptly and lays them on the coffee table. He closes his eyelids, though, reminding me that I'm not the only one with insecurities.

Shifting to face me, he skims a hand up my arm, following the line of my shoulder to my face. His fingers slip behind to the nape of my neck and burrow into my hair. He leans closer, pressing his forehead to mine, and simply holds that position.

I relax into him, enjoying the contact. I close my own eyes to experience a bit of the world as he does. Even in the dark like this, there's a sense of connection between us. Not just the physical connection of our foreheads touching, or the soft brush of our exhalations, but a different kind of connection, something intangible. In the dark like this, there's just the two of us, and it's easy to block out the rest of the world.

When his fingers begin to massage my neck muscles, I moan with pleasure. Without a word, he tilts his head and kisses my left temple. I savor the gentle contact, and his lips brush over my eyelids, dropping little kisses. The stress of the afternoon catches up with me, and my mind and body crash.

Jamie shifts position on the sofa, leaning back against the cushions, and pulls me into his arms. "Just rest," he murmurs, his lips in my hair. "Close your eyes and relax."

I lean against his chest, savoring the warmth and the strength of his body. I'll let myself rely on him, just for a few minutes, before I have to get up again and face the world.

26

Jamie

Molly falls asleep in my arms, resting against my chest, and I'm in no hurry to wake her. I think the events of today really knocked her for a loop.

I'd like to show Todd what it feels like to be frightened, to be intimidated, to be at someone else's mercy. The fact that he had his hands on Molly – hell, his fingers around her God-damned throat – makes me want to break something. Preferably something on his body. I'm trying to remain calm, for Molly's sake, but damn it, I just want to make him suffer for what he's done to her.

Molly makes a quiet sound in her sleep, a cross between a moan and a sigh, and she snuggles closer to me. I can't help my body's physical reaction to the feel of her warm body pressed against mine. I close my eyelids and inhale deeply, taking in the scent of her. My body responds with a mind of its own, and I can feel myself getting hard. Damn it. I have to shift a little to make room for my dick.

My body's response is inconvenient, to say the least. I don't think she'd welcome it right now, and it's pretty damn uncomfortable for me. Still, I have to admit it's a bit gratifying. Molly is the first woman I've had any sexual interest in since my accident. Since the explosion, I lived in isolation, first in a hospital, then in Shane's house, rarely coming into contact with anyone other than family and friends and McIntyre Security staff. Meeting Molly changed all that. Now I just have to convince her to give us a chance.

I understand why she's hesitant to enter into another relationship. Her failed marriage to Todd, and his asshole behavior to her now, probably soured her on men altogether. I get that. But we're not all assholes. I'm sure she knows that, but right now she can't see the forest for the trees.

But even if she were open to the idea of dating again, that doesn't mean she'd want to date *me*. I'm defective. Although I can take care of myself and handle most situations, there will always be some things I can't manage on my own.

I know she worries about what Todd might try to do to me. Hell, I'd love for him to take a crack at me. That's all the justification I'd need to break every bone in his body. I'm pretty sure Molly has no clue what I'm capable of. Maybe I should show her. Maybe I should arrange to give her a demonstration of my physical capabilities in the boxing ring.

If she saw me go hand-to-hand with someone like Jake, someone who's a real freaking bad ass, maybe she'd reevaluate me as a potential partner. I'll have to call him and set something up –

maybe at the wedding.

I'm still stunned she agreed to go with me to the wedding. I was so sure she'd say no. It was all I could do to remain calm when she said yes. Of course, she agreed we'd go as friends. But still, having her there *with me* is a big step in the right direction. If we can spend more time together, maybe she'll see that I have a lot to offer her.

I reach up to rub my eyes and stop myself just in time. It's an old habit, rubbing my eyes, and I still have the urge to do it when my eye muscles are tired, like they are now. To distract myself, I relax and pull Molly closer. She's still out cold, and I'm enjoying the chance to hold her. Of course, I'd rather be holding her in my bed, both of us naked, but this will have to do for now. Anything more is wishful thinking at this point. But I'll wait. I've got all the time in the world.

I brush her hair back from her face, letting the strands slide through my fingers. I love playing with her hair; I love the texture of it, the weight and the waves. I have an indistinct image in my mind of a woman with brown hair and brown eyes, about five-eight, probably around one-hundred-fifty pounds or so if I had to guess. But I can't see her face. I'll *never* see her face, but I try not to dwell on that. If we were to get married and have kids, I'd never see their faces either. It's a shame we didn't meet before the accident. At least then I'd have a memory to carry with me.

Molly's cat jumps up on the sofa and starts purring as he rubs against my thigh.

"Hey, buddy," I say when he bumps his head against my hand. "Sorry I can't pet you right now. I've got my hands full. Maybe later." *I'm sure as hell not letting go of Molly to pet the cat*. "No offense, pal, but priorities. You understand, right?"

Molly stirs, making a sleepy sound that goes straight to my dick.

"Who are you talking to?" she says, barely awake.

"Your cat. I'm sorry we woke you. Go back to sleep."

She sits up, and sadly I have to let her go.

"I fell asleep," she says, moaning as she stretches. "How long was I out? Please tell me I didn't snore."

I laugh. "You were asleep for about an hour, and no, you didn't snore."

"Oh, thank God. What time is it?"

I ask my phone for the time, and it obliges me. Four-thirty. It'll be time for dinner before long. "Why don't you come over to my place for dinner? I'll cook something quick and easy. You can relax."

She hesitates and I'm afraid she's going to say no. I know what she's thinking... slippery slope and all. We keep getting closer and closer, every time we see each other.

"Molly, it's just dinner, not a commitment. Besides, you need to eat. We both do."

She laughs nervously, and I know I was right. She's afraid we're getting too close.

"Okay," she says. "Dinner sounds good. I am hungry."

I gently lower Charlie to the floor and sit up, reaching for my glasses. I stand and lift my arms, stretching my back, which is a bit stiff after having been in the same position for so long.

"Why don't you go ahead," she says in an odd voice, making me wonder if she's going to change her mind.

"Molly – "

"I just need a few minutes to freshen up. I'll be right over. Do you have your cane – oh, yes, it's by the door."

"Okay. I'll see you in a few minutes. As long as you promise not to change your mind."

"I promise."

27

Molly

The moment Jamie's out the door, I lean back on the sofa and run my hands through my hair. *Oh, my God!* When he stood and stretched, his shirt rode up, exposing his waist. I'm sure it wasn't intentional, but I got a front-row view of his muscled abdomen, lightly furred with brown hair. I saw so many muscles I couldn't count them all. All I know is that my gaze went right to his happy trail, which disappeared beneath the jeans hanging low on his hips. I can only image what's beneath those jeans.

Seeing him like that, in a moment of weakness, lit a fire deep in my belly that I thought had been extinguished for good. I honestly thought Todd had killed my desire for intimacy. Just now, I'd wanted to reach out and grab him and pull him back down on the sofa with me. I'd wanted to wrap myself around him and feel him sink deep inside me.

As Chloe would say, what fresh hell have I gotten myself into? How can I continue to spend time with him and not *want* him? And knowing he's interested in me just makes resisting him that much harder.

I head to the bathroom to make good on my promise to freshen up. I run a comb through my sleep-mussed hair, brush my teeth, and splash water on my face, all the while staring at myself in the mirror.

Do you have any idea what you're doing?

What does Jamie see in me? He doesn't even know what I look like – but maybe that's a blessing. I guess I'm moderately attractive, although I'll never win any beauty pageants. And I'll always be struggling to lose an unwanted ten or fifteen pounds.

After setting Charlie's dinner out for him, I lock up my apartment and head down the hall to Jamie's place. Standing outside his door, I steel myself against temptation and take a deep breath.

Just friends, I remind myself. *Just friends.*

But why? asks a little voice in my head. *Why not more than friends?*

Because Todd! And because I'm missing a couple of key body parts, that's why.

But the little voice in my head isn't satisfied with those answers. *He's not afraid of Todd. And maybe he won't mind so much about your missing body parts. You'll never know unless you tell him.*

* * *

"Now you're just making me look bad," I tell Jamie as I sidle up beside him at the stove.

I'm so glad he enjoys cooking. One of us should. I'd be happy to do the dishes every night, if he'd cook the meal.

He's just taken two foil packets out of the oven and laid them on the cutting board to unwrap. Inside each packet is a baked chicken breast on top of a little mound of cut-up roasted new potatoes. The chicken, which he seasoned with rosemary, garlic, oregano, and thyme, smells delicious.

"Well, I will admit I'm trying to impress you," he says, sticking a meat thermometer in one of the chicken breasts. The thermometer beeps. "It's ready," he says.

I watch as he carefully dishes the food onto two plates, arranging everything just so.

When he reaches for a serving fork, he brushes the back of his hand against the hot baking dish he'd just taken out of the oven. "Shit!" he hisses, jerking his hand back. His hand is curled tightly into a fist, and I can tell from the grimace on his face that it hurts.

"Here, put your hand under cold water," I say, moving around him to turn on the faucet. "Come on."

He follows me to the sink and holds his hand under the stream of water. His jaw is clenched tightly, his lips flattened. His nostrils flare as he breathes hard.

"Do you have any aloe?" I say. "It does wonders for the pain."

"Don't bother," he says, gritting his teeth. "The pain's fading. I'll be fine."

"You don't sound fine."

I glance up at him, and he turns his face away, as if he's embarrassed. That's when I realize... it's not the pain that's bothering him. He's angry because he burned himself. "It was an accident," I tell him. "It could happen to anyone."

I watch the muscles in his jaw clenching and flexing as he grinds his teeth. Reaching up, I brush his hair gently, then lean close enough to kiss his arm where it meets his shoulder. "No one's perfect, Jamie. Not even you."

That earns me a smile, and he relaxes his fist under the stream of water. I grab a clean hand towel from the cupboard and pat his hand dry, careful not to touch the burn.

"Is it feeling better?"

"Yes." He laughs. "If I knew burning myself would earn me a kiss, I would have done it long before now."

* * *

He bumps his shoulder against mine. "Food's ready. Can you grab the bottle of red wine in the fridge? I'll carry the plates."

While I bring the bottle of wine to the table and open it, Jamie carries in the plates, then goes back to the kitchen to fetch the dinner rolls.

"Jamie, thank you. This is a really nice dinner. You didn't have to go to all this trouble for me, you know."

He smiles, looking pleased. "It's no trouble. You had a rough day. You needed a good meal."

The food is amazing, cooked and seasoned perfectly. I have to admit, he's a better cook than I am.

"How's your hand?" I ask him.

He flexes his hand and closes it into a fist. "Much better now. I think I'll live."

When we're finished eating, we clear the table and clean up in the kitchen together. I enjoy this little moment of domesticity with him. Housework is always more enjoyable when there are two sets of hands.

The kitchen is cleaned up in no time, and I don't know what to do. I should leave, I suppose. I've taken up all of his afternoon and part of his evening. I'm sure he has work to do. But the thought of leaving him and going back to my empty apartment holds little appeal.

"I should go," I say. "You've probably got stuff - work - you need to do."

I'm feeling torn. Part of me wants to leave before I get even more attached to him, and part of me hopes he'll insist I stay a while longer. In the back of my mind, I'm worried about Todd showing up this evening. I don't know if the police have arrested him yet or not. Or if they did, if he's managed to get out on bail. Here, I feel safe.

"Molly, are you okay?"

How does he read me so well? "I'm fine."

"You don't sound fine." He lays his hands on my shoulders, and I'm sure he can feel the tension in my body. I'm fairly radiating with it. "Are you worried?" he says. "About Todd?"

"A little bit, yes."

He frowns. "You're worried he'll try to get into the building tonight?"

"He has a knack of getting into places he shouldn't be. And I don't know if he's been arrested or not yet, and if he was, how soon he'll get out on bail. He's going to be so angry." Just the thought of how he'll react when he's arrested makes me shudder.

"You're welcome to stay here tonight. I have plenty of room."

"Thanks, but I don't want to inconvenience you."

"It's no inconvenience. You can have my bed, and I'll take the sofa. Or, if you'd feel more comfortable, I'll stay with you at your place. I can sleep on your sofa."

"I wouldn't mind staying here tonight," I say. My belly is happy and a glass of wine has warmed my body. I feel like tempting fate tonight. "Just this once."

* * *

I'm curled up on the sofa next to Jamie, and we're twenty minutes into a sci-fi movie when Jamie's intercom buzzes, announcing the arrival of a visitor. I nearly jump out of my skin when Gus shoots to his feet and runs to the door, barking.

Jamie laughs and pats my knee. "It's okay, it's just Jake." He pauses the movie. "His team must be done installing the security system in your studio."

Jamie walks to the intercom and speaks to his brother, then buzzes him up. A few moments later, there's a firm knock on the door.

Jake steps inside the apartment, his presence a bit overwhelming in the small space. Dressed in all black, as he is now, he's incredibly intimidating. I wonder if he's married, or has a girlfriend. I can't imagine being on the receiving end of all that intensity.

Jake takes off his black leather jacket and hangs it over the back of one of the dining table chairs. He's wearing a T-shirt, also black, and it accentuates his muscular build. There's a black handgun holstered to his chest.

"The system's in and functioning," he tells us in his slightly gruff, deep voice, as he absently reaches down to pat Gus on the head. Then he pulls a packet of folded papers out of his jacket pocket and lays it on the table. "Here are all the instructions you'll need, Molly, including your passcode. We've installed a couple of panic buttons in strategic locations in your shop. If you hit one of those buttons, the police will be on your doorstep in no time."

"Thank you," I say.

Jamie nods. "I'll walk her through everything tomorrow. Thanks, Jake. I appreciate you doing this on such short notice."

"No need to thank me, bro." Then he turns those obsidian eyes on me. "You okay, Molly?"

I nod. "Yes, thanks."

"If anyone bothers you at your shop, you just push one of the panic buttons and help will be on the way, I guarantee it. No more worries, okay?"

I smile gratefully. "Okay."

Jake glances at the flatscreen panel on the wall. "What are you guys watching?"

"Aliens," Jamie says. "Molly's never seen it before."

Jake looks at me like I'm from another planet. "Seriously? You've never seen Aliens? My brothers and I were weaned on Aliens."

I shake my head, laughing. "I've never really been a big sci-fi fan."

"Jamie will fix that," he says, grabbing his jacket and pulling it on. "Well, enjoy your movie, kids. I've got to get back to work."

"This late?" I say, surprised. It's got to be nearly nine o'clock. "Aren't you done for the night?"

Jake shakes his head. "Surveillance work is never done. I've got to go relieve one of the teams in the field. We're keeping tabs on a drug distributor who's trying to muscle his way into the city. Fun stuff."

When the movie ends, and most everyone in it is dead courtesy of slobbering aliens, I'm pretty sure I've carved permanent scars into Jamie's arm. I've been holding onto him for dear life for the past hour and a half, digging my nails into his arm every time one of those disgusting monsters popped out of nowhere to kill someone. Gus slept blissfully unaware of the carnage while I was on the verge of having a heart attack.

"Oh, my God," I say, leaning back against the cushions as the credits roll. "That was absolutely horrifying. I'll never sleep now."

Jamie laughs. "Oh, come on! It's just a movie."

"That's easy for you to say. I hate scary movies."

"Okay. Next time, we'll watch a chick flick. Your pick. How's that?"

I smile. "That would be wonderful. Thank you."

I unfold myself from Jamie's cozy sofa and get to my feet to help him clear away our glasses and the empty popcorn bowl. Apparently, we both have a soft spot for buttery, salty popcorn.

When we're done cleaning up, Jamie comes up behind me and lays his hands on my shoulders, squeezing gently. His touch sends shivers down my spine.

He kisses the back of my head. "It's getting late. I'll make up your bed."

* * *

While Jamie takes Gus out for a late night potty break, I run back to my apartment to get my toiletries and some pajamas. I'm relieved to find Charlie waiting for me at the door – which lets me know the coast is clear. I reach down to pet him. "You're such a good watch kitty, you know that?"

Charlie responds with a plaintive meow.

"Are you feeling neglected? Do you want to sleep over at Jamie's too? I'll ask him about it. Maybe you can come next time."

I placate Charlie with a handful of kitty treats. Then I take a moment to brush my hair and teeth, and wash my face.

I grab my overnight bag and fill it with just the bare necessities… toothbrush, hairbrush, a change of clothes, and a T-shirt to sleep in.

After petting Charlie one last time, I lock up my apartment and head back to Jamie's place. Just as I reach his door, he and Gus come in the front entrance and jog up the stairs.

"Got everything?" Jamie says, as he follows me into his apartment.

"Yes."

He reaches out and touches my arm, then leans close to kiss my forehead. "Come. I'll show you to your bed."

More slippery slope. *Just friends* don't kiss each other, do they?

28

Molly

Jamie shows me to his bedroom, which is very neat and sparsely decorated. There's a king-sized bed against the longest wall, with a night stand and lamp on each side. There's a tall chest of drawers and a closet, and that's it. There are no rugs, no mirrors, no decorations of any kind on the bare walls. I guess that's to be expected. He can't see them to appreciate them, so why bother?

The bed is neatly made with crisp white sheets and a blue comforter. The bedding is turned down, and it looks very inviting with four pillows propped against the mahogany headboard.

"I put out fresh sheets and pillowcases," he says. "And there's an extra blanket in the closet if you get cold. Please help yourself."

"It's perfect."

"I'll be right down the hall on the sofa. If you need anything in the night, just call for me. I'll hear you."

"Are you sure you'll be all right on the sofa?" I'm not sure it's long enough to accommodate his six-foot-two height.

"Molly, in the military I slept under shrubs in the desert in freezing temperatures. Trust me, the sofa is perfectly fine."

He starts to back out of the room, and I feel a sharp pang. I don't want him to leave.

"Jamie, wait!"

He pauses, but says nothing.

I'm selfish. I want him to sleep in here with me. Just sleep. Is that too unfair of me to ask?

I'm tired of cuddling with spare pillows. I want to cuddle with *him*. I want to fall asleep in his arms. But cuddling might lead to touching, and touching might lead to exploring. And I'm *not* ready for that.

"Molly?" he says, waiting patiently.

"Never mind. Good night."

"What's wrong?"

"Nothing. I'm just tired."

He sighs as he comes toward me. "You are such a terrible liar."

He reaches for me, and because I can't stand it another moment, I slip my arms around his waist.

He makes a rough sound deep in his throat, part pleasure and part pain. His arms tighten around me, drawing me close, and I can feel his lips in my hair. The heat of his body warms me, and the scent of him makes me want things I shouldn't.

"Why are you fighting this?" he murmurs against my temple. "I feel it. Surely you do too. This can't be one-sided – please tell me it's not. Life couldn't be that cruel."

I swallow against the lump in my throat. "It's not," I breathe.

"Oh, thank God."

And then he kisses me. Gently at first, tentatively, as if he expects me to push him away. But it's late, and I'm tired of fighting my feelings. I need his comfort. When I kiss him back, it's the green light he's been waiting for.

His mouth closes over mine, hungrily nudging my lips open and sealing our mouths together, mingling our breaths. When I stroke his tongue with mine, his arms tighten around me, and he kisses me with a sudden, raw hunger that sets my body on fire.

When he finally breaks our kiss, he takes a step back, putting some distance between us. His chest is heaving. He runs his fingers through his hair and exhales heavily. "Damn. I was just going to give you a good-night kiss. I'm sorry, I got carried away."

"I'm not sorry."

"You're not?"

"No."

His brow furrows. "Molly, are you sure?"

"I'm sure I want you to kiss me again."

He grins. "I can do that. Is that all you want from me? Kisses?"

"Right now, yes. And I don't want you to sleep on the sofa. I want you to sleep in here with me. Just sleep, though."

His nostrils flare as my words sink in. "Are you sure?"

"Yes."

"All right. I can do that."

He leaves me alone in his bedroom while he goes to the bathroom to get ready for bed. I hear the shower come on.

I quickly strip out of my clothes and, leaving on my prosthetic bra, I pull on my sleep shirt. Then I turn off the lights and crawl into bed beneath the covers.

While I'm waiting for him, I have time to think about all the reasons why I shouldn't do this. We've already established we have a mutual attraction. He's made it clear that he wants me, and I want him, so there's very little to keep us apart. We're both adults. We're both single and unencumbered. What's keeping me from taking a chance with him?

A light knock on the open door announces his return. "Can I come in?"

I smile. He's such a gentleman. "Yes."

He walks into the room and heads for the foot of the bed. "Now's your chance to change your mind. I promise, no sex. But I can't promise I won't hold you or kiss you."

I laugh. "That's what I'm counting on... the holding and the kissing."

He climbs on the bed and crawls toward me, caging me in. It's dark in the room, but there's enough light coming through the curtains that I can see he's wearing a pair of flannel PJ bottoms. His chest and arms are bare and just a foot above me. His chest is a work of art, muscles carved like stone. His shoulders are broad enough to block out the rest of the world, and those arms... his biceps. I can feel the heat of his body and smell him. He smells like soap and clean male skin.

My belly clenches painfully. "You showered," I say, feeling a little bit at a disadvantage.

"Yeah. Just a quick one. I wanted to make a good first impression."

I laugh. "It's a little late for first impressions, don't you?"

He smiles. "Okay. How about a first impression as a bed mate?"

"Well, that's true." I run my fingers down the center of his chest, past his pectorals to his abdomen, which is nicely bisected with ridges of muscle, and he shivers. "You smell good."

He laughs. "Thanks. I'm glad you think so." Then he drops his face to the crook of my neck and inhales. "You smell good too."

He kisses me then, just a gentle kiss, sort of a getting-to-know-you kiss. Then he drops down beside me, lying on his side to face me. His finger skims across my forehead and then down my nose to my lips. "So, tell me the ground rules for tonight," he says.

"Kissing and holding are okay. No sex."

He nods. "No sex. Got it. What about touching? Holding involves touching. Is that permissible?"

"General touching is okay, the friendly type. But no genitals. No breasts." *Especially no breasts.*

"Gotcha. Touching is okay, but don't touch the good parts. So, basically, we're looking at a PG-13 sleepover. Is that right?"

More laughter. "Yes. Basically."

"Okay. I can do that."

And then he leans close and kisses me, on the lips twice, very PG-13 type kisses. Then his lips travel across my cheek to behind my left ear, which makes *me* shiver. His lips travel down the side of my throat, to my shoulder, and he takes his sweet time kissing his way across my collar bone to the other side.

I tense up when he lays his arm across my chest to pull me closer. His arm is laying right across my breasts, and I don't know if he can tell they're prosthetic or not. As sensitive as he is to touch, I'm afraid he can.

"What's wrong?" he says, pulling his arm back.

"Nothing. Nothing's wrong. Just, we said no breasts, remember?"

"I just laid my arm across your chest. Was that a violation?"

"Yes." *Please don't ask me why.*

"When you said no breasts, I assumed you meant no fondling,

no copping a feel, not just *don't touch them at all.*"

"It was don't-touch-them-at-all."

"Oh."

He sounds disappointed, and my heart starts pounding. *Slippery slope, here we come.*

"Molly?"

"Yes?" *Please don't ask.*

"What are you not telling me?"

My heart begins to hammer painfully. *Slippery slope. Please don't ask.*

"Molly?"

I swallow so hard even I can hear the tell-tale sound. "What?" I say, wincing at the break in my voice. This was such a huge mistake. What was I thinking?

"Molly, just tell me," he says. "Get it off your chest. God, sorry, that came out wrong. Pardon the pun."

My stomach sinks like a stone. *He knows. He already knows. But how?*

I push him away and sit up, shoving back the covers and swinging my feet to the floor. "This was a mistake. I have to go."

"Wait!" he reaches out to grab me and ends up fisting the back of my nightgown. "I'm sorry. I didn't mean to rush you. I was just hoping... since we're alone and in bed.... Molly, talk to me, please. You don't have to hide anything from me. I, of all people, understand."

He knows. I feel sick to my stomach. I try to stand up, but he's still got a hold of my nightgown. "Jamie, please let me go."

"No."

"No?" I say, flabbergasted.

"No. You need to talk to me. I know you're scared, but you don't have to be, and I'm not going to let this hang over our heads any longer, putting unnecessary distance between us. You're too important to me."

"*Unnecessary* distance?"

"Yes, unnecessary. Okay, if you won't tell me, how about if I tell you what I think's going on?"

"Okay." I know I sound defensive, but I can't help it. "Go ahead, Mr. Know-It-All. Tell me what's going on."

"It's about your breasts."

I feel like he knocked the wind out of me, and I can barely breathe. "What about them?"

"Did you have a mastectomy?"

I'm shocked to hear him say the words. "How did you know?"

"Molly, it's okay. You can tell me."

"Yes, I did have a mastectomy. A *double* mastectomy, in fact. I was diagnosed with breast cancer two years ago, and I chose to have both breasts removed."

He sits up and reaches for my hand to pull me back onto the bed. "I'm so sorry, sweetheart."

I've started down this path, so I might as well continue. The words rush out of me, strung together between shaky breaths. "And I opted not to have reconstruction, so my chest is flat. I don't have breasts, I have scars. I wear a specially designed bra that includes prosthetic breast forms. Is that how you found out? Could you tell?"

"It's not obvious – "

"Could you tell?"

"Yes. The other night, when we hugged, I could tell."

I let out a long, heavy breath. "And you didn't say anything?"

"I was waiting for you to tell me. When you were ready."

"I wasn't ready to tell you tonight!" My throat tightens painfully. "You forced the issue."

"I know. I'm sorry."

I tug on my hand. "Will you let go now? I want to go back to my apartment."

"Molly, please don't go. You've had a traumatic day, and you promised me a sleepover. I'm going to hold you to it."

"You still want me to stay? Even after all this?"

"After all what?"

"You know what! My body is defective!" My voice just keeps climbing, but I can't help myself. "I'm missing a couple of body parts that, as far as I can tell, most men think are pretty crucial to their happiness."

"I'm defective too," he says, his voice gone quiet. "Besides, I've always considered myself more of an ass man. You do have an ass, right?"

"Oh, my God!" I snort, nervous laughter overtaking me. "You are insane!"

His voice turns serious. "Please don't leave. Okay?"

My laughter dies a quick death, and suddenly I feel exhausted. I honestly just want to crawl into bed, cuddle with Jamie, and pass out. "Okay."

He tugs me back down onto the mattress and pulls the covers over both of us. Then he rolls me on my side and spoons with me. His arm goes around my waist, and he draws me against him. To my surprise, I feel his erection prodding me from behind.

"Sorry about that," he says, drawing his hips back just a bit. "I can't control that, so just ignore it and go to sleep."

I chuckle. I don't know how he expects me to just fall asleep while he's plastered to my body. How am I supposed to ignore the fact that we're in bed together, both of us half undressed, both of us attracted to the other? Especially now the cat's out of the bag, and Jamie doesn't seem overly fazed by the news.

Still, even though he knows about my surgery, it doesn't change anything. He may think it's okay in the short run, but surely he'd become dissatisfied in the long term. Once reality sets in – like it did for Todd – he'll change his tune. And then I'll have lost the budding friendship we have developed.

He means too much to me as a friend to lose him. I *like* him. I don't just have a crush on him, I *like* him. And I don't have so many friends that I can afford to lose one. I have Chloe, yes, and she's a wonderful friend, but I can't really cuddle with her the way I'm doing now with Jamie.

I lay my arm along the top of Jamie's arm, and we link fingers.

He squeezes my fingers. "Promise me you'll never be afraid to tell me anything."

"I promise." I can say that without qualms because he knows all of my secrets now. He knows about my crazy ex, and he knows about my surgery. There's nothing else.

29

Jamie

Molly's in my bed, finally asleep in my arms, and yet I'm not sure I've made any progress with her.

It took her nearly an hour to fall asleep. She just couldn't relax. At one point, I was tempted to offer her a glass of warm milk. All I could do for her during that time was be there for her and show her that it didn't matter to me that she doesn't have breasts. I imagine that would be a showstopper for some guys, sure. Apparently, it was for that asshole of an ex-husband of hers. But it's not for me.

After what I've been through, after losing my sight and learning how to live my life all over again, I've learned that it's who people are at their core that matters – not their exterior packaging. Hell,

I can't even see Molly – I have no idea what she looks like beyond a general description. But that's not important to me. What's important are the things that I do know about her... she's intelligent, kind, artistic. And she's courageous – God, is she courageous.

And then there's that intangible something about her that I find so attractive. When she speaks, my whole body lights up. I feel like I've finally come home after years of wandering. I can't explain it, and I don't question it. It just is.

I've met a few women since my accident, and none of them had this kind of effect on me. I'd started to think I was incapable of desire, or even wanting someone in my life. Now it's like my body has awakened from a deep sleep, and I'm starting to think about the future. I'm starting to think about wanting a wife, a family one day. And I want those things with Molly.

She's been through a lot herself, and she's learning to cope with the curve balls life threw at her too. She's been hurt, betrayed by the one person who was supposed to be her champion. Todd failed her, but I won't. Now I just need to make her see that.

I might have jumped the gun tonight by pushing her into telling me about her mastectomies, but I don't regret it. Now that it's out there, we can deal with her feelings and move forward. At least that's my hope. I'm not giving up.

I figured it out from a simple hug. The density of her breasts wasn't quite right. I'd suspected for a while, but I didn't say anything because I wanted her to tell me herself. I suspected her lack of breasts was the reason she was keeping me at arm's length – at least one of the reasons. I already knew her concerns regarding her ex.

I understand what it feels like to be defective... to be missing pieces of yourself that others take for granted. Sure, I'm self-conscious about my eyes. That's why I always wear my glasses around other people. And I know she's got to be self-conscious about her breasts.

Frankly, the fact that she's lost her breasts isn't an issue for me. I mean sure, they're nice to have. What red-blooded man doesn't crave the pleasure of pillowing his head on a pair of soft breasts? But in the grand scheme of things, I'd rather have her without breasts than not have her at all. Now I just have to convince her of that.

* * *

I awake around six-thirty when I feel Molly begin to stir. I've learned to tell time in the early morning by the sound of the birds in the back courtyard. The birds are up just before sunrise, and they're consistent as hell. I would confirm the time, but if I ask Siri, I'll wake up Molly for sure. I don't want to disturb her. I'm hoping if I lie really still, maybe she'll fall back to sleep, and we can have a couple more hours in each other's arms.

I'm lying on my back, and she's tucked into my side with her arm across my bare torso. We slept like this all night, with our bodies intertwined in one way or another. One of us would shift, and the other would follow, seeking the comfort of a physical connection.

Suddenly she tenses, withdrawing her arm from my chest and pulling away. She slides off me and brushes back her hair. I lie still, listening to her movements, wondering what she'll do. Will she stay or will she run?

She runs.

I'm disappointed when she leaves the bed and slips quietly out of the room. A moment later, I hear the bathroom door close. A few minutes later, I hear the toilet flushing, then the sound of water running.

I don't say a word when she returns to my bedroom, opens her overnight bag, and digs around in the dark.

"You can turn the light on, you know," I tell her. "It won't bother me."

"Oh." She sounds nervous. "You're awake. I hope I didn't wake you."

"No, you didn't. I'm usually up at this time."

"I tried to be quiet."

I sit up in bed, stretching my arms and back. The sheet is pooled at my waist, covering my erection. I hope she can't see it. She already feels awkward this morning. I don't want to make it worse for her.

"Did you sleep well?" I say, hoping to put her at ease.

"Yes." She sounds surprised. "You don't have to get up on my account. I'm just going to get dressed and head home."

"How about some breakfast before you go?"

When she doesn't answer right away, I know she's about to bolt. "Scrambled eggs and bacon? Toast? Or waffles?"

Right on cue, her stomach growls, and we both dissolve into laughter. "I'll take that as a yes," I say. "Just let me get dressed. There's a Keurig machine in the kitchen if you want to make some coffee or tea."

She's dressed now and just slipping on her sneakers. "That sounds perfect. I'll be in the kitchen."

* * *

As I throw on a pair of jeans and a T-shirt, I come to terms with the fact that gaining Molly's trust is going to take some doing. She's not ready for a relationship. She's still too deep in flight mode thanks to her asshat ex. I really hope I get an opportunity to express my displeasure with him soon. All I need is five minutes alone with him, and I guarantee he'll never darken her doorstep again.

As soon as I pull on clean socks and grab my sneakers, Gus jumps to his feet and stretches.

"Come on, buddy," I tell him. "Let's go water the tree out front."

As Gus and I head down the hall to the kitchen, I'm relieved to smell freshly brewed coffee. She hasn't run yet. That's a good sign.

"I have to take Gus out, then I'll start on breakfast," I tell her, taking Gus's harness off the hook on the wall. "We'll be right back."

"Take your time," she says. She's seated at the kitchen table, sipping her coffee, and she sounds a lot calmer than she did when she first woke up.

As Gus waits by the door, I walk over to Molly and put my hands on her face, orienting myself. "Good morning," I say.

Then I lean down and kiss her lightly, tasting vanilla latte mixed with mint toothpaste. I figure I might as well start laying the ground rules. We're not going backward after last night. She can't pretend I'm nothing more than her next door neighbor, not after spending the night in my bed.

"Good morning," she says.

I can hear the smile in her voice. She's starting to relax.

"Do you like the coffee? Beth insisted on stocking my cupboard with all sorts of fancy blends. Me? I'm just a plain coffee kind of guy."

"It's good. I could get used to having coffee like this every morning."

"Well, you know where to find it, don't you?" I kiss her again, just a light grazing of our lips.

* * *

The entire time Gus and I are outside, I'm afraid Molly's going to bail on me. When we return, I open the door to the smell of bacon frying.

She didn't bail.

I find her standing at the stove. I move in behind her and lay my hands on her hips. I lean close, my nose in her hair. "You're making breakfast."

She shivers. "You made dinner last night, so I thought I should make breakfast."

I step back to give her room and lean against the kitchen counter.

"Thank you for last night," she says in a quiet voice. "I needed... a friend."

She's still categorizing me as a friend. I guess I still have a long way to go. "There's no need to thank me, Molly. I want to be here for you."

"Well, I appreciate it."

I listen to her going through the motions of making breakfast. Cracking eggs, whisking them, pouring them into the pan. The bacon is done, and while the eggs cook she makes toast. I make a cup of black coffee for myself and brew a second cup for her. Finally, when everything's ready, we sit at the table to eat.

Just as we're nearly finished eating, Molly's phone rings. She picks up the phone and accepts the call. "Hello?"

Silence.

"Yes, this is she." *Pause*. "Oh, Officer O'Grady. I'm fine, thank you." ... "Yes." ... "You did?" ... "I see. Yes, thank you. I will." ... "Goodbye."

Molly sets her phone down on the table and is silent. The apartment's so quiet you could hear a pin drop.

"Well?" I say.

"I suppose you caught the gist of that. That was Officer O'Grady. She said she and Officer Sullivan went to Todd's condo this morning and arrested him. He's at the Cook County Jail awaiting arraignment on charges of violating a restraining order. Also assault and battery charges."

She sounds calm as she delivers the news, but I know better. It's times like this that I wish I could see her expression. Then maybe I'd have an idea of what she's thinking. "Are you okay?"

"I'm not sure," she says, getting up from the table. I hear her walk toward the kitchen. She rinses out her coffee mug and sets it in the sink.

I follow, waiting by her side for some indication as to what she's feeling. When I hear her breath catch on a quiet half-sob, I realize she's holding back tears.

I reach for her. "Come here."

She doesn't hesitate for a second. She melts into me, her arms going around my waist as mine wrap around her.

"He's going to be so angry," she says. "Todd's an attorney, and he knows the system. It'll only be a matter of time before he's out on bail."

As I rub my hand up and down her back, I can feel her trembling. She's afraid. "I'll call Shane. Maybe his attorney can prevent Todd from getting bail."

"I doubt Shane's attorney can work miracles. Todd knows what he's doing. He's a master manipulator, and knows the system inside and out. He'll get his way. He always does."

"I'll make sure you have protection," I tell her. "If Todd's released, I guarantee you protection. Please, don't worry."

Molly pulls away and wipes her face. "Sorry." She brushes her hand over my sweatshirt. "I got you all wet."

"I don't mind."

She takes a deep, cleansing breath. "I should get going back to my place. Charlie's probably dying of starvation."

Without saying a word, she collects her phone and her overnight bag and purse.

I follow her to the door. "Do you want me to go with you to your studio this morning? To show you how to use the new security system?"

"Jake left instructions. If I run into any problems, I'll call you, okay?"

"Okay." I hate that she's leaving, but I'll be seeing her again soon. Unless she changes her mind about the wedding. "You're still coming with me tomorrow, aren't you?"

She hesitates. "Um, sure. I'm still going."

"I'll arrange for a car to pick us up at ten tomorrow morning."

"Sounds good. Thank you. I'll see you, Jamie."

And... then she's gone. She's running, but hopefully not far or for long.

I sigh as I head down the hall to my office. My editor sent me a whole file of edits to review. I might as well get caught up on work.

30

Molly

After feeding Charlie and grabbing a quick shower, I dress for work and head to my studio. Even though Todd's in jail, I still feel like he could jump out at me at any time. He's made me paranoid, and I hate that! I don't want to live in fear of him and what crazy thing he might do next.

Thanks to the nifty user guide Jake left for me, I'm able to figure out how to set and turn off the security system in my studio without too much trouble. There's a control panel right behind the sales counter, along with a panic button, and there's another control panel in the back, along with another panic button. There are motion detector lights and video surveillance cameras at the back door in the alley, and all kinds of high-tech gizmos throughout the two rooms.

I have no clue what all this cost, and I'm afraid to ask. But I have to admit, it does help me breathe a little easier. Todd won't be able to sneak in again.

* * *

Saturday morning rolls around before I'm ready. I'd packed my weekend bag the night before, and my dress for the wedding is hanging in a garment bag on the back of my closet door. I tried on the half-dozen dresses I have before deciding on a Wedgewood blue, shin-length satin dress with a high neckline. It has a lacey overlay that makes it a bit more dressy than something I'd normally wear. It's the best I could come up with on short notice.

I leave out plenty of food and water for Charlie. I know he'll miss me, but I'll make it up to him when I get back.

My heartrate picks up when I hear Jamie's door open and close. Not wanting to appear too eager, I force myself to sit on my sofa and wait. A few moments later, there's a knock on my door.

After taking a deep breath, I peek out the peephole. It's Jamie. He's got Gus with him, as well as an overnight bag and a garment bag.

"Hi," I say, after opening the door. "What's in the bag? Will you be wearing a tuxedo?"

"Yes. I'm one of the groomsmen."

Charlie races into the room to greet Jamie, but he comes to a sudden halt when he gets a look at Gus. Charlie approaches Gus cautiously, and the two of them sniff each other. Gus seems pretty chill about the whole thing, and Charlie seems to take pretty quickly to the dog, purring as he rubs against Gus's chest.

"My cat likes your dog," I say.

Jamie smiles. "That's a good sign. Are you ready to go? Our ride is downstairs."

"Yes. I'll just grab my stuff." I give Charlie one last pat on the head and tell him to be a good boy. Then I bring my bags out into the hallway. Jamie takes them from me so I can lock up.

Jamie insists on carrying his bags and mine, along with holding Gus's harness. "Lead the way," he says.

I head downstairs, with Jamie and Gus following behind.

Outside, there's a black SUV waiting for us at the curb. Our Uber driver gets out of the vehicle when he sees us, and opens the rear passenger door. "Good morning. I'm Keith, your driver."

"Good morning," I say, returning the young man's welcoming smile. "Thanks for the ride."

"Not a problem." Keith approaches Jamie. "I'll stow all this in the back. Can the dog ride in the back?"

"Sure," Jamie says, leading Gus to the rear of the vehicle.

Once Gus is safely situated in the back, Jamie opens the rear passenger door and climbs in beside me. He reaches for my hand and links our fingers together. "Did you sleep okay last night?"

"Yes."

"Todd's still in jail?"

"As far as I know, yes."

Jamie squeezes my hand gently. "You can relax this weekend and just have a good time, okay? Nothing to worry about."

I appreciate that he's trying to put me at ease. I return the squeeze and lean into him as we pull into traffic.

* * *

It's nearly eleven o'clock when we arrive at Shane's estate. We stop at both of the security checkpoints, and Jamie talks to the guard through the intercom to gain entrance. Up at the house, there are at least a dozen cars parked around the perimeter of the circular drive. Our driver pulls up to the front entrance to let us out.

There's a small crowd assembled outside the house, including the groom and the future bride, who are welcoming new arrivals. I recognize Elly and her husband, George. And Lia and Jonah.

We say hello to Shane and Beth. Elly greets Jamie with a big bear hug, wrapping him in her arms and squeezing tightly. When she releases him, she gives me a bright smile. "Molly, hello, dear!" she says, hugging me as well. "I'm so glad you came," she whispers in my ear.

Our driver grabs our belongings from the back of the SUV and sets them on the front steps. Gus hops out of the vehicle and races up the steps to greet the bride-to-be.

"I'll carry up your bags, Molly," George says, smiling at me. "Come, I'll show you to your room. It's right next to Jamie's."

* * *

I wondered what the sleeping arrangements would be this weekend. I didn't know what his family thought of me being here, or what, if any, relationship they thought we had. I find it very interesting that they put me in the suite right next to Jamie's.

We follow George up the stairs and down a long corridor. George shows me to my room first, and he points out which suite is Jamie's.

My room is beautiful and spacious. There's a king-sized bed in the center of the room, against the back wall, a fireplace with a stone hearth, a little sitting area, and a balcony overlooking the rear of the house with a front-row view of Lake Michigan.

I hang up my clothes in the closet and put my toiletries in the bathroom, which resembles a high-end spa, complete with a sunken hot tub that easily seats several people. And this is just one suite out of how many? Good grief.

As I step out of the bathroom, my attention is diverted by a knock at the door.

"Come in," I say.

The door opens, and Jamie and Gus walk in.

"Getting settled in?" Jamie says.

"Yes. This room is gorgeous."

Jamie reaches for my hand. "Come downstairs with me. I'd like to introduce you to my parents."

Oh, dear. I am *so* not ready for this.

* * *

The house is decorated beautifully. It's all very tasteful, with lots of candles and fresh flowers. The dining room table, which seats a ridiculous number of people, is decked out with platters filled with every type of finger food imaginable. No one will go hungry this weekend, I'm sure. There's a beverage bar manned by a barista, with every choice imaginable, including fancy coffees, soft drinks, beer and liquor.

The wedding is scheduled to start at two in the afternoon, so we have plenty of time to wander around and explore before we have to get dressed.

Jamie and I continue through the spacious foyer to the great room, where Jonah is setting up his guitars, and the guys are arranging folding chairs into neat rows.

Jamie catches Jake's attention. "Where are Mom and Dad?"

"In the back, by the windows."

Jamie takes my hand and leads me to his parents.

The resemblance between Jamie and his father is easy to see. Calum McIntyre is tall, with a strong build, broad shoulders, and graying brown hair and beard. His brown eyes are so similar to Jamie's.

His mother, Bridget, reminds me of Lia, petite, although there are definitely strawberry hints in her blonde hair, and maybe some strands of gray. Her eyes are a clear, bright blue, and she has freckles. Now I know where Jamie gets his.

Jamie introduces us, and his parents greet me warmly.

"It's a pleasure to meet you, Molly," Bridget says, holding my hand in both of hers. She gives my hand a light squeeze before letting go.

When Jamie's parents are called away for picture taking, we stand at the glass wall, basking in the warm sunlight streaming through the glass. The view from here is stunning, and it saddens me that he can't see it.

So I describe it to him, telling him all about this clear, cold, crisp day, about the sky that is a piercing blue, like his mother's eyes; and the fat, buoyant clouds of pure white that resemble giant cotton balls.

He puts his arm around my shoulders and draws me close. "When you describe things to me, I feel like I can actually see them."

I lean my head against his arm, reveling in the closeness.

"Are you glad you came?" he says, murmuring close to my ear.

His warm breath ruffles my hair, making me shiver. "Yes."

"Good. I'm glad you're here. Will you help me with my tux when it's time? I'm terrible with ties."

"Why don't I believe that?" I say, laughing. "I think you're good at just about everything you try."

He chuckles as he reaches for my hand. "No, it's true. I can't tie ties. I swear it."

I link my fingers with his, enjoying the connection. I still don't believe him, but I'm not going to turn down the opportunity to help him get dressed. "Yes, I'll help you."

* * *

We mingle for a while, and Jamie introduces me to a few more people I don't know. Gina Capelli, the woman catering the reception, her brother Peter Capelli, a restaurateur. Beth's brother, Tyler. Beth's friend Gabrielle, who's organizing the event.

Beth looks radiantly happy today. And it's nice to see Lia and Jonah again. I'm thrilled when I learn that Jonah's going to play and sing.

I'm pleasantly surprised to see Beth's bodyguard, Sam. He's confined to a wheelchair, his left leg in a cast. And there are bruises on his face, as well as healing cuts. But I'm so glad he's on the mend.

Jamie introduces me to an older guy named Cooper, who works for Shane. They're apparently also close friends, and Cooper lives with Shane and Beth. Cooper hovers protectively over Sam, never wandering far from his side, and I think there might be something going on there. I'm a bit surprised at the difference in their ages, but based on the way Sam follows Cooper with his gaze, it seems their admiration is mutual.

About an hour before the ceremony is scheduled to start, Jamie suggests we go upstairs to change. We walk up the curving staircase to the second floor and head toward our rooms.

Stopping at my room, Jamie says, "Why don't you get dressed and come to my room when you're ready?"

"Okay."

There's something about the act of getting dressed up, knowing that Jamie's waiting for me, that gives me butterflies. I clean up quickly and change into my undergarments and matching silk stockings. Then I slip my dress over my head and watch it settle into place.

I pull my hair up into a simple twist, apply just a touch of mascara and eye shadow, and slip on my shoes. Then, as my stomach does somersaults, I head next door to Jamie's room.

"Come in," he says, when I knock lightly.

The sound of his voice makes my spine tingle. I open the door and step inside, stopping dead in my tracks when I see him standing there in nothing but his black trousers. He's in the process of removing his white dress shirt from the garment bag. His feet are bare, as is his chest. He's also not wearing his glasses for a change, and I can't help wondering if he took them off for my sake.

My God, no man has the right to look that good. It's just not fair.

His trousers are unbuttoned and hanging low on his hips, and I can see the waistband of his black boxer briefs.

"Oh, I'm sorry!" I start to back out of the room, but he calls me back.

"Wait! Don't go. Come help me with this shirt. I'm having trouble with all these damn pins."

I close the door behind me and meet him at the foot of the bed. "Here, let me," I say, taking the shirt from him and removing all the straight pins that are keeping the starched, white shirt in pristine condition.

I dispose of the pins in the trashcan, then unbutton the shirt and hold it out to him. “Here you go.”

I’m pretty sure he doesn’t need help putting on a shirt. “What else can I help you with?” I say.

31

Molly

It's the cuffs that give me the biggest headache," he says, buttoning up his shirt. Once he's got it on, he hands me a pair of sterling silver square cuff links with the initials JEM engraved on them.

"What does the 'E' stand for?" I say.

"Edward."

I smile. James Edward McIntyre has a nice ring to it.

I wait patiently for him to tuck the shirt into his trousers, trying not to stare below his waist. Once he has zipped up his pants and secured his belt, he holds one wrist out to me so I can attach his cuff link.

"Yes." It's torture standing so close to him. He smells so good.

Whatever cologne he wears should be made mandatory for all men, because it's absolutely edible. "Hold still," I tell him.

The top three buttons of his shirt are still undone, and standing so close to him makes me hyper aware of him as a man… his height, his warmth, the scent of his skin and cologne. It's very unsettling as my body responds helplessly.

"You okay?" he says. "You're being awfully quiet."

I swallow hard. "I'm fine."

After I attach the first cuff link, he hands me the second one. And while I'm working on that one, he distracts me by skimming his fingers over my hair.

"You put your hair up," he says.

Then he gently fingers one of the tendrils I left hanging loose, making me shiver.

I notice his throat contracting as he swallows. "What are you wearing? Describe it to me."

"A dress."

He chuckles. "Funny. Try again."

"It's Wedgewood blue satin, shin-length, with a lace overlay."

"In English, please."

"It's blue. Sort of a medium to medium-light blue, with a hint of gray."

He nods. "That's better. What else?"

"My shoes are gray, just basic pumps with a slight heel."

"You do seem a bit taller. What else?"

"Chandelier earrings with tiny seed pearls. That's it. Nothing fancy."

He fingers my earrings as I finish attaching the second cuff link.

"There, all done," I say.

He cradles my face in his hands and closes his eyelids. "God, I wish I could see you."

"Don't worry, you're not missing much," I say, trying to keep the mood light.

He frowns. Then his hands tighten on my face, and he presses his mouth to my forehead. "Molly, you have no idea how wrong you are."

He trails kisses down my face until his lips settle on mine. He seals our mouths, his lips nudging mine open. When I gasp in surprise, he slips his tongue inside to stroke mine. I taste mint toothpaste and Jamie. When I make an involuntary sound, something that sounds a lot like a whimper, he tightens his arms on me. I lose myself in him, slipping my arms around his waist and splaying my hands on his firm back. He pulls me closer and deepens the kiss.

I suddenly wonder why we're putting clothes on when we should be taking them off. We're standing right at the foot of a big bed. It would be so easy to fall into it and give in to something I think we both want.

Someone knocks on the bedroom door, and I jump.

"Wedding party downstairs in ten minutes for photos," says a booming male voice. "Shake a leg, buddy!"

"That was my dad," Jamie says. He sighs. "I've got to go."

I release Jamie and step back. My face is hot, and I know I'm flushed.

"I'll find you after the ceremony," he says.

"Okay."

I quickly help him with his cummerbund and gray vest and tie his gray silk tie for him. My dad taught me how to tie ties when I was a little girl, and I always tied his. I feel a sense of deep satisfaction helping Jamie with the finishing touches.

He pulls on his tuxedo coat and grabs his cane. "I'll see you after the ceremony." Then he kisses me one last time before he leaves the room.

With Jamie off to do wedding party stuff, I wander downstairs alone. It's half-past one, so the ceremony doesn't start for another half-hour. I have some time to kill.

I head to the great room, where I see Beth and Shane standing on the dais at the head of the room, along with Cooper, who's wearing a no-frills black suit and tie. It looks like they're doing a bit of rehearsing.

Shane's already wearing his tuxedo, but Beth's still in casual clothes. He looks incredibly handsome. Beth's a lucky girl.

Shane takes Beth's hands in his and pulls her close. He glances at his watch, then says something to Beth that makes her smile. She reaches up and fiddles with his tie, beaming radiantly. It's so obvious that they're madly in love. I almost feel like an intruder watching them together.

I wander into the kitchen, where Elly is helping Gina Capelli put some final touches on a beautiful three-tiered wedding cake.

"That's a gorgeous cake," I say.

Gina smiles at me. "Thanks. It's pretty, but it's a pain in the ass to work with."

"Everything's wonderful," I say. "The food, the cake. You're very talented."

Beth's friend Gabrielle waltzes hurriedly into the kitchen. "Has anyone seen Beth?" Her long, curly red hair is styled in an elaborate up-do, with sprigs of baby's breath woven through the strands. Her complexion is pale, like cream, and her face is sprinkled with freckles.

"She's in the great room," I say. "With Shane. They're rehearsing."

"Oh, thanks! Sorry, gotta run. Beth needs to get dressed."

I hang out in the kitchen with Elly and Gina, trying to be helpful when I can. When I hear Lia's boyfriend playing something soft and lovely on the guitar, I take my cue and head into the great room to take a seat.

The guests begin to fill the rows of chairs quickly, and Shane and his brothers take their places at the head of the room. Cooper's standing on the dais, front and center. It looks like he's going to officiate the ceremony. Shane's standing next to Cooper, then it's Jamie, Jake, and Liam. Jamie looks so handsome up there in his tux, and so bad-ass in his dark glasses. How can one family have so many attractive sons? Of course, if you look at their father, who's seated in the front row on the right side, you can easily see where they get their good looks.

The photographer takes a few more pictures of the groom and his party. Then the lights dim a little, and the photographer steps out of the way as a hush comes over the room.

Jonah starts playing Pachelbel's *Canon in D*, the tempo slow and the melody lilting, and I feel my throat tighten with emotion. The bridal party enters the great room. First, Gabrielle, then a young woman with a sweet, round face, chin-length dark hair, and bright blue eyes.

Finally, the bride enters the room on the arm of her brother, a dashingly handsome man with dark hair and blue-green eyes, dressed in an austere black tuxedo.

The wedding ceremony is simple and lovely. Beth looks so happy as she recites her vows to Shane, and as he recites his vows to her, his gaze never once leaves her face.

After the ceremony ends, the guests wander out into the foyer and the dining room while the guys immediately start clearing away the folding chairs. I slip out into the foyer, but stay close so I can watch Jamie, who's helping with the chairs.

Beth comes out of the dining room.

"Beth, hi! Congratulations!" I give her a hug. Not surprisingly, she's practically giddy with happiness. "It was a beautiful ceremony, and you look radiant."

Her smile is genuine. "Thanks, Molly. I'm so glad you came."

"I wouldn't have missed it for the world. And this place – holy cow! It's magnificent."

"Where's Jamie?" she says, glancing around.

I nod toward the great room. "He's helping his brothers clear away the chairs."

"You guys came together, right?" she says.

"Yes."

"Are you going to dance with him?"

I make a face and laugh. "God, no. I'm not dancing. I'm just here to watch and eat cake."

32

Molly

After the chairs are put away and the photographer takes more pictures, everyone reconvenes in the great room to proceed with the wedding activities. I haven't really attended that many weddings, so I'm not sure what all's involved.

Shane and Beth enter the great room, and the guests greet them boisterously, hooting and hollering and applauding. Beth's turning all shades of pink as Shane leads her to the front of the room.

Gabrielle hands Beth the wedding bouquet. "Turn around and throw the bouquet behind you to the single ladies." Then Gabrielle turns to us. "All right, all the single ladies up front."

Lots of good-natured ribbing takes place as the single women are pushed and prodded to the front of the crowd.

"Don't forget Lia!" Shane says, pointing out his sister, who's doing her best to blend into the background.

"Yeah, come on, Lia," Jake says, pushing his sister next to me in line.

Laughing, Beth turns her back to us. She says something to Shane I can't quite make out, and he says, "Fire away."

Beth tosses the bouquet behind her. The flowers are heading straight for Lia, and she reaches out and catches the bouquet before it hits her squarely in the face.

"Oh, hell no!" Lia says, shoving the bouquet into my hands. "Here, you take it!"

I don't want it any more than Lia does, and I try to pass it back to her. "That's okay," I say. "You can keep it."

But Lia lifts her hands, saying, "Not a chance," leaving me stuck with the flowers, to the sound of well-intentioned laughter.

"Now it's the guys' turn," Gabrielle says, ushering all the bachelors to the front of the room, including Jamie and all the rest of Shane's brothers. Even Sam gets in the action when Miguel Rodriguez pushes his wheelchair into the line-up.

Laughing, Shane points out several men who aren't in the bachelor line who apparently should be. "Hey, Cooper, Tyler, you're single. Get up here! You too, Peter!"

Cooper growls back at him, and everyone breaks into laughter.

Gabrielle directs Beth to a chair in the center of the room and instructs Shane to kneel down in front of her and remove her garter so he can toss it to the line of bachelors.

Shane kneels down in front of Beth, and when he slips his hands up beneath her wedding gown, the crowd hushes in anticipation of the big reveal. His heated gaze is locked on hers as he slips the garter oh, so slowly down her leg and pulls it free. Then he stands and raises the garter belt into the air like it's a trophy. But instead of throwing it, he kisses it, then grins as he tucks it into the front pocket of his trousers.

"Sorry, guys," he says. "There's no way in hell I'm letting this go." Then he bends down to kiss Beth. "I don't share."

"Party pooper," Gabrielle chides him, as more laughter ensues. "All right, next is the first dance featuring the newly married couple."

The room goes quiet as Jonah begins to play *Everything* by Michael Bublé. Shane gallantly holds out his hand for Beth, and then he sweeps a very nervous Beth into their first dance. "Don't look at them," he tells her. "Look at me."

A hush falls over the room as everyone watches them dance. Eventually Beth relaxes and seems to be enjoying herself. Their gazes are locked on each other's, and neither of them pays anyone else any attention.

I find myself holding my breath as they move across the room. It's so obvious that they're madly in love with each other. Of course, I'm happy for them, but I'm also a little envious. Todd and I were never so wrapped up in each other the way these two are. I would give anything to have that with someone. And then I glance at Jamie, and my heart constricts. Maybe I have found that kind of love, or at least the potential for it, if I can stop being afraid and start taking a chance.

As their dance comes to an end, Shane pulls Beth close, and the two of them stand in the center of the room, with eyes for no one but each other. When he lowers his head and kisses Beth, there's an audible sigh in the room.

"I love you, Mrs. McIntyre," he says.

I think there are tears in his eyes.

"I love you, too," Beth says, her voice barely audible.

As Jonah ends the song, everyone breaks into applause.

Then, Gabrielle steps forward and grabs my hand, pulling me into the center of the room. I forgot all about Lia handing me the bouquet. I think that means I'm supposed to have the next dance. I feel the blood drain out of my head when I realize that I'll be expected to stand in front of this room full of people.

"Next is the dance with the lucky lady who caught the bouquet. Normally, she'd dance with the lucky gentleman who caught the garter belt, but since Shane was stingy...." Again, more laughter. "Poor Molly doesn't have anyone to dance with," she says, scowling at Shane for messing up her plans.

For a moment, I'm relieved, thinking I'm off the hook. But then Jamie steps forward, dashing my hopes.

"I'd be honored to dance with Molly," he says, removing his dark glasses and slipping them into the pocket of his tuxedo. "That is, if she'll have me."

I glance around the room, first at Jamie, then at Beth, who's watching me sympathetically. She knows I don't want to dance. But now I'm on the spot, in front of everyone. As I glance at Jamie, my heart hurts. I don't want to dance in front of a room full of people, but I can't turn him down in front of everyone. He even took his glasses off for me.

I have no choice. I can't say no without hurting Jamie, and there's no way I'm going to do anything that would hurt him. How can I stand here and be such a coward when he's putting himself out there for me? I smile at him, touched at his courage and his kindness. "I'd love to, Jamie."

As Jonah starts strumming the opening chords of one of my favorite songs – *All of Me* by John Legend – I move toward Jamie, and he meets me halfway. His arm sweeps around my back, and he takes my hand in his and begins the dance.

A brand new hush falls over the room, making me acutely aware of how closely everyone is watching us. I catch a glimpse of Jamie's mom, who has tears in her eyes. I feel queasy.

"You're shaking," Jamie says. "Just relax. It'll be over before you know it. And I promise not to step on your toes."

"It's not that. Jamie, your mom looks like she's about to cry."

He smiles, and I see tiny crows' feet crinkling around his eyes.

"She worries about me," he says. "She's just happy to see me doing something so normal."

I squeeze his hand. "By the way, you look very handsome."

He grins. "Thank you."

And I could swear he's blushing.

I work hard to maintain the smile on my face for the sake of all the onlookers, as we're still very much the center of attention. Knowing everyone's eyes are on us is nerve wracking. I don't know how long I can do this.

His arm across my back is warm and solid, and he grips my hand firmly, using it to steer us in the right direction.

"Warn me if we're on a collision course," he says, laughing.

But I don't think there's any danger. We have the whole floor to ourselves, with plenty of room to maneuver. Jamie dances perfectly, leading me across the room with confidence. He keeps his face on me, and I enjoy seeing him without his glasses.

I glance up at Jamie and tease myself, for just a moment, by thinking that we could have something special. He's extraordinary, and he doesn't do things in half measures. But I honestly don't know if I can let go enough to trust someone with my heart – more specifically, with my body. I did that once, and it didn't turn out well. My *husband* betrayed me – the one who had pledged to forsake all others. I don't think Jamie would ever betray me – it's just not in him to do something like that. But the idea of trusting someone, risking my heart again, terrifies me. Jamie deserves someone as courageous as he is, and I feel like a fraud standing here with him. He deserves someone whole, someone brave.

When the song comes to an end, I go up on my toes to kiss his cheek. "Thank you for the dance."

And, before I turn into a blubbering fool in front of everyone, I walk out of the room without looking back. If I look back and see Jamie's expression, I'll lose it for sure.

33

Jamie

As I listen to the sound of Molly's footsteps fading in the distance, I slip my glasses back on. The only reason I took them off was for her.

She couldn't get out of here fast enough. I try hard not to take it personally. In hindsight, I put her on the spot by asking her to dance in front of a room full of people. She probably didn't want to dance, but she said yes so she wouldn't embarrass me in front of everyone. I screwed up. I should have asked her in private.

With an exasperated sigh, I run my fingers through my hair and try to regroup. I put myself in her shoes. She's self-conscious about her body – that much I know. It must have been difficult for her to stand up in front of the entire room and dance. She has no reason to be self-conscious because she looks beautiful. I know this because nearly a dozen people have told me so today. Elly, my mom, my dad, all three of my sisters. My brothers. Beth.

The funny thing is, it doesn't matter to me what she looks like. Physical appearance just isn't relevant to me now. It's the person inside the physical body that I can connect with – not the exterior.

But her fears aren't driven by logic – they're emotional. I get that. She's scarred, both emotionally and physically, too, I suppose.

I need to find a way to convince her that I honestly don't care about her mastectomies. I mean, yeah, breasts are nice. They're soft and they smell so damn good. And nipples are sweet when they pucker up like little pink berries. But in the bigger scheme of things... in my life right now, it's not that important. I'd far more rather have someone in my life who makes me feel good – someone I can talk to and laugh with. Someone I can snuggle up with and spoon and touch and caress. There's *so much* we can have together that the little bit we can't have doesn't matter.

And then there's Todd. I know she's afraid that Todd will come after me, but honest to God, unless he has a gun, I can handle Todd with my bare hands. Molly has no idea what I'm capable of physically, but that's easy enough to rectify. I'll ask Jake to help me give Molly a demonstration. Maybe that will help relieve some of her concerns about my safety. There's a fully-equipped martial arts studio down on the lower level. Jake and I – and maybe Liam if I can wrangle him into it – could put on a show Molly won't soon forget.

But first, I need to find her. I need to apologize for putting her on the spot, and I need to convince her that I mean what I say. I need *her* in my life. I don't require a pair of breasts to be content.

* * *

I know this house like the back of my hand. I don't need Gus, or my cane, to find my way upstairs to the suites, and to my own room.

Jake intercepts me on the stairs as I'm going up. "Hey, you need some help?"

"No, thanks. Well, actually, yes, I do need your help a little later this evening. I need a favor."

"Sure. What is it?"

"I need for you to spar with me in the ring later. I want to put on a demonstration for Molly."

"Are you going to show off a little? Maybe do a few party tricks?"

"Something like that. Molly's worried that Todd might try to hurt me. She doesn't realize that I can fend for myself in a physical confrontation. I want to show her."

"Gotcha. Sure, no problem. Just give me a holler, and we'll do it. Do you want Liam too?"

"Yes. Ask him."

* * *

I reach Molly's door and knock.

Nothing.

I knock again. "Molly? It's Jamie."

I hear footsteps, and then the door knob turns and she opens the door. I can't help wondering if she's been crying.

"Can I come in?" I say.

"Sure." She takes a step back, and I walk inside.

Yeah, she's been crying. I can hear it in the thickness of her voice. I close the door behind me. "You've been crying. Are you okay?"

She gives me a tearful laugh as she closes the door behind me. "I'm okay," she says.

"I owe you an apology."

"Jamie – no, you don't. I owe you one."

"What happened downstairs? Why'd you walk away?"

"It was just too much. Everyone was looking at us, and your mom... she was crying. I think quite a few people in that room are convinced there's something going on between us."

"Isn't there?"

She makes a pained sound of protest. "Jamie, I told you, we can't. *I* can't."

"Why not? You can't tell me you don't feel anything for me. So why can't there be something between us? Is it because of this?" I take off my glasses and wave them at her before slipping them into my jacket pocket.

"Oh, my God, no!" she says, clearly insulted at the insinuation that she'd reject me because of my blindness.

"Then why?"

"You know why!"

"I want you to tell me. Is it because of your body, or because of Todd? Because personally, I don't see either issue as a problem. I told you, I don't care about your breasts, and I also told you I'm not worried about Todd."

She makes a frustrated sound – something that sounds an awful lot like a growl – and I have to bite my lip not to laugh. Here she is, all twisted up inside over things I think are nonissues.

"Molly." When I reach out for her, my hands come into contact with soft fleece fabric. "You changed?"

"Yes. I'm done for the evening. I thought I'd stay here in my room and relax, maybe watch a movie."

"I was hoping you'd come downstairs with me. There's something I want to show you."

"Do I have to get dressed up again?"

"No. You can wear whatever's comfortable. I'll be changing into workout clothes for this."

"Oh?" She sounds intrigued.

"Yeah. Come with me. Please."

"Okay," she says, sounding curious.

I'm going to give her a show she won't soon forget, and I hope at least one of her concerns will be laid to rest. Then, I'll just have to convince her that I mean what I say when I tell her I don't care that she doesn't have breasts.

* * *

While Molly goes into the bathroom to change, I message Jake:

We'll be on our way downstairs. Are you ready?

His answer:

Anytime

A few moments later, Molly comes out of the bathroom. "Okay, let's go see this thing you want me to see."

We walk down two flights of stairs to the lower level, where there's a completely outfitted workout room. It's all here... free weights, weight machines, treadmills and stationary bikes, a boxing ring, and mats for martial arts. As we approach the workout room, I pause with Molly outside the observation window. I know Jake's in there. I can hear him hitting the punching bags – warming up.

"Who's in there?" I ask her.

"Jake and Liam."

"Let's go in." I open the door for Molly, and she walks inside. I can hear Jake punishing the bag with rapid-fire punches, grunting with exertion.

"Oh, my God," she says, and I presume she's watching Jake.

I don't have to see my brother to remember the intensity with which he works out, driving himself to the limits of his endurance. I'm sure he's already hot and sweaty, and if he's not wearing gloves, then his knuckles are bloody.

"Is he wearing gloves?" I ask.

"No," she says in a subdued, slightly-horrified voice.

"Typical. Jake's a brute."

"Hey, guys," Liam says as he approaches. "What's up?"

"I thought I'd go a few rounds in the ring with Jake," I say. "You want to referee?"

"Go a few rounds doing what?" Molly says, sounding worried.

"Sure," Liam says. "Let's do it."

"Do what?" Molly says, her voice suddenly an octave higher.

At least now I have her attention.

34

Molly

I don't know what's going on, but none of it seems like a good idea. Jake is beating the hell out of a punching bag, his thick, muscled arms churning like pistons. He's not wearing gloves, and his bandage-wrapped knuckles are smeared with blood.

Of all Jamie's brothers, Jake's the biggest. He's wearing a pair of black board shorts and a sleeveless black T-shirt. There's a tattoo on his left side. It looks like a date, but I can't quite read it from here.

Liam throws a towel at Jake. "Dude, wipe the blood off your hands and rebandage. Jamie wants to go a few rounds."

Jamie pulls off his sweatshirt, and underneath it he's wearing a black T-shirt tucked into his sweatpants. He kicks off his sneakers and pulls off his socks. Then he hands me his glasses. "Would you hold these for me? I don't want to break them."

"What? No!" I say, taking his glasses. "What are you doing?"

Liam climbs into the ring and calls to Jamie. "Over here, man."

Jamie zeroes in on the sound of Liam's voice and walks to the ring. Then he steps up onto the platform foundation of the ring and slips between two ropes. Jake's right behind him, wrapping fresh bandages on his hands.

"What are the rules?" Liam says, as his two brothers face off in opposite corners of the ring.

"There aren't any," Jake says, grinning at Jamie.

"Wait a minute!" I say, approaching the ring. I have no idea what's going on, but I don't like it one bit. "What are you guys doing?"

"We're sparring," Jake says, giving me a *duh* look. "What does it look like?"

"You can't do that!"

Jake gives me another exasperated look. "Why not?"

"Are you kidding me? Because Jamie can't see!"

Jake shrugs. "So? It never stopped him before."

Jamie turns in my direction. "Molly, it's okay. You don't have to worry about me."

And then I realize what he's doing. He's trying to prove that he's capable of protecting himself physically. This is because of Todd! I climb up onto the platform and grab hold of the ropes near Jamie. "Jamie, please! You don't have to do this. Please come out of there."

"Are we going to do this or not?" Jake says, sounding annoyed. "I don't have all night."

"Stop pressuring him!" I say.

Liam comes up beside me and lays his hand on my shoulder, giving me a consoling pat. "Molly, it's okay, really. You don't have to worry about Jamie."

"Yeah," Jake says. "If anything, worry about *me*."

"All right, take your places, gentlemen," Liam says, climbing into the ring with his brothers.

Jake moves back into the corner opposite of where Jamie's standing. Jamie steps forward into the ring, and stands with his arms at his sides, completely relaxed, looking like a sacrificial lamb.

"Okay, go," Liam says. "May the best man win."

"That would be me," Jake says, coming out of his corner.

My heart is in my throat, nearly choking me as I watch Jake stalk across the mat toward Jamie. This is so wrong! So unfair! I shake my head, wanting to bash both their heads in for being foolish.

The door behind us opens.

"Ooo, just in time!" Lia says.

I glance back as Lia and Jonah stroll into the room.

"Lia, make them stop!" I say.

She rolls her eyes at me like I'm nuts. "Why would I do that? This will be the most fun I've had all day."

"Molly, you'd better get down from there," Lia says, grabbing my hand and pulling me back down to the floor. "They get crazy sometimes."

I watch as Jake stalks barefoot in a wide circle around Jamie, as if looking for an opening. Jamie closes his eyelids and cocks his head slightly, as if he's listening. But there's nothing for him to listen to, except the faint shuffling of Jake's bare feet on the boxing ring floor.

As Jake continues to circle Jamie, Jamie moves with him, turning to keep his brother in front of him. I can't possibly see how this is a good idea.

Suddenly, moving faster than I ever could have imagined, Jake strikes out at Jamie, but Jamie sidesteps the blow and turns the table on Jake, twisting to grab his brother from behind and throw him to the floor. Jamie follows him down and pins him to the mat with an unbreakable hold on his shoulders and a knee in the middle of his back.

Jake slaps the floor, and Jamie leaps back, letting his brother up.

Jake chuckles. "Lucky first strike," he says, taunting Jamie.

Then, without pausing even to catch his breath, Jake comes at Jamie with a roundhouse kick. Jamie intercepts Jake's foot before it makes contact, redirecting his momentum and driving him back down to the mat.

"Ooo, man!" Lia yells, hanging on the ropes along the side of the ring. "Brutal!"

Jake jumps to his feet, then comes at Jamie from behind and gets him in a choke hold. He's squeezing Jamie so tight his arm muscles are bulging. He's got to be cutting off Jamie's air.

"Stop it!" I yell. "Let him go."

Lia laughs as Jamie reaches back and strikes his brother's groin. Jake grunts with pain, and Jamie follows through by pivoting and striking his brother in the abdomen with a solid punch that knocks the air out of Jake.

This isn't sparring! These guys are trying to kill each other. My heart stops in my chest and I can't breathe.

Jake takes advantage of the lull in the action to jump Jamie from behind, throwing him to the floor. Jamie twists to his back, catching Jake's legs with a swift kick and knocking his brother to the ground. They roll across the mat, struggling for control, and

Jamie ends up on top, lying on top of Jake, who's face down on the mat. Jamie threads his arms under Jake's brawny shoulders and behind his neck, trapping him in a choke hold.

"Had enough?" Jamie grunts, breathing heavily.

Unable to get enough air to speak, Jake slaps the mat twice. That must be some sort of surrender signal, because Jamie releases him and jumps back out of reach.

"He kicked your ass, Jake," Lia says, climbing in the ring with them.

I glance at Jonah, who's standing beside me shaking his head. He simply shrugs. "Never get in the way of McIntyre siblings when they're having their fun," he says.

Jamie holds out his hand and hauls Jake to his feet.

"Shake it off, pal," Lia says to Jake as he tries to catch his breath.

Jake wraps his arms around Lia and lifts her high in the air, then throws her over his shoulder so that she's hanging face down, laughing as she struggles to get free.

I glance at Jonah again, and he just shakes his head. "Like I said, don't get in their way. You could get clobbered by mistake."

When Jamie climbs down from the boxing ring, he says, "I need a shower, badly."

Jake laughs and throws a hand towel at him. Jamie catches it midair before it can hit him in the face. *How in the hell does he do that?*

This close to Jake, I can see the tattoo on his side better: March 5, 2005. I wonder what the significance of that date is.

"Molly?" Jamie says, facing my general direction.

I realize he's trying to zero in on my location. "I'm right here."

Sure enough, he walks right to me, and when he gets close, I reach out and touch him. He is hot and sweating, and he's breathing hard.

"Come upstairs with me?" he says.

"Yes."

"But first, can you help me find my shoes and socks?"

* * *

We leave the workout room and head for the stairs.

"Everything all right?" he says, walking behind me with his hand on my shoulder so I can guide him.

"Yes."

"You've been awfully quiet since the ring."

You mean, since your brother tried to kill you? I want to say, but I bite my tongue. Obviously, this is normal behavior for these guys. "I don't want to talk about it right now."

"Okay," he says.

I'm preoccupied by what I just saw downstairs. How in the world did Jamie do that? How could he anticipate his brother's every move and meet it so effectively with a counter move? The man's blind, like completely blind. It makes no sense.

I stop in front of the door to his suite and open it. He grabs my shoulders and walks me into the room, nudging the door closed with his bare foot. He tosses his sneakers and socks to the floor. "What's wrong?" he says.

I shake my head, exasperated. "I don't even know where to start."

"Start anywhere you want," he says. And then he whips his T-shirt off and tosses it onto the floor.

My eyes widen at the sight of his magnificent chest up close and personal. That fiend! He did that on purpose! "No fair. You're cheating!" I say.

He laughs. "I have no idea what you're talking about."

"Bullshit! You're trying to dazzle me with your magnificent body, and that's not fair."

He smiles. "Magnificent? Do you really think so?"

"Oh, stop. You know perfectly well what you look like, and yes, it's magnificent."

He unbuttons his jeans and lowers the zipper. "You don't mind if I shower, do you?"

"Don't let me stop you," I say, daring him to follow through with his threat to strip in front of me.

35

Molly

I don't know what possessed me to say that, but knowing him as I do, I shouldn't have been surprised when he drops his jeans, leaving himself standing there in nothing but a pair of black boxer briefs.

Oh, my God. Magnificent doesn't even begin to do him justice. He's so far out of my league, but he doesn't even realize it.

"Want to join me?" he says, moving closer.

I can smell his maleness, which is accentuated by his vigorous workout downstairs. He's hot still, and he's sweaty, and he's sexy as hell.

"Jamie, how did you do what you just did downstairs? How is that even possible?"

His lips quirk up into a half-smile. "I told you my senses have sharpened to compensate for lack of sight. Hearing, touch, even smell – every sense is heightened. Even something as miniscule as a shift in air pressure, wind speed and direction... I can feel it. Plus, I know how Jake fights. He's a brute. All brute strength and no finesse. Normally that works well for him, but I can anticipate his moves and I can tell where his strikes are coming from as they come."

Jamie pulls me into his arms. "Come shower with me."

His words are part invitation, part question, and part plea. I gaze into his face, scanning his profile. He's still a little flushed from the physical activity. If he went hand-to-hand with Todd, Todd wouldn't stand a chance – I realize that now.

I have to say it gives me a little bit of comfort to know that Jamie can handle a physical attack. "I know why you did it," I tell him.

His lips flatten. "I wanted to demonstrate that you don't have to worry about Todd hurting me. I can handle myself. Now, enough about Todd. Come shower with me."

"I can't."

"Why not?"

"You know why." I don't want to be naked in a shower with him. I don't want him coming into contact with my chest.

"Molly." His voice is a mixture of censure and impatience. "You know I don't care."

"Well, I do. I'm just not comfortable – "

Jamie turns me in his arms, standing behind me, and wraps his arms around me and pulls me close. I can feel his erection pressing against the fabric of his boxers. His hands come to rest just beneath my breast forms. "I dispelled your fears of Todd hurting me.

Now I have to dispel your fear of me touching your chest."

I try half-heartedly to break away. "Jamie, let me go."

His lips press against the back of my head. "It's just a shower. I won't touch your chest without your permission. I promise." He dips his head and kisses the side of my neck, making me shiver. "Come on. I need help washing my back."

"Ha. If you can do the things I saw you do tonight, you can wash your own back."

"Well, technically I can, yes. But it would be a lot more enjoyable if you did it for me. If you wash mine, I'll wash yours."

"Are we still talking about backs?"

"Sure. If that's what you want."

"You're incorrigible." The idea of taking a shower with him is very tantalizing. And if he keeps his promise and washes my back, and not my front, I think I can handle that. "If you promise... just my back."

Jamie holds up three fingers and gives her a Boy Scout salute. "Scout's honor."

"Were you really a Boy Scout?"

"Of course I was." He kisses the back of my head. "Now, you're overdressed. Let me help you."

36

Molly

I know I'm playing with fire when Jamie lifts my shirt up over my head and tosses it onto his bed. I shiver, chilled by the sudden exposure. Thankfully, he bypasses my bra and reaches in front of me to unsnap my jeans.

"I can't believe I'm agreeing to this," I mutter.

He leans against my back, his big body warming me, and lowers my zipper. What are we doing here? I wonder, as he tugs my jeans past my hips. This slope keeps getting slipperier and slipperier.

"Come on, it'll feel good. I promise."

I step away from him and pull off my socks and shoes, then kick off my jeans.

Jamie holds my hand and pulls me along with him into the

bathroom. The room is dark when we step inside. Jamie flips on the light, then he grabs washcloths and towels from the linen closet and sets them out for us.

When I think about how I left him on the dance floor, walking out of the room as my emotions were swamping me, I feel ashamed. I'm such a coward.

His warm hands settle on my bare shoulders. "Ready?"

I decide to leave my hair up, because I don't want to deal with having to dry my hair right now. I remove my panties and bra, fold them, and put them on the counter where they'll stay dry. My breast forms are not waterproof. "Yes."

We step into the warm spray and wet our bodies. Then Jamie sticks his head beneath the water and grabs a bottle of shampoo and quickly washes his hair.

When he's done, he squirts some body wash into his hand and creates a lather. "Turn around. I'll wash your back."

I do what he says, and he starts massaging my shoulders and neck with soapy hands. Then he moves down my arms and back to my hips.

"I think you should give us a chance," he says. "I know what your concerns are, and I think I'm done a good job demonstrating that they're unfounded. I think I deserve a chance."

I laugh. "You've laid out a very logical argument."

"Thank you. Does that mean yes?"

He's gone to so much effort. How can I say no? Especially when we want the same thing. I sigh.

"Yes?" he says, interpreting my sigh. "Baby steps?"

"All right. Baby steps."

"Excellent." When I feel his lips on my neck, I shiver.

He squirts more soap into his hands, creates a lather, then

reaches around to wash my belly. His hands slowly migrate up toward my chest area, stopping just shy of my ribcage. He's just inches from my scars.

I tense. "What happened to *baby steps*?"

"Sweetheart, you need to get used to me touching your body. All of it, including your chest. There's nothing to be afraid of."

Very slowly, his fingers move up my body, rubbing slow soapy circles on my skin.

"That's easy for you to say."

"I take my glasses off for you because I trust you. I don't do that for anyone else."

Now he's not fighting fairly.

"Molly." His lips graze my ear, and his voice is low and warm. I just want to close my eyes and sink into him. "Please don't be afraid. You can trust me not to hurt you."

He's right. I can trust him. He's one of the most trust-worthy people I've ever met. "Okay, fine!" I stand stiffly in his arms as his hands slide further up my torso to my scars.

He runs his hands gently across my chest, tracing my scars, traveling the dips and rises of my body. I close my eyes and surrender to the inevitable. The only place I want to be is in his arms, and the only way to get there is to let him make it right for us.

"Do you trust me?" he says.

"Yes." I trust him with my life. So why shouldn't I trust him with my self-esteem?

As I relax back against him, he draws me close. "Close your eyes and relax."

As a blind man, he learns through touch. He's very tactile, so it comes as no surprise that he wants to explore my scars. He skims the tips of his fingers along the path of each scar, measuring the distances. My heart is thundering painfully, and I really want this to be over. I keep reliving Todd's censure of my decisions and choices. I keep feeling Todd's dissatisfaction over and over.

But as Jamie's fingers gently explore my chest, it strikes me that Todd never once touched me like this. He never made the slightest effort to learn my new body. We did have sex a few times after my surgery, but he always requested that I keep my nightgown on the entire time. He didn't want to be reminded of my *imperfections*, as he called them. In the beginning, I didn't see them as imperfections as much as evidence that I'd overcome a challenge life threw my way.

Once I'm able to relax a bit, I melt against Jamie and allow myself to feel the pleasure of his touch. When his fingers drift south, I realize his inspection is over. It's done. He discovered what he wanted to know, and now he's moving on to a very different part of me. I feel a sudden weight lifting off my shoulders, as if the one big thing I've been afraid of is suddenly not so scary anymore.

Instead, his fingers are grazing the skin of my abdomen, past my belly, to my belly button. My belly clenches tightly at the sudden change in direction of his thoughts and fingers, and my body switches gears quickly from panic mode to arousal mode.

I am fully aware of the heat of his erection pressing against my lower back. My thoughts focus on that firm pressure, and I imagine what it would feel like to have all that strength and heat inside me. I'll bet he makes love with the same hyper-awareness that he has for everything he does.

Am I ready for this? I'm not a casual sex kind of person. If I share my body with someone, it's because he's already captured my heart and soul.

Jamie's fingers slip between my legs and touch my wetness. I gasp, arching my back in response. It's been so long, it's a shock to feel someone touching me there.

"It's okay," he murmurs, as his lips skim along the sensitive skin of my neck and shoulder. He plies me with gentle, sucking kisses that heat up my skin and set my body on fire. I have only a second to wonder if his kisses will leave marks on my skin when his finger dips inside me.

It's been a long time for me, and it's a tight fit, even for his finger. Jamie gently works his finger inside, and I begin squirming and mewling.

"God, you're so tight," he says, dropping a heated kiss on my shoulder. "Tell me if I hurt you."

When his thumb presses on my clit, I see fireworks behind my eyelids. *This is really going to happen!* "Jamie, if you didn't bring condoms, I'm going to kill you."

He laughs. "Not a problem. Everything's taken care of." He trails kisses up and down my sensitive neck as his thumb strokes my clitoris. His finger is deep inside me now, stroking a tender spot. I'm practically panting now as the pleasure swells deep inside me.

I don't realize how tense I am until he whispers in my ear, "Relax into me. I've got you."

I melt into him, allowing him to support me as my knees go weak. His finger keeps stroking, and his thumb keeps pressing delicious little circles into my clit, stealing my breath and my sanity.

When pleasure detonates deep inside me, my body stiffens and I bite back a cry. He wraps his arms around me, holding me steady beneath the spray of warm water until the pulses subside.

"What do you say we dry off and move to my bed?" he says.

"I think that's a good idea, before I fall down."

"Don't worry, I won't let you fall."

Jamie shuts off the showerhead, then grabs the towels and hands me one. We both dry off and wrap ourselves in the big towels, then step outside the shower stall.

"Come to my bed?" he says, putting his arms around me.

"Okay."

He smiles, then leads me by the hand out of the bathroom and to his big bed. As I climb beneath the bedding, he opens the top drawer of the bedside table and pulls out a brand-new box of XL condoms. He opens the box and pulls out a strip, then lays it on the nightstand.

I think about making some sarcastic statement about the fact that he brought an entire box, but the thought of that XL gives me a moment's pause.

I catch a quick glimpse of his size just before he crawls into bed with me.

My entire body is trembling. "Um, Jamie. It's been a while for me."

He stills. "Me too."

His words sink in and I realize he's just as nervous about this as I am. "Have you been with anyone since your accident?"

"No. I've never trusted anyone enough."

37

Molly

His confession guts me, and I realize this is just as big a milestone for him as it is for me. And while I've been self-absorbed with my own issues, I haven't considered his. We're both wading into new territory. We're both going out on a limb and trusting someone else not to hurt us.

I reach out and put my hands on his face, brushing my thumbs along his cheeks just above his beard. He lowers his eyelids and relaxes into my touch.

"Jamie?"

"Yes?"

"Come here."

I guide his face toward mine with a gentle pull, and he follows.

What starts out as a simple kiss quickly turns into something a little bit out of control. It's like someone flipped a switch. Now that we've given each other the green light, there's nothing standing in the way.

Jamie looms closer, sliding his fingers into the hair at the base of my skull, tugging firmly, not enough to hurt, but definitely enough to get my attention. He pulls off my hair tie, and my hair falls to my shoulders. I draw in a nervous breath, and he takes advantage of my open mouth to slip his tongue inside.

He lifts his mouth just enough to speak, his voice low and rough. "I won't ask for anything more than you're comfortable with. We don't have to have sex if you're not ready. We can just sleep together. But either way, I want you to stay the night with me. Please."

How can I say no? He's saying all the right things, the things I need for him to say. He's not pushing me. He's not asking for more than I'm ready for. And I know I can trust him to keep his word.

"All right," I say, my voice barely more than a whisper. My heart's beating triple time, thundering against my ribs. I feel like I'm stepping blindly off a great precipice. I can only hope that he'll be there to catch me.

I lie back, and Jamie hovers over me, kissing and licking his way into my mouth. His hands are holding my face, angling our mouths for the perfect fit. My arms slip around his torso and I stroke his back, feeling the taut lines of his muscles.

We kiss until we're breathless. He finally lifts his mouth to trail kisses down my neck to the sensitive pulse point at the base of my throat. I shiver, and he chuckles quietly. But when he keeps moving lower, I tense.

He pauses and pulls back. "What's wrong?"

I just wish he'd bypass my chest altogether.

When I don't answer, he lies down beside me on his side, his head propped on his hand. "Hey, talk to me."

"I just – I'd prefer it if you didn't touch my chest."

"Why?"

"Because."

"Molly, your chest is part of your body, and right now, I want to explore every inch of it." He lays his free hand in the center of my chest, his fingers splayed. "I want to be able to touch you, all of you. I don't want areas that are off limits."

And then, to prove his point, he traces the path of one scar with the tip of his index finger. Then he skims past my sternum and traces the scar on the other side.

Gently, he explores the dips and valleys on my chest, and I shudder from the onslaught of unfamiliar sensations. No one has touched my chest except for me, and the sensations are overwhelming.

"Jamie – "

"Can you feel me touching you?"

I shiver. "Yes."

"Does it hurt?"

"No. It just feels... weird. Some parts are still numb. Others are overly sensitized."

I close my eyes when I feel the sting of tears forming and my throat tightening up. His touch is so gentle, so reverent as he explores every inch of my chest. Todd was repulsed by the way I look.

I cry out when he gently kisses the center of one of the depressions. "I'm sorry I wasn't there for you," he says. "I wish I'd been there to help you through it."

My throat closes painfully, and I squeeze my burning eyes shut.

I don't even realize I'm crying until he croons, "Shh... don't cry." He brushes the tears from my cheek. "Everything's okay. You're okay."

"I'm sorry." My voice cracks. "I didn't mean to spoil tonight."

"You didn't spoil anything."

"It's just..." I stop and take a deep, shaky breath. "I was so sure no one would ever want me again."

He grips my chin and turns my face toward his, giving me a gentle smile. "I guess you were wrong." And then he kisses me, his lips steadying mine, our kiss flavored by the salt of my tears.

Jamie shifts lower on the bed, kissing his way down my abdomen, past my quivering belly. He buries his nose in the cloud of curls between my legs, and his hot breath there is shocking.

I reach down and nudge him back. "Jamie – "

He lifts his face. "What?"

"What are you doing?"

The expression on his face nearly reduces me to tears of laughter. "Really? You have to ask?"

I laugh. "I know what you're doing, silly. Just not why."

He slides between my legs and uses his broad shoulders to nudge my thighs apart.

"Jamie...."

"Relax."

"That's easy for you to say. I can't just rela – "

When his hot tongue flicks my clitoris, I screech and buck my hips off the mattress. I'm already sensitive and primed from the orgasm he gave me in the shower. He uses his hands to pull me back down, and then he traps my thighs open with his arms.

He lifts his head to me, and I know he's not actually looking at me, but still I feel the weight of his expression. "Lie still."

"You just love pushing my boundaries, don't you?"

He laughs. "Maybe just a little bit. But you push mine, too." He raises his eyebrows, and I get the point.

His glasses. Yeah, I guess I do push his boundaries too. So, I lie back down and close my eyes, resigning myself to this physical torture.

When his tongue returns to my clit, I gasp, sucking in a deep breath. The sensation is too much! I'm not used to this. Todd never went down on me, and only one boy I dated briefly in college did. It makes me nervous. And the pleasure is so intense, it's hard to relax.

I feel his finger at my opening, testing the wetness there. He dips his finger inside, then out again. With each foray, his finger slips deeper inside me, stroking me methodically, making me squirm. My attention switches from his tongue on my clit to his finger deep inside me. He has no trouble finding the sweet spot, and he works that spot, rubbing me over and over, until suddenly something's happening all over again. I feel an impending wave deep inside me, swelling like a tsunami that's growing in intensity.

I can't contain the whimpers and high-pitched keening sounds coming out of me. Afraid that someone in the house will overhear me, I grab the pillow beside me and press it to my face to muffle the sounds. When the wave detonates like a bomb deep inside me, I cry out into the pillow, shuddering from the impact.

I can feel Jamie crawling up the bed, and a moment later the pillow is pried out of my hands. Then he lies next to me and rolls me into his arms. I'm breathing like I just ran a marathon.

Jamie kisses my forehead. "Are you okay?"

"I'm not sure."

He laughs.

"I just wasn't... prepared for that," I say, breathless. "I didn't know it could be like that."

"*What* could be like that?" he says.

I'm thirty-five years old, and I really don't want to confess that I've never had an orgasm during sex before. Oh, sure, I've given myself plenty of orgasms in the privacy of my own bed, but no one's ever given *me* one before. And two of them in a span of ten minutes? Never.

"You've never come before?" he says, sounding shocked.

"Not with a partner, no. And never twice."

He grabs the sheet from the foot of the bed and wipes his beard, then he crawls over me, caging me in. I gaze up into his face, amazed at how beautiful he is. He takes my breath away. When he lowers his head to kiss me, I taste myself on his lips, and while I feel like I should be embarrassed, I find it secretly thrilling... like I've marked him somehow as my own. Jamie McIntyre is wearing my scent on his skin. He smells like *me*. *Dear God.*

Suddenly, all I can think about is having him inside me. I reach for his erection, wrapping my fingers around his heated thickness. "I want you. Inside me."

His brow furrows. "Are you sure? We don't have to – "

"Yes, I'm sure."

Jamie reaches for the strip of condoms on the nightstand table. He sits back on his heels and tears open a packet, then rolls it onto his erection. I can't help watching, fascinated by the size of him. Fully erect, he's much bigger than I imagined. I'm not sure how that's going to fit inside me.

When he comes over me, he reaches between my legs and nudges them apart, then settles between them, nestling his hips between my thighs. I can feel his fingers between my legs as he guides himself to my opening.

My legs are trembling when he says, "Just relax."

As he nudges the head of his penis inside me, I can feel my body opening to him. I'm already so soft and wet there – now I know why he went down on me. It was to make sure I was ready to take him.

I gasp as he slowly presses inward, the big head of his cock pressing inexorably deeper, one centimeter at a time. He rocks forward a bit, then pulls back and then sinks further, repeating this gentle rocking motion until he's finally seated all the way. His movements are controlled and measured, but even so, his body's trembling same as mine.

If he hasn't been with someone since his accident, it's been at least several years for him. His body must be on sensory overload same as mine.

I suck in a shaky breath when he's in. It doesn't hurt, exactly, but I can tell my body's being stretched to its limits.

He dips his head and finds my mouth, giving me a gentle kiss. "Okay?"

"Yes," I breathe.

He begins moving, so slowly at first, pulling all the way out and then sinking back in. He's holding himself up so that he doesn't crush me, his arm muscles taut and bulging, and I can feel the tremors in them shaking the mattress.

I slip my hands up his arms, stroking him gently, my fingers following the contours of his muscles and bones. There's so much strength in these arms, so much power, and yet so much gentleness too. When he groans, I feel the vibration in my bones.

Jamie's a walking contradiction. He can be so gentle, and yet I know what he's capable of. I saw him just this evening in hand-to-hand combat, and it was brutal. I've read so many stories about SEALs and their physical capabilities and stamina, and it's nothing short of awe inspiring. To have all that strength and intensity focused on me is humbling.

After shifting his weight to his elbows, he reaches for my hands and links our fingers together, clasping our hands tightly and pressing them into the pillow on either side of my head. He's got me completely caged in, and I've never in my life felt so safe, so sheltered. Right now, I feel like nothing and no one can touch us. Not Todd, not my own insecurities, nothing. Even Jamie's blindness no longer seems very significant, as he's proven over and over how capable he is in spite of his lack of sight.

Jamie's seals his lips to mine, drinking in my cries and my gasps as I respond to each thrust of his body. As my body makes way for him, I begin to relax and enjoy the feel of him surging inside me. With each thrust, his length strokes me inside, stirring up all kinds of delicious sensations. My body is still tingling from my orgasm, and I can tell he's close to his. His breathing gets heavier with each thrust, and he squeezes my hands harder. I look up at him, and the grimace on his face steals my breath. His jaw is tightly clenched as are his eyelids, and he's gritting his teeth. I get the impression he's trying to hang on as long as he can. If it's been a while for him, too, then I'm sure he's desperate to release.

On reflex, I tighten my muscles on him as he surges inside. He moans in response, and then his entire body tenses. He throws his head back, arching his taut neck muscles, and cries out in agonizing pleasure.

As his thrusts slow with each residual pulse of heat from his cock, I pull my hands free and gently stroke his back, comforting him as his body is wracked with tremors. He tucks his face in the crook of my neck, his breath hot and heavy, and then kisses my shoulder.

"Are you okay?" he says, his voice low and rough.

He pulls out gently, then rolls to his side to face me. His short hair is tousled and damp from the shower. I reach up to brush it out of his eyes.

"I'm wonderful," I say, watching his expression as his body comes down from the high. "Are *you* okay?"

He laughs. "At least I didn't embarrass myself this first time. I think I lasted at least five minutes."

He leans down to find my mouth and kisses me gently. "I didn't hurt you?"

"No." At least not more than should have been expected. "I'm fine. In fact, I'm better than fine."

Jamie carefully removes the condom and heads to the bathroom to dispose of it. Then he returns to bed and crawls in beside me, pulling the sheet and the comforter up to cover us.

"I need a minute," I tell him, extricating myself from the bedding. I head into the bathroom to pee and clean up. I find several packages of new toothbrushes in the cabinet, so I brush my teeth. My hair is already beyond help, and my lips are red and swollen. There are love bites on my neck and shoulder. I look well loved, and that makes me smile. I never expected to find myself in this place again.

I have nothing to wear to bed, and Jamie's naked, so I guess it doesn't matter. I head back to bed and climb in beside him.

"Come here," he says, pulling me into his arms.

He lies on his back and draws me close, so that I'm resting my head in the crook of his shoulder. His arm is around me and he strokes my back lightly, his fingers skimming up and down my spine. His other hand comes around me to join the first, sliding down to palm my butt cheek.

I shiver.

"You're going to stay all night, right?" he says.

I yawn. "Yes. I'll stay."

"Good." He tightens his hold on me. "I want to wake up with you in the morning and do this again."

We lie there together, quiet and peaceful. My body is still quaking from my orgasm and from the feel of his body surging into mine. I imagine he's feeling something very similar.

After a while, I ask him the question that's been in my mind for a long while now. "Why me?"

"Hmm?" He sounds half asleep.

"I'm just wondering why you're interested in me. Usually, a guy meets a woman, he likes how she looks, and he becomes interested in her. But you can't see me. Oh, sure, you have a general description of what I look like, but it's got to be vague in your head. I don't even have breasts to attract you."

He chuckles and strokes my butt cheek. "Told you, I'm an ass man. You have a fine ass."

"I have a big ass, you mean." I laugh. "I'm serious. Why me?"

He's quiet for a long while, and I start to wonder if he just doesn't have an answer or if, more likely, he's dozed off. Then he sighs.

"I've asked myself that a million times, and I'm not sure how to answer it, but I'll try." He pauses again, this time brushing my hair back from my hot face, tucking the strands behind my ear.

"I like what you do to my senses," he says. "I experience the world differently now than I did before. Before, it was a pretty smile that caught my attention. Now, it's different. My other senses have taken over – sound, smell, feel." He runs the tip of one finger down the side of my face, following the curve of my cheekbone to my jawline, then down my throat. "I like who you are. I like how I feel when I'm with you. You're a good person, kind, intelligent, courageous, creative, talented. But it's also how you make me feel when I'm with you."

"And how is that?"

"You make me feel good." He brushes his lips against my temple, dropping a light kiss. "When I'm with you, it's like you're a magnet, drawing me in. When I'm away from you, I wonder when I'll see you again. When I'm with you, I don't want to leave. When I met you, it was like my body reawakened from a long sleep. It was like something inside of you called to something inside of me."

He sighs heavily and tightens his hold on me. "Does that sound crazy?"

"No."

"Good. Because the something inside of me doesn't want to let go of the something inside of you."

I shiver when I feel his lips in my hair at the back of my neck. He's so tactile, and my body acts like it can't get enough of the touching. I lay my hand over his and stroke my fingertip along the path of a thick vein.

I'm starving for the affection he's giving me, but I don't want to mislead him. As much as I care about him, I never want to risk him getting hurt. And knowing how well Todd can work the system, I'm afraid he'll be out on bail any time. In fact, he might already be out. He's going to be furious with me for calling the police on him, and if Todd finds out Jamie was involved in that decision, he'll retaliate.

"I met Shane's attorney this afternoon," I say. "Do you think he would check on Todd's status for me?"

"Troy's staying overnight. We can ask him to look into it first thing in the morning."

"Thank you."

"Don't worry about Todd, okay? I'll take care of him."

38

Molly

When I awake, I'm surprised to find myself alone in Jamie's suite. A moment later, the door opens and he and Gus stroll in. Jamie's dressed in jeans and a sweatshirt and is wearing his jacket.

"Good morning," I say, stretching languidly in bed. I feel tenderness deep inside me, reminding me of what we did last night.

He smiles at me. "Good morning. I just took Gus outside for a pee break. Have you been awake long?"

"No. I just woke up a few minutes ago."

Gus runs to the side of the bed to greet me, and I scratch behind his floppy ears.

I shiver. "His ears are cold."

"There was a light dusting of snow overnight. It's pretty frigid this morning."

Jamie takes off his jacket and hangs it on a wall hook. "Ready to go down for breakfast? Elly has a hot buffet set out in the dining room. I saw Troy this morning. He said he'd make some calls and get back with us."

Jamie crawls up the bed on his hands and knees, and I fall back in bed as he hovers over me. "I'm cold too," he says, plaintively.

To prove his point, he sticks his ice-cold nose in the toasty warm crook of my shoulder, making me squeal. "Jamie!"

"Good morning," he says. And then he kisses me.

He tastes like mint toothpaste and smells faintly of soap, deodorant, and clean perspiration. I slip my hands up underneath his sweatshirt to find his skin deliciously warm from his outing. Feeling brave, I push his shirt up and lean up to kiss the center of his chest. "You smell good."

"So do you," he says, burying his nose in my hair. Just as he bends down to kiss me, his phone rings.

"That's Troy," he says, sitting back on his heels to answer his phone. "Troy. Hi."

I wonder how he knows who's calling?

"Sure," he says. "We were just about to head downstairs for breakfast. We'll meet you there."

Jamie ends the call and pockets his phone. He kisses me once more. "Let's go. Troy will meet us in the dining room."

"*After* I get a quick shower," I say, climbing gingerly out of bed, making a pained sound when I feel a twinge deep inside me.

"Are you all right?" Jamie says, as he sits on the side of the bed.

"I'm fine. Just a little sore, that's all."

I swear he's struggling not to smile as I head into the bathroom.

* * *

Lia and Jonah are just leaving the dining room as we enter. Lia takes one look at us and gives me a knowing smile.

"Hi, Molly. Sleep well?" she says.

"Yes, I did." I nod and smile back, trying to look innocent.

I don't think she's buying it.

"You look well rested, Jamie," she says. "Did you sleep well too?"

"I did."

She glances from me to Jamie, then back to me, with a thoughtful look on her face. "Um, Molly?"

"Yes?"

She points to her own throat. "You've got something on your neck."

My hand shoots up to cover my throat, and I realize Jamie must have left a mark on my skin. I'm thirty-five years old, and I have a hickey.

Jamie doesn't say a word.

Jonah rolls his eyes at me and shakes his head. "Enjoy your breakfast, guys," he says, steering Lia out of the room. "Don't mind us."

"Well, that was embarrassing," I say, as we make our way into the dining room. There's a long buffet along the wall filled with trays of hot food. The dining table is currently empty.

I look at Jamie, and he's trying hard not to laugh.

"Oh, you think it's funny?" I ask him.

He grins. "Maybe. Just a bit." Then he laughs. "Yeah, it's funny. I'm not sorry, you know."

"Not sorry about what?" Troy says, as he walks into the dining room. "I'm starved. What's there to eat?"

"Anything you want, Troy," Elly says, walking in through a kitchen access door. She smiles warmly at me. "Good morning, Molly, dear. Did you sleep well?"

"Yes, I did. Thank you."

"And you, Jamie?" Elly's doing her best to suppress a grin, and I suspect she knows that I slept in Jamie's bed last night. Apparently, the news has gotten around.

"Yes, ma'am," he says.

Elly checks the status of the coffee pot. "Good. Grab yourselves some plates and help yourself to whatever you want. If there's something you need that's not here, just holler and I'll get it for you."

Troy fills his plate and pours himself a cup of coffee.

I touch Jamie's sleeve. "Why don't you tell me what you want, and I'll get it for you."

He hesitates for a moment, and I suspect it's because he doesn't like to be waited on. But I also think part of him likes the idea of me doing something for him.

"Thanks," he says, taking a seat across the table from Troy.

Jamie gives me his order – scrambled eggs, sausage, waffles, and coffee – and I fill a plate for him. Then I get the same for myself and sit down beside him.

"I'm afraid I have bad news," Troy says, consulting a message on his phone. "Todd Ferguson's already been released on bail."

My stomach drops, and I suddenly lose my appetite. *He's out. Todd's out of jail.*

"I'm sorry," Troy says. "But Molly, the restraining order still stands. If he violates it again, the court won't be so lenient with him a second time."

I try my best to smile. "Thank you, Mr. Spencer."

"Call me Troy, please."

Troy quickly finishes his meal and takes his leave, telling us he's heading back to the city now. He promises to monitor Todd's case and let us know of any further developments.

"You're not eating," Jamie says, when we're alone again.

"I'm not hungry."

"Molly, you need to eat something."

"I can't. I feel like I'm going to be sick." My mind is racing as the ramifications of what I've done sink in. Todd's going to be furious, and he'll know Jamie was involved. He's going to retaliate. My pulse starts racing as my mind goes through all the possible outcomes. "Will you be okay on your own? I think I'll go up to my room."

"Don't go," Jamie says, reaching for my hand. "You don't have to face this alone. I'll be right by your side, I promise."

That's what I'm afraid of. I tug my hand free of his and stand. My thoughts are racing as I think of all the ways Todd can target Jamie. It's a little late now, but I've got to do what I can to protect Jamie. "That's the problem, Jamie. I don't want you by my side. I don't want you anywhere near me."

He doesn't say a word as I walk out of the dining room and head up the staircase to the second floor. My words were cruel, and I hurt him. I didn't want to, but I can't keep sticking my head in the sand. Todd's going to retaliate. There's absolutely no doubt in my mind about that, and Jamie's vulnerable. I can't be with him every second to protect him.

I feel sick as I walk down the hallway to my room. I should never have let things go so far with Jamie last night. I should never have slept with him. It's my fault he's in this position. If anything happens to him, I'll never forgive myself.

Once I'm in my room, I pace anxiously, my mind racing through every possible contingency as I try to search for a way to keep Jamie safe. Maybe there's something I can do or say to Todd to convince him that Jamie had nothing to do with me calling the police. Maybe if I take the blame, Todd will redirect his ire toward me and not Jamie.

I stop pacing when I hear a knock at my door. I freeze.

There's another knock, and then Jamie's low voice sounds muffled coming through the door. "Molly? Honey, please talk to me. I know you're worried, but we can work through this together."

He waits patiently for a reply. When I don't give him one, he says, "Molly, please?"

I can't bear to listen to the plea in his voice, so I go into the bathroom, close the door, and turn on the faucet. I stare at my reflection, at a woman who looks scared. I am scared, not for myself, but for Jamie.

What have I done?

39

Jamie

I stand outside Molly's suite for half an hour, hoping she'll change her mind and talk to me. I know she's scared. I suspect Todd has convinced her that he's a formidable foe. Personally, I think he's nothing more than a bully. In the meanwhile, Molly's hurting, and it's driving me crazy that she won't let me help her.

When it's obvious she's not going to let me in, I head back to my suite to grab my swim trunks. I need something to do – something physical to help me burn off some of this tension. Otherwise I'll do something stupid like break down Molly's door. Somehow I don't think that would be helpful right now.

Gus and I head down to the lower level. I change in the locker room, then head out to the pool. Maybe an hour of hard laps will help.

I've done about fifty laps when I hear the doors to the pool room open. Gus runs to greet the new arrival, practically squealing with excitement. There's only one person he gets *that* excited for, and that's Beth.

I continue swimming hard, my arms cutting through the water. I'm not sure what to say to Beth, or how much to tell her. She's still recovering from a recent traumatic experience, and she's pregnant. I certainly don't need to add to her worries. Shane definitely wouldn't appreciate that.

She sits at the side of the pool and puts her feet in the water, gently kicking them. "Are you just going to ignore me?" She sounds hurt.

I come to a stop and tread water, pushing my wet hair out of my face. This just isn't my day to make the women in my life happy. "I'm sorry. I'm just not in the mood to socialize."

"I'm not here to socialize with you, dummy," she says, making me smile. "I'm here to see how you're doing."

I realize Beth's probably been watching me all weekend to see how I fared with Molly. "I'm fine."

"That's bull," she says. "I saw the expression on your face last night, after your dance with Molly ended. You weren't fine."

Ahh, so Beth doesn't know about Todd being out on bail. She thinks I'm preoccupied by the fact that Molly walked out of the wedding reception last night after our dance. She must not know that Molly and I spent the night together. Maybe it's for the best. "She walked away from me without a word."

"Jamie – "

Gus starts barking excitedly again, alerting me to another new arrival.

"Wow, Lia wasn't kidding," Molly says as she comes into the pool room. "There's actually a pool in your house."

Relief that Molly has come out of her self-imposed seclusion sweeps through me. And I'm thrilled that she's come looking for me.

"Hey, Molly!" Beth says. "Why don't you join us? There's a closet full of brand new swimming suits in the locker room, in every size and style imaginable. Help yourself."

I hear footsteps moving around the side of the pool. Then Molly says, "Thanks, but swimming's not really my thing. But I'll hang around and watch, if you guys don't mind the company."

I swim in Molly's direction, wondering if her breast forms are waterproof. I doubt the pool chemicals would be good for them. Surely there are water-resistant breast forms out in the market. We'll have to get some.

"Of course I don't mind," I tell her. "I'd love the company. Is there something else you'd rather do?" I suggest that we watch a movie in the home theater or go out for a walk, go see the docks, the barn, the horses. Personally, I'd vote for the walk. It would get us out of the house and away from prying eyes so we can discuss her fears.

"I would love a walk," she says. "But don't let me interrupt your swim. I can wait until you're done."

I'm sure Beth would understand if I go with Molly, but I don't want to leave Beth alone in the pool room. We have rules about civilians swimming alone, especially pregnant ones.

I hear the doors open again, then a familiar voice. "I figured I'd find you down here," Shane says. I'm sure he's talking to Beth. "How's the water?"

"It's perfect," she says, kicking her feet in the water. "Come on in."

I hear running feet hit the concrete floor, followed by a splash.

"Looks like my swim buddy is here," Beth says, laughing as Shane breeches the water and splashes her.

And that's my cue. With Shane here to safeguard Beth, I'm free to take off with Molly. I haul myself out of the water near where Molly is standing. "Since Beth is adequately occupied with her swim buddy, I'll dry off and change, and we'll go for that walk."

"I'd like that," Molly says.

I grab my towel off the back of a lounge chair and dry off. Then I call Gus to me and put his harness on him. "Come on, buddy, let's go get dressed. I won't be long, Molly."

I hear Molly take a seat on one of the lounge chairs as I head to the changing room to dress. I want to get her alone someplace where we won't be interrupted – like the barn.

We kissed the last time we were in the barn. I wouldn't mind a repeat of that.

* * *

We drop Gus off in the kitchen with Elly.

"We're going out for a walk," I tell her.

"Make sure you're back in time for lunch. I've got a celebratory luncheon planned. Shane and Beth are the guests of honor, so make sure you're here for it."

"We will be," I assure her.

Elly gives me an impromptu hug. She doesn't say anything, but then again she doesn't need to. She's happy for me. And for Molly.

Elly releases me, then hugs Molly too. "You kids have fun," she says in a shaky voice, trying to pretend that she's not on the verge of tears.

Molly and I bundle up for the cold outside temps and trudge through the light snow to the barn. She takes my hand, and I match my stride to hers, navigating the uneven terrain with the help of her quiet verbal cues. We work well together.

When we reach the barn, I open the side door and hold it for her to walk inside. I follow her in, closing the door behind me to keep out the cold wind.

It's warm in the barn, and the interior smells like hay and grain, leather, and manure.

Releasing my hand, Molly walks down the central corridor, past each of the horse stalls, to the open double doors that lead to the pasture. I lean against one of the stalls, giving her a few minutes to collect her thoughts.

She's quiet. Too quiet. I'm afraid I know where this is going. She's going to play the noble card and tell me it's too dangerous for us to be together. The problem is, I'm not sure how to pull her back from there. I figure it's best to get her talking, so we can get this out in the open and I can work on countering her argument.

I cross my arms, getting ready for a battle. "Just say what's on your mind, Molly."

She kicks at the straw littering the hard dirt floor before she turns to face me.

She takes a deep breath, and when she speaks, her voice is thick with unshed tears. "I'm sorry."

God, I hate that she's hurting like this, and all because she feels like she has to protect me. "Sorry?" I say, pushing away from the wall. "For what?"

"For letting things go so far between us. I shouldn't have done that, and I'm sorry."

"Hell, I'm not sorry. Molly, what happened between us was mutual. There's no blame to be had – not by either of us."

"Yes, there is, because I know Todd. I know how persistent he can be. Ever since his affair ended, he's been obsessed with me coming back to him. He'll see you as an impediment to that goal."

I scoff. "I am more than ready to take on your ex, Molly."

"Jamie, be serious."

I stalk across the aisle toward her and she takes several steps back. The sound of her boots scuffing against the ground helps me pinpoint her location easily. I clasp her shoulders and press her against the wall. "I am being serious."

As I lean close, she sucks in a breath and raises her hands to push me back. "Jamie, no. We have to stop. Listen, I've been giving this some thought, and I think I have a solution."

"We don't need a solution, damn it, because there's no problem!"

"Wait a minute and hear me out," she says. "I've decided to move out of the apartment building. I'll sublet my apartment for the remainder of my lease and find another place, maybe in Rogers Park or Old Town. Some place far from you. Hopefully that will direct Todd's attention away from you."

I squeeze her shoulders in exasperation. What I really want to do is shake some sense into her. I expected her to run. I just didn't expect her to run that far. "No," I say.

"No?" She sounds part incredulous and part affronted.

"You heard me. You're *not* moving out of your apartment."

"Jamie – "

"I mean it." I press my hands to the wall, one on each side of her head, and cage her in. I dip my head so that our foreheads are touching. "Did last night mean anything to you?"

She sucks in a startled breath. "Jamie, we can't – "

"Did it?"

At first she doesn't answer, and I'm afraid she won't. But eventually she gives in. "Yes."

"That's all I need to know." I lower my mouth to hers and swallow her gasp, sealing our mouths together and drinking in the sounds she makes, soft moans, faint whimpers. When she opens her mouth, I slip my tongue inside to stroke hers.

She grasps the front of my coat and pulls me closer, her mouth as greedy as mine. My hands move to cup the sides of her head, and I thread my fingers through her hair and hold her in place.

I whip off my glasses and stow them in my coat pocket so that there's no barrier between us. "Look at me and tell me you don't want me," I say, challenging her directly.

I wait patiently, giving her a chance to formulate an answer. I realize I'm pushing her, maybe too hard, so I soften the tone of my voice. "If you can honestly tell me you don't want me, I'll back off right this minute. No hard feelings, no harm done."

Still, she says nothing.

"But, you see, I think you do want me, just as much as I want you," I tell her. "And I'm not going to lose this – lose *you* – because of Todd. You've got to trust me, Molly. There's nothing for you to be afraid of, I promise."

She lifts her hands to my face, tentative and gentle. Then she leans forward to kiss me, her soft lips clinging to mine. She's trembling. "I'd be lying if I said I didn't want you," she whispers.

I close my eyes as relief sweeps through me. I don't know what I would have done if she'd called my bluff. "Then stop trying to push me away for my own sake and trust me to handle Todd."

"All right," she says, in a quiet voice. She sounds far from convinced, but at least she's willing to give me a chance.

I wrap my arms around her and pull her closer. I press myself against her, gritting my teeth at the exquisite pleasure. I'm sure her pulse is racing like mine. I could try to talk her into coming back to my suite with me, but I don't want to move from this spot. Are we too old to make out in the barn?

As I kiss her, I drink in her sighs and soft moans. The sounds coming from her make me harder, painfully so, and all I can think about is getting her home.

"Let's go home," I say.

"We can't go yet. Elly's planning a special luncheon for Shane and Beth. We can't miss that."

I huff out a breath. "All right. But afterward, we're going home."

"Okay."

40

Molly

By the time we make it back to the house, the dining room is filled with happy, excited guests. Beth and Shane are the center of attention, of course, and they're surrounded by family and friends. It looks like most everyone is here, except for a few conspicuously absent people. Namely, Sam isn't here, and neither is Cooper.

According to Lia, Sam took off for parts unknown, and Miguel left with him. Cooper's still here at the house, but holed up in his suite. Shane's attorney, Troy, left already too.

The food is delicious, and there's leftover wedding cake, which is divine. Gina, the one responsible for the delicious food and the cake, makes a wonderful toast to the newlyweds.

Jamie's parents are here, and his mom, Bridget, is happily chatting with Beth's mom, Ingrid. It's one big happy family reunion of sorts.

Jamie's seated on my left, and Lia's on my right, with Jonah beside her. Lia's the life of the party at our end of the table. I never know what's going to come out of her mouth. Jonah just sits back and watches her with obvious affection. I sneak a few glances at Jamie when I think no one's looking, but Jamie's mother and Elly catch me a few times.

Eventually, the party starts to break up. It's late Sunday afternoon and most of the guests need to think about packing up and heading back to their respective homes. Apparently, Beth and Shane are going to stay for a few days and enjoy some relaxing privacy on the estate as they celebrate their wedding.

Jamie and I head upstairs, hand-in-hand, and we go to our respective suites to pack our belongings. Jake offers to drive us home, and he pulls his SUV up to the front of the house, and Elly's husband, George, helps us load our bags and Gus into the back of the vehicle.

* * *

Back in Wicker Park, Jamie carries all our bags up to our apartments, and I take Gus for a quick walk to stretch his legs and let him take care of business.

I walk past Chloe's tattoo shop, which is closed. I pass my shop, too, and just peek in through the front windows at the dark interiors to make sure everything looks all right.

Gus and I walk a few more blocks just enjoying some quiet time alone. When I'm with Jamie, I'm so focused on him that there's little room in my head for anything else. He has a knack for occupying my thoughts.

It's starting to get dark, so we turn back toward home. Gus is his usual happy and curious self, wanting to stop and sniff every light pole, mailbox, and planter we encounter.

I just happen to glance across the street and see a black sports car parked along the street. The car catches my attention because it's the same model Todd drives. Immediately my heart starts pounding, even as my brain chides me for overreacting and tells me to calm down. That car model is a dime a dozen in Chicago.

When the tinted driver's window slowly goes down, though, there's a familiar face staring back at me.

What's he doing here? If he just got released from jail on bond, why in the world is he risking rearrest by showing up in my neighborhood? He has no business here. Both his law office and his condo are way across town in Lincoln Park.

I ignore him and keep walking, although I pick up my pace. "Come on, Gus. Let's get home."

Out of my peripheral vision, I see Todd crossing the street on a path to intercept me on the sidewalk. I stop when he falls into step beside me.

"Is that his dog?" Todd says, scowling at Gus. "You're walking the guy's fucking dog?"

"You're in violation of the restraining order," I say, maintaining my calm.

He rolls his eyes at me. "What are you going to do, Molly? Call the police again? I was out on bail in 24 hours the last time. The next time, I'll be out in half that time."

I swallow hard and shake my head. "You won't get bail next time."

"Bullshit. I have connections, Molly, and you know it. I'm a fucking defense attorney. You can't touch me."

I don't believe a word he says – he's just trying to intimidate me. I resume walking, keeping my gaze straight ahead, trying to ignore the pounding of my heart. I can see my building from here, and I'm relieved to see Jake's SUV is still parked out front. Jake steps out from behind the vehicle and walks around to open the driver's door. My heart sinks. *He's leaving.*

Just before he climbs into the vehicle, he glances my way and makes eye contact. I raise my hand in a half-hearted wave, willing him to notice that I'm not alone. Jake's never seen Todd before, so he wouldn't recognize him, but maybe he'll put two and two together.

I'm practically holding my breath to see what Jake's going to do. To my utter relief, he closes the driver's door and walks around to the sidewalk, facing me, his hands on his hips as he watches our approach.

The moment Jake takes a step in our direction, Todd turns and jogs across the street, heading quickly back to his car.

"Is everything all right?" Jake says, when he reaches me. He's talking to me, but his gaze is tracking Todd's movements.

I take a deep breath. "No, not really."

"Was that your ex?"

"Yes."

"I thought he was in jail for violating the restraining order?"

"He was released this morning on bail."

Jake's eyes narrow as he watches Todd drive past us. "Cocky son-of-a-bitch," he says.

"He thinks he's above the law. That the laws don't apply to him."

"Narcissistic bastard."

I laugh. "Yes, he is."

Jake puts his arm across my shoulders. "Come on. I'll see you to your apartment. Jamie needs to know about this."

Jamie. That's my real concern. I don't think Todd would actually hurt *me,* but I know he'd hurt Jamie. "I'm afraid for Jamie," I say. "I think Todd's out to hurt him."

Jake chuckles. "Is Todd armed?"

"I don't think so. In all the years we were together, he never showed any interest in getting a gun."

"Then I wouldn't worry about Jamie," he says. "If it's hand-to-hand contact, Todd doesn't stand a chance."

When we approach my building, the door opens and out steps the young man who lives in the first-floor apartment. Based on the towering stack of boxes he's holding, it looks like they're moving out. The guy props the door open with a brick.

"Hey, pal, don't prop the door open," Jake says, retrieving the brick and setting it inside the foyer. "This building has a secured entrance. Leaving the door propped open kind of defeats that, right?"

"Oh, sure, gotcha," the young man says, continuing down the steps to his DIY moving van.

Jake walks me inside and up the stairs. He watches down the stairs as my neighbor carries several boxes out the door, letting it swing shut behind him.

Jake frowns. "I don't like having other occupants in the building. They might do something stupid, like prop the door open."

I laugh. Jake has no idea how right he is. "Mrs. Powell is forgetful, and she's let Todd into the building several times, thinking he's my husband."

My bags are sitting right outside my door. I unlock my door, then turn back to Jake. "Thank you," I tell him. "For the ride home and for coming to my rescue just now."

"No problem. Any time." He gives me a bear hug and pats my back. "I'm glad you came to the wedding. Jamie's been alone for a long time. It's good to see him happy."

Speaking of Jamie, I hear his door close and watch him walk toward us.

"I'm taking off now," Jake says, clapping his brother's upper arm. "Why don't you ask Molly who she ran into outside?"

Jamie turns toward me. "You saw Todd?"

"You kids have a nice evening," Jake says, heading for the stairs. "You, too, Gus."

Jamie takes hold of my hands. "Tell me what happened."

"I saw Todd outside a few minutes ago. He was parked on the street, and when he saw me walking with Gus he came over and spoke to me."

Jamie's brow furrows and he shakes his head. "Your ex is nuts. He's just asking for jailtime."

"He thinks he's above the law. He thinks he'll get off again if I call the police."

"He's wrong." He pulls me into his arms and kisses the top of my head. "Can I come in and hang with you for a while? We could watch a movie, maybe order carryout later. I'll bring a bottle of wine."

I slip my arms around his waist and melt into him, loving the solid warmth of his body. "I'd love that."

* * *

It's my turn to pick the movie, so we watch one of my favorites – *Pitch Perfect*. I can watch that movie over and over without getting tired of it. I figure Jamie will be entertained by the music and it won't matter so much that he can't see the action. We crash on the sofa, with Gus lying on the floor and Charlie stretched out along the back of the sofa.

Partway through the film, Jamie stretches out on his side along the sofa, and I lie in front of him. He wraps his arm around my waist and holds me close. Throughout the movie, I hear him humming along with the familiar melodies, his voice a rich baritone that makes my insides quiver with delight.

We're both too comfortable and cozy to want to go out again tonight, so we order Thai food and have it delivered. When the food arrives, I run downstairs to collect it, while Jamie gets a bottled of chilled red wine from his apartment. We spread our feast out on the coffee table and enjoy our food with red wine sipped out of fluted wine glasses.

When we're done eating, we nestle back onto the sofa again. He's engaged in the movie, but occasionally I feel his lips in my hair, or along the back of my neck, which makes me shiver.

"What's it like?" I ask him, leaning back against him. "Listening to a movie when you can't see what's happening on the screen?"

"It's pretty easy to follow the story," he says. "Filmmakers invest a lot of resources into their soundtracks and special effects. I can pretty well figure out what's going on just by listening to the audio effects." He laughs. "To be honest, I saw this movie twice with Lia when it first came out years ago. Mom wouldn't let her go to the theater alone, so I offered to take her. So this one, I actually saw."

I can easily picture Jamie as a big brother taking his little sister to the movie theater. I'm sure he was a very good big brother – very protective of his younger siblings. I'm sure he'd make an equally good father one day.

"Do you ever think about having kids?" I ask him.

He tightens his arm around my waist. "Sure. I grew up in in a big family. I always figured I'd have a family of my own one day."

My bottom is tucked against his groin, and I'm hyperaware of how his erection is pressing against me. When his fingers drift south and slip beneath the waistband of my sweats and into my panties, I suck in a breath, and my insides start quivering.

He laughs softly. "Don't mind me. Just enjoy the movie."

When his index finger slips between the folds of my sex, sliding through my wetness, I gasp. "That's easy for you to say."

My mind short circuits at that point, and I lose all track of the movie. I press my face in to Jamie's bicep, which is currently my pillow and concentrate on just trying to breathe as his finger strokes my clitoris, teasing me, arousing me, body and mind. I grow wetter, achier with each brush of his finger. He rubs tiny circles on the little knot of flesh between my legs, fairly vibrating with pleasure as I squirm in his embrace.

I close my eyes and whimper helplessly as the pleasure builds. "Jamie."

"Hmm?"

He brushes my hair aside with his chin to expose my throat for hot, deep kisses. I know he's definitely going to leave marks as he sucks on my skin.

His finger is relentless in its torment of my clit, circling my flesh and teasing it, pressing and stroking. My hips start moving on their own, lifting to meet his touch, to increase the pressure right where I need it.

"That's it," he murmurs, his voice low and hoarse.

I'm clearly not the only one affected here. I can feel his hot breath on the back of my neck and the muscles in his arms are taut.

He nudges my legs farther apart so he can glide his finger into my opening, which is flushed and slippery. He curls his finger inside me, stroking the front wall of my sex, jacking up the pleasure until I'm practically panting. I can't help the sounds coming out of me, and they quickly escalate into breathless gasps and whimpers.

"I want to feel you come, just like this," he says.

"Jamie – "

He lowers his mouth and sucks on the tender skin beneath my ear. Tingles course through me from the sensation of his mouth on my sensitive skin. Combined with the swelling pleasure deep inside me, it's more than I can bear.

My body stiffens helplessly as an orgasm sweeps through me, leaving my insides melting and my heart beat racing.

Jamie rolls me to my back and looms over me, drinking in the sounds I'm making. He coaxes my mouth open and slips his tongue inside, stroking mine, sucking gently as my hips rock through the residual tremors of pleasure.

He pulls his finger out and sucks it clean, which blows my mind.

"Can I stay the night?" he says, his voice little more than a deep rasp.

He's clearly aroused and very much on edge. I reach between us to caress his erection. My fingers outline the length and shape of him through the fabric of his sweatpants, and he groans as he presses his face into my neck.

"Is that a yes?" he says, part laugh, part groan. "God, it had better be. I don't think I can take much more."

41

Molly

Of course you can stay," I tell him, smiling as he kisses me.

Then he sits up and reaches for his sneakers, which are under the coffee table. "I've got to take Gus out for a walk," he says, dropping a quick kiss on my lips. He puts his glasses on. "I'll be right back."

This is happening so fast. He's going to wheedle his way into my life, into my bed, and into my insecurities. I'm going to be helpless against him.

I leave the door unlocked for him, since he'll be back in just a few minutes. I head to the bathroom to get ready for bed. I'm shaking, literally, from head to toe.

I slip on a pale blue silky nightgown that just barely covers my thighs. It's sleeveless and sexy. Even though Jamie can't see the nightgown, it might boost my confidence to wear it.

After putting out a night-time snack for Charlie and refilling his water bowl in the kitchen, I turn off all the lights and head to my bedroom to wait for Jamie.

I'm surprised at how nervous I am. It's not like we haven't done this before, and he's already explored the terrain of my chest. But still, I feel cold and shaky.

When I hear the apartment door open and close, I feel butterflies in my belly.

He comes down the hall and pauses in my open bedroom doorway. The apartment is dark, and the only light comes through my white lacey bedroom curtains. I can make out the outline of his body, but that's all, as he stands there watching me silently.

"Gus settled for the night?" I say, hoping to break the awkward silence. I don't know what he's waiting for. An invitation?

"I wouldn't know."

At the sound of that unexpected voice, I shoot up in bed, grasping the sheet and comforter to my chest. "What are you doing in here?"

I reach for the lamp on the bedside table and switch it on, momentarily blinded by the light. Todd's standing in my bedroom doorway dressed from head to toe in black. His pale hair is mussed and his light blue eyes are bloodshot.

My heart slams into my throat, threatening to choke me. And then the real fear sets in. Jamie's going to be back here any second, and he'll be caught unprepared.

"Get out!" I yell, hoping that Jamie might hear me and be forewarned.

Todd just gives me a look as he walks into my bedroom. "Where's your boyfriend?" he says.

"I don't know what you're talking about. I don't have – "

He grabs the bedding and rips it out of my hands. "Don't lie to me, Molly. I know you're screwing the blind guy."

He crawls onto the bed, looming over me, and when I try to slide out from under him and roll to the other side of the bed, he grabs the back of my nightgown and drags me back. "Not so fast, you little slut. I'm not through with you."

"Todd – "

He backhands me, knocking my head back against the headboard. Bright flickering lights blind me for a moment, disorienting me. Then he tugs me down so that I'm lying on my back, and he shoves my nightgown up around my waist. Since I was anticipating Jamie coming to bed, I'm not wearing any panties.

"Stop it!" I scream, trying to push his hands away.

He grabs me around the throat, wrapping his long fingers around my neck and cutting off my air. I grab his wrist and try to pull his hand off me, but he's too strong.

I can feel my face turning red from the lack of oxygen, and I struggle in vain to pull his hand off my throat.

He reaches with his free hand to unbuckle his belt, then unfastens his jeans.

This can't be real. This can't be happening. Who is this monster? He's not the same man I married a decade ago. When I hear his zipper going down, I redouble my efforts to get free. I'm not going to let him rape me.

My eyesight starts fading to black around the edges, and I'm afraid I'm about to pass out from lack of air. In a desperate measure, I raise my head and bite his forearm as hard as I can, sinking my teeth relentlessly into his flesh. I taste blood, and my stomach turns. But it works. As Todd releases his grip on my throat, I suck in a huge lungful of air.

"You bitch!" he yells, slapping me hard enough to make my ears ring.

He grabs my wrists and pins them above my head, then looks around the room frantically. I think he's looking for something he can use to secure my wrists.

I buck my hips, trying to dislodge, but he's too heavy for me to budge.

A moment later, the light goes out, and we're in the dark. My apartment is eerily silent all of a sudden, and I realize the electricity is off. At first, I'm at a complete loss. Then it dawns on me. *Jamie. He must have flipped the breaker. He doesn't need the light.* Throwing the apartment into total darkness gives him an advantage.

"What the fuck?" Todd says, sitting upright on me. He releases my wrists and jumps off the bed.

I hear him pull something out of his back pocket, and then I hear the tell-tale flick of a switchblade opening.

"Jamie!" I scream, trying to warn him.

"Shut up!" Todd hisses at me. He leans close and I can feel the edge of the knife against my cheek. "If you make another sound, I will carve you up."

But I have to warn Jamie about the knife. Hand-to-hand combat is one thing, but Jamie needs to know if his opponent is armed.

"He has a knife!" I yell at the top of my lungs.

"God dammit!" Todd growls.

And a moment later, I feel the sharp tip of the blade pierce the edge of my cheek. As he swipes down, intending to carve a line in my cheek, I turn my face, trying to get out of his reach.

A moment later, I hear a deafening roar, and Todd is lifted off the bed and tossed to the floor.

I scramble off the bed, landing on the floor between the bed and the wall, away from the struggle I hear ensuing on the opposite side of the bed.

"Molly, get out!" Jamie yells.

Then I hear Todd cry out sharply. "You fucker! I'll kill you!"

"Molly, go!"

42

Jamie

Come on, Gus, let's make it quick," I say to the dog. "Molly's warm and toasty, and she's waiting for me."

We head down the stairs to the foyer, and I hear a lot of activity coming from apartment 1B. A young man is breathing heavily as he walks out the building's front entrance. It sounds like he's carrying a heavy load.

As I reach the door, I find it propped wide open with something heavy. Irritated, I kick what feels like a brick out of the way and let the door swing shut.

"Hey, man, leave it open," the guy says. "I've still got a lot of shit to carry out."

"Don't leave the door propped open," I tell him.

"Yeah, whatever," he says, trudging down the steps toward the street.

He's probably got a rented moving truck parked at the curb.

I walk Gus a hundred feet or so from the building to one of his favorite trees and wait for him to finish his business. It's cold outside, and Molly's waiting for me in her warm bed, hopefully naked. And right now, that's where I want to be. "Hurry up, pal," I mutter as Gus sniffs loudly.

Once Gus is done, we head back toward the building.

"Gus, find the stairs," I tell him, and he leads me up the front stoop. When we reach the front of the building, I feel a strong draft of warm air coming through the open door. *Dammit.* I told him not to prop the door open.

I bend down and grab the brick, intending to toss it in the trash can. My downstairs neighbor comes stomping out of his apartment, carrying another load. It sounds like he's carrying a noisy box of pots and pans.

"I told you not to prop open – " I stop mid-sentence when I hear a scream from the second floor – a shrill female cry. *Molly!* I shove Gus's harness into the guy's hand and tell him, "Take care of my dog and call 911! Now!" And then I run up the stairs toward Molly's apartment.

Her door is unlocked and I crack it open, listening. I can hear the muted sounds of a struggle coming from the bedroom.

I slip into the apartment, shutting the door behind me, and open the electrical panel in the corner of the living room, throwing the main breaker to shut off electricity to the apartment. I can operate just fine in the dark; Todd Ferguson can't.

As soon as the power is cut off, I hear Molly scream, "Jamie!"

Todd hisses, "Shut up!"

Molly cries out in fear. Then Todd tells her, "If you make another sound, I will carve you up."

He's got a knife. If he has a knife, chances are he probably doesn't have a gun. Good.

"He has a knife!" Molly screams in a hoarse voice.

"God dammit!" Todd growls.

Then my blood runs cold when I hear Molly cry out in pain. If he cut her, I'll kill him!

I move quickly across the living room and down the hallway toward her bedroom. Her apartment is identical to mine, so I can easily navigate the floor plan. When I enter her bedroom, I hear them scuffling on the bed.

I grab hold of Todd's jacket and lift him off the bed, tossing him to the floor. Then I follow him down, pinning his hand - the one wielding the knife - to the floor.

"Molly, get out!" I yell.

Todd struggles to get to his feet, but I pin him to the floor with a knee to his chest.

"You fucker!" he growls, heaving for breath. He tries to buck me off, but I outweigh him. "I'll kill you!"

"Molly, go!" I yell. Whatever happens here, I don't want her to hear it.

My mind registers the sound of Molly running from the room in her bare feet. Once she's gone, I'm at liberty to take action. I reach for Todd's knife hand, grasping his wrist and twisting it, wrenching it back until the bones snap. Todd screams, the sound high pitched and desperate.

"Not so tough now, are you?" I say, panting from the exertion of holding him down. I figure I have fewer than five minutes before the cops arrive.

I reach for the knife with the intention of relieving Todd of his weapon, but he grabs for it with his other hand. He swings his arm toward me with the intention of stabbing me in the back. It's a classic mistake in close-contact fighting – don't let your own weapon be used against you. He's not taking into consideration that if he follows through on his intended arc and misses my back, he'll bury the knife in his own chest.

Yep, classic mistake.

As he takes his swing, throwing all of his strength behind it, I roll away at the last second. His hand continues on its path with enough momentum to bury the knife deep in Todd's chest.

He grunts when the knife pierces his ribs and tunnels into his heart. His desperate gasps for air sound wet as his lungs fill with blood. I think he'll suffocate before his heart stops beating.

I sit back on the floor, breathing heavily myself, as I listen to his labored gasps.

"You should have left her alone, asshat," I say, feeling no remorse. "You have no one to blame but yourself."

He tries to speak, but his words are garbled by the blood filling his throat. He grabs at the knife in desperation, trying to pull it out, but it's lodged in there firmly.

I can hear the sirens now, wailing in the distance, as the police descend on our location. I pull my phone out of my back pocket and voice dial Shane.

"Hey, brother, what's up?" he says, sounding a bit groggy.

"Did I wake you?"

"Yeah, but no problem. You wouldn't call this late unless it was important. What do you need?"

"A little help would be nice. I just killed Molly's ex-husband. Well, technically, he killed himself. Basically, he fell on his own knife. Classic beginner mistake."

There's an ominous silence over the phone line as Todd's gurgling breaths slow. I give him two minutes, tops.

Shane's voice is impressively steady and calm. "Did you just say –"

"Yeah. I did. Can you send Troy over to our building? And a coroner. We're going to need a body bag."

Shane exhales heavily. "I'm on my way. Hold tight."

Ferguson didn't even make it two minutes. When the gurgling breaths stop, I reach over to feel his carotid artery. Nothing. No pulse. No breaths. Nothing. He's gone.

A moment later, I hear Molly's footsteps coming down the hallway. She's moving cautiously.

"It's okay, honey," I say. "The coast is clear."

She hovers in the doorway. "Are you okay?"

"I'm fine. Are you okay?"

She laughs shakily. "I am now. Are you sure you're all right?"

I climb to my feet and blow out a heavy breath. "Yeah, I'm sure." I meet her in the open doorway. "We should probably turn the power back on. The cops will need the lights on to do their jobs."

It's pitch black in the apartment, so I lead Molly by the hand back into the living room. I sit her down on the sofa, then head for the breaker box to flip the breaker back on. Immediately, the refrigerator starts humming again, and the furnace starts back up. Molly switches on the lamp on the end table beside the sofa.

I take a seat on the coffee table directly across from her so I can run my hands over her body. "Are you hurt?"

She lifts her fingertips to her face and hisses a pained breath. "He cut my face, but I don't think it's bad. There's not much blood." She takes a deep breath. "What about Todd?"

"He's no longer a problem."

"Oh."

"Yeah. He stabbed himself in the chest."

Police officers sweep into the apartment, yelling at us to freeze.

"It's okay," I tell them. "It's over. The intruder's body is in the bedroom." I point down the hallway. "The only door on the left."

I've got hold of Molly's hands, and they're trembling. I move to sit beside her on the sofa and pull her into my arms.

"I've called for an ambulance," one of the officers says. "She's going to need medical treatment."

"How bad is it?" I ask, dreading the answer.

"Well, I'm not an EMT, but it doesn't look too bad to me. She may need stitches. Her throat is badly bruised too. The squad's on its way."

Molly's apartment turns into Grand Central Station not long after that. Two Chicago detectives arrive, along with a forensics team, and finally the coroner.

Then Shane walks in, in the middle of a heated phone conversation with Troy Spencer.

Apparently he brought Jake with him as well.

"Jamie, what the hell?" Jake says as he walks into the apartment. Jake sits on the other side of Molly. "Let me see your face. Jesus, you're lucky. One inch higher, and he might've taken out your eye. That's going to need stitches. But don't worry, it'll just add character to your face – make you a little more bad ass than you already are."

She laughs nervously. "I'm not a bad ass. Jamie's the bad ass."

"Hey, bro, how the hell did Ferguson get in?" Jake says.

"The tenants downstairs are moving out, and they kept propping the door open. I closed it when I left to walk Gus, but the kid must have propped it open again once I was gone. Ferguson must have slipped inside when I was walking Gus."

"We're going to have to do something about the security in this place," Jake says. "Having other tenants is a problem without proper door security. It seems silly to add a doorman twenty-four-seven. It would make more sense to move you guys to a secured building."

While Jake's talking, Molly leans into me. I can feel her body shaking, and I'm afraid she's in shock. I put my arm around her and draw her close, kissing her temple. "Just rest."

43

Molly

The EMTs check me out and assure Jamie my injuries aren't serious. But it looks like I'll need to go to the ER for treatment.

Shane gets the okay for Jake to drive us to the hospital, rather than having me ride in the ambulance. We all get in Jake's SUV, which is parked a block down the street, and head to the Cook County Hospital ER. Shane and Jake are in the front seat, and Jamie and I sit in the back. I'm absolutely exhausted, dead on my feet, and I find myself falling asleep in the backseat leaning against Jamie. His arm is around my shoulders, warm and solid, and I feel safe.

It still hasn't sunk in that Todd's dead. I suppose I should grieve that my former husband met a violent end, but the man he'd become lately bore little resemblance to the young man I married in college. I don't know what happened to him over the years. I guess he changed so gradually that I didn't realize that monster he'd become until after the divorce, when he insisted that I come back to him.

I sigh heavily, feeling a little overwhelmed by the evening's events. But the important thing, though, is that Jamie and I are all right. Jamie saved me from attempted rape, and he didn't get injured in the process, despite the fact Todd was wielding a wickedly-sharp knife.

Jamie tightens his hold on me and leans over to kiss my forehead. "How's your cheek?" he murmurs, his lips pressed against my brow.

"It stings. And it feels hot."

"It needs to be cleaned. God knows where that knife has been."

When we arrive at the hospital, Jake pulls up to the entrance to the emergency room. Shane gets out of the vehicle, and Jamie helps me out.

"You two go sit down," Shane says. "I'll sign Molly in."

Jamie and I find seats in the waiting room. Jake joins us before long and offers to go get us coffee.

Lia and Jonah arrive at the ER not long afterward and spot us across the room.

"Are you all right, Molly?" Lia says. She gets a good look at my cheek. "Damn. And your throat, too. Did that fucker choke you?"

"Yes."

Lia shakes her head in disgust then looks at Jamie. "Please tell me you took care of that."

Jamie nods. "I did."

"Good," Lia says. "Beth sends her love. She wanted to come, too, but Shane put his foot down and said she needed to stay home and rest."

Troy Spencer arrives wearing jeans and a University of Chicago sweatshirt, and carrying a slim black briefcase. "Jamie, when you get a chance, we need to talk."

For the first time, I wonder if Jamie could get into trouble for what happened. Todd was the intruder. Jamie was my rescuer. Surely he's not in legal trouble because of what happened. Todd stabbed himself.

When the receptionist calls my name, Jamie accompanies me to the registration desk. I check in, and then an attendee takes me back to the treatment area where a nurse cleans and sterilizes the cut on my face.

I'm seen shortly afterward by a doctor, who applies some type of adhesive to the cut, to hold the edges together while it heals. Jake was right. I was lucky. Very lucky. It could have been so much worse. And I'm not just talking about the cut on my face. If Jamie hadn't arrived when he did, Todd would have raped me. And worse yet, Jamie might have gotten hurt. He grappled bare-handed with a man holding a knife.

The ER doctor sends me home with a prescription for pain medication and ointment to put on my cut, to help minimize scarring while it heals. My throat is badly bruised, but he doesn't think any lasting damage was done to my vocal chords.

"Your throat will be sore for a few days, and your voice will be a little hoarse until the swelling goes down. Just get lots of rest and drink plenty of water. You'll be good as new in no time."

* * *

I was dead on my feet by the time I was finally discharged.

"Do you guys want to come back to our place tonight?" Shane says. "We've got plenty of room. Or, if you'd rather, I can let you use one of the guest apartments in my building." Shane pauses for a moment, as if delivering bad news. "Molly can't go back to her apartment. It's an active crime scene, and it's off limits until the police complete their investigation. And once they're done, her bedroom will need to be professionally cleaned before she can enter that room."

"What do you want to do?" Jamie asks me. "We could go to my apartment. Or, sleep in one of Shane's guest apartments. What would you prefer?"

"Charlie. I don't want to leave him in the apartment alone tonight."

"We could take him with us to my apartment, and sleep there tonight. Then, in the morning, we'll decide what to do next."

I nod. "Let's do that. I don't like leaving him alone in that apartment. He's probably traumatized."

"Are you sure, Molly?" Shane says. "I've got an apartment you can use for as long as you need it. I can send someone to retrieve your cat and bring him to you."

"I'm sure. Thank you, Shane. I just want to go home, and Jamie's apartment is the closest thing I have to home right now."

Jamie smiles and reaches for my hand, lacing our fingers. "Let's go."

Jamie and I practically carry each other out to Jake's SUV, which is waiting for us outside the automatic doors. Jamie helps me stay upright, and I do the navigating, steering us clear of any pedestrians and other obstructions.

"We make a good team," I say.

"Yes, we do."

* * *

My apartment's not very big, but it takes us fifteen minutes to find Charlie. At first, the furry little orange guy is nowhere to be seen. When he doesn't greet us at the door, I panic a little, fearing that he might have slipped out of the apartment during all the chaos tonight.

"Charlie?"

We step inside the apartment, and I turn on a light. "Charlie? It's okay. You can come out."

Nothing. My heart starts pounding at the thought that he's lost.

I check everywhere... the kitchen, the pantry, the spare bedroom, the bathroom. I check all his favorite hiding places. Nothing.

I'm just about to break the police seal on my bedroom door to see if he got trapped in my room. Perhaps he was hiding under the bed or in my closet when the police sealed the room. I really don't want to go in there to look for him because I know what I'll see... a huge pool of blood on my wood floors, where Todd died.

I knock quietly on my bedroom door, putting my ear to the wood panel to listen for a meow. *Nothing.*

I'm really starting to panic now, thinking that he must have gotten out of the apartment.

I knock once more on my bedroom door and call him, but there's no response from inside the room.

"Looking for this little guy?" Jamie says, coming down the hallway with Charlie cradled in his arms.

Jamie's scratching Charlie's ears, and Charlie is obviously in heaven, turning and twisting his head to soak in all that attention.

I burst into tears as I reach for Charlie, surprising even myself. It's all just been too much. "Where did you find him?"

Jamie wraps one arm around me and pulls me close. "I found him hiding under the sofa. It took a bit of coaxing to get him to come out."

"He must have been scared to death, with Todd coming into the apartment, and then all those strangers."

While Jamie entertains my cat, I gather up what I'll need tonight and tomorrow... my toiletries, a few cans of cat food, and the little package of cat treats. I dump the litter box and pour fresh litter into it. I can't grab a change of clean clothes or any pajamas as I can't go into my bedroom. I'll just have to make do with what I have for now.

Jamie carries the cat litter box – which is heavy – and I carry Charlie and everything else. When Jamie opens the door to his apartment, Charlie jumps down and runs inside to be greeted by an exuberant Gus, who's clearly very happy to see his little buddy.

"Where should I put this?" Jamie says, holding up the litter box.

"How about in the laundry room? That's where I keep it."

Jamie sets the cat litter box down in his laundry room – in the same spot where I keep it in mine. We're hoping the similarities will help Charlie settle in to the strange place easily. While I spoon Charlie's food into a dish, Jamie refreshes the water in Gus's bowl, then offers Charlie a few of the cat treats and gives him another scratching behind his ear.

As I watch Jamie going out of his way to make my cat feel comfortable, I'm reminded of the fact that in all my ten years of marriage, Todd refused to even once consider getting a pet, no matter how much I wanted one. And here's Jamie going out of his way to make my cat feel welcome.

"You're amazing," I say.

Jamie looks up and grins. "Why is that?"

"Because you're nice to my cat." Once again, I burst into tears, absolutely mortified at how short my emotional fuse is tonight.

He rises to his feet and pulls me into his arms. "It's late, and you're tired. Let's get you to bed."

"That sounds wonderful."

I head to the bathroom to get ready for bed while Jamie locks up the apartment and turns out the lights. Just as I'm wondering what I should wear to bed, he raps on the bathroom door.

"I've got a T-shirt for you to sleep in," he says.

I open the door to see him standing there holding a T-shirt, looking a little sheepish, I might add. "Thank you." I strip out of my clothes and remove my bra – and my breast forms along with it – and slip his big T-shirt over my head.

He follows me into the bedroom and pulls back the bed covers so I can crawl into bed.

It feels so good to be lying down. I stretch and moan. "I'm so tired I can barely think straight."

Gus drops down on his dog bed in the corner of the room with a heavy sigh. Charlie jumps up onto the bed and curls up next to me.

"Aren't you coming to bed?" I say.

"I need to wash up first. I'll be back soon."

Jamie switches off the bedside lamp and heads for the bathroom. I relax into the comfortable bed, snugging with Charlie, listening to the shower in the other room.

Just relax. Todd's gone. He can't hurt you or Jamie anymore.

I'm tired, and my energy wanes quickly. I'm half asleep when Jamie crawls into bed beside me, his skin warm and slightly damp from his shower. I roll to face him, and he draws my arm across his chest. One of my legs slips in between his and I press a kiss to his chest. He smells so tantalizingly good, so male. He runs the fingers of his free hand up and down my bare back, gently stroking me, setting off tingles wherever he touches me.

Part of my mind is focused on Jamie's touch, but the other part is still fixated on what happened this evening. "He's really gone?" I say, my voice little more than a whisper in the quiet darkness.

"Yes." Jamie's hand slides up to massage the nape of my neck. "Are you okay?"

I swallow hard. It's difficult to answer that question when my mind is reeling with all the *what-ifs*. "He cut me. On purpose."

"I know. I'm sorry, Molly."

"You have nothing to be sorry about."

"If I'd gotten back from walking Gus sooner, I might have prevented him from getting into the building."

"Jamie, you saved me."

"Yes, but he still managed to hurt you." Jamie's hand tightens on my neck. "It makes me nuts to think what he might have done to you."

The only thing I'm worried about now is Jamie. "What happened with Todd – that was self-defense, right? You couldn't be charged with anything, could you?"

"You don't need to worry. Troy says he's already reviewed the police reports, and he says there are no charges pending against me. It truly was self-defense, Molly. I never even touched the knife. He stabbed himself."

My cheek is throbbing, both from the cut and from where Todd backhanded me. I'm sure I'll have a lovely bruise for quite a while. I gently examine the area around the cut. "What's one more scar, right? I already have so many."

Jamie rolls me to my other side so he can press up against me from behind. His arm comes over me, lying protectively across my chest. "You're beautiful, Molly. One tiny scar on your cheek won't change that. It will just add to your allure."

I laugh. "How do you know I'm beautiful? You can't even see me."

He presses his lips to the back of my head. "I can see you just fine. Now go to sleep while you still can."

I'm pretty sure his comment is in reference to the growing erection I feel pressing against my lower back. "I can't sleep," I murmur. "My mind is racing."

"Mine too," he admits. "If I'd been even a couple of minutes later..."

"Don't," I say. "You did get there, and you stopped him."

Jamie's hand slips up beneath my T-shirt and he begins stroking my chest, his gentle fingers following the path of my scars, traveling across my sternum to the other side. When I stiffen self-consciously, he kisses the side of my neck. "It's okay. Relax."

"I can't. That makes me nervous."

"What? Me touching your chest?"

"Yes."

"Why? Don't you like to touch my chest?"

"Yes, of course I do, but that's different."

"I'll stop if you really want me to, but I think you should let me touch your chest."

"Why?"

"Because you need to learn that every inch of your body is beautiful to me, whether it's perfect or not."

I feel hot tears leaking out of the corners of my eyes. "Here I go again," I say, sniffling. "I just can't seem to stop crying tonight."

Jamie turns me to face him, my face against his chest. "That's okay. You go ahead and cry. I don't mind."

* * *

I must have fallen asleep with my face pressed against Jamie's chest. When I awake, it's daylight outside. I'm facing away from Jamie, and he is spooning closely against my back.

"Good morning," he murmurs into my hair when I begin to stir. "Did you sleep well?"

"Yes." Once I fell asleep, I slept deeply all night. I reach for my phone on the nightstand to check the time. "It's nine-thirty. I should be at work already."

"I figured you needed as much sleep as possible."

"I need my clothes from my bedroom, but I can't get in there."

"Troy texted me this morning. He said the police would be done with their investigation by noon, and that you could have access to the room at that time. I don't want you to go in there until after the room's been cleaned, though. That should happen later this afternoon – Shane's already made arrangements. In the meanwhile, you can either hang out here and wait, or you can go to work wearing what you had on yesterday."

"I want to go to work, at least for a little while. And I need to see Chloe. I need to tell her what happened before she finds out some other way."

Jamie kisses the spot behind my ear, making me shiver. "All right. I'll get dressed and take Gus out for a walk while you get ready. I'll make you some breakfast, and then I'll walk you to Chloe's shop, and then on to your studio. While you're at the studio, I'll come back here and work."

When I wash up in the bathroom and put my clothes on, I find Jamie in the kitchen at the stove, scrambling eggs and frying bacon.

"Bacon, eggs, and toast?" he says.

"Yes, please."

"Coming right up. You can make yourself a cup of coffee with the Keurig machine there, if you'd like to."

"Thank you." I see his own cup of black coffee sitting on the counter.

One delicious caramel latte later, I'm standing in the kitchen sipping my coffee as I watch Jamie prepare breakfast. He's very methodical and precise, and everything's laid out carefully on the counter top.

"Are these eggs done enough for you?" he asks, pointing at the skillet with the spatula.

"Yes, they're perfect."

"Salt and pepper?"

"Yes, please." I can't help chuckling.

"What's so funny?" he says.

"No guy has ever made me breakfast before, other than you."

"Oh. Well, they're idiots then. Don't they know how to impress a woman?"

44

Jamie

Molly's very easy to please. All it takes is crispy bacon, a bit of scrambled eggs, and some lightly buttered toast, and she's putty in my hands. It's all part of my evil plan to prove to her that I'm good boyfriend material. I may have my limitations, but I make up for them in other ways.

After we feed Gus and Charlie, we both brush our teeth in the bathroom and head out to the tattoo shop.

* * *

"What did that crazy motherfucker do to you?" Chloe says.

"Molly, your poor face! Oh, my God, I could kill him!"

"There's no need," Molly says. "He's dead."

"What!" Chloe's screech is deafening.

"He died of an accidentally self-inflicted stab wound to the chest."

"What in the hell is an accidentally self-inflicted stab wound?" she says. "Were you there?"

Molly nudges me, and I realize Chloe's talking to me. "Yes. I was there."

"When Todd accidentally stabbed himself?" She sounds incredulous.

"Yes."

"Was he, by any chance, trying to stab *you* at the time?"

I chuckle. "Yes."

"I see," Chloe says. "And he just happened to miss and hit himself instead? Well, I always suspected Todd was an idiot. Now I know." Then her voice softens. "Molly, your poor face."

"They're just bruises," Molly says. "And one small cut. They'll heal."

After assuring Chloe that Molly's okay, we leave her still fuming at Todd and walk the short distance to Molly's studio. I go in with her. The shop's not open today, but she wants to work on paintings in the back room. I figure I'll hang here for a while until she gets settled in to her work.

I listen as she takes off her coat and hangs it on a hook. Then she starts to gather her supplies – glass jars, brushes, fresh water from the faucet.

"I guess I'll go home and do some work myself," I tell her a little while later. I hate leaving her here alone. But I keep telling myself, Todd is dead. *She'll be safe. But will she be okay?* "I'm only a phone call away," I say. "If you need me for any reason at all, just call me, okay?"

"Okay."

"How about if Gus and I come pick you up at five and take you out to dinner?"

"I'd love that," she says, lifting up on her toes to kiss me.

"By the time we get home from dinner tonight, your bedroom should be cleaned up."

When she doesn't reply, I say, "Are you okay?"

She exhales heavily. "The idea of going back to my apartment isn't very appealing. I want my *things*, but I don't want to be *there*."

I nod. "I figured as much. Why don't you stay with me, in my apartment, for the time being? We'll move your stuff into my place this evening."

"Thank you. I'd like that. You don't mind?"

I laugh. "Are you kidding? I've been doing everything I possibly can to get you into my life. No, I don't mind."

* * *

On the way back to my apartment, I stop in for a quick chat with Chloe. She's Molly's best friend, and that makes her important to me. When I enter the tattoo parlor, I find her on the phone, and clearly not in a good mood.

"What do you mean sometime next week? I have no fricking heat, Mr. Carver! In case you haven't noticed, it's pretty damn cold outside! It's winter!"

I step up to the counter and wait for her conversation to end.

"Well, that's no excuse. It's so cold I can't even bear to take a shower in my own apartment. You're the landlord, for crying out loud. You're supposed to fix the things that aren't working, and my heat's not working!"

She's quiet for a moment, listening to the other party of the call. I can just barely make out the muffled voice of a man. It doesn't look like her landlord is giving her good news. "I'm calling the housing authority if you don't do something about the heat."

She ends the call and sets her phone down on the counter top with an exasperated sigh. "I should just move. My lease is up next month anyway, and the place is a total dump." She takes a deep, cleansing breath as she abruptly switches gears. "Howdy, handsome," she says, her tone brightening instantly. "What brings you in here?"

I listen intently, but I can't tell if we're alone in her shop or not. I hear a couple of muted voices, but it sounds like they're coming from a back room.

"It's okay. We're alone," she says. "Say what's on your mind."

"Molly's having a rough time processing everything that's happened."

"No kidding," she says. "The guy was her husband, for crying out loud. They were happy once. Then he had to go and turn into a freaking monster."

"I was hoping you would keep an eye on her. Maybe stop over and check on her this afternoon? I'll be back at five to take her to dinner."

"Sure, of course I will."

Chloe gives me her mobile number, and I send her a text so she'll have my number as well.

"Thanks," I say. "If she needs anything, call me."

* * *

When I get back to the apartment building, there's a spat of activity going on out front. I hear a lot of people – men from the sound of it – carrying a lot of heavy stuff.

"Find the door, Gus," I say, and Gus leads me up the stone steps. Inside the lobby, I hear an unfamiliar female voice coming from the left – from Apt 1A. Mrs. Powell's apartment.

"Be careful, that's very fragile!" the young woman says.

"Hello," I say. "Can I help you?"

She pauses near me. "Oh, hi. I'm Cheryl Powell. I'm moving my grandmother out of her apartment and into my house."

"Ah, Mrs. Powell."

"Yes." The young woman lowers her voice, speaking barely above a whisper. "I'm afraid she can't live on her own anymore. It's just not safe. Her memory's just not what it used to be."

"I'm sorry to see her go," I say, not knowing what else I can say. Mrs. Powell let Todd into the building on several occasions, always confused and thinking Todd was Molly's husband, so I can't say I'm sorry to hear she's moving out.

"Well, it's for the best. I'll be able to care for her better if she's living with me."

Mrs. Powell comes out of her apartment, fussing at one of the movers. She stops abruptly. "Oh, hello, dear," she says.

I assume she's talking to me. "Hello, Mrs. Powell."

"He's the nice young man I was telling you about, Cheryl. He's married to the young woman who lives upstairs."

"That's nice, Grandma. Come back inside the apartment while we pack up the last of your stuff."

After Mrs. Powell has shuffled back into her apartment, the young woman says, "Sorry about that."

"No problem," I say, laughing. "It's not a bad idea."

* * *

Gus and I head up the stairs. When I open the door to my apartment, Charlie's there to greet us, purring loudly as we enter.

"You guys entertain yourselves. I've got work to do."

I'm having trouble focusing on this new novel I'm writing. My mind keeps wandering back to Molly. I hope she's doing okay. Maybe I shouldn't have left her alone today. I didn't want to smother her, but maybe it's too soon for her to be alone all afternoon.

I lean back in my office chair and put my feet up on the desk. I review the last chapter I dictated to get caught up, then proceed with dictating the next chapter.

An hour later I'm still at it, actually making some decent progress, when my editor, Kara, calls just to check up on me. She calls me once a week to touch base and see how things are going.

After a couple of hours of productive writing, an idea occurs to me. I pick up my phone and call Chloe.

"Wow, twice in one afternoon," she says. "I must be doing something right. What's up, stud?"

"How would you like to move into our apartment building? The two units on the first floor are both opening up. I think Molly would love having you downstairs."

"Seriously?"

"Yes, seriously. You said your current lease is up next month. Now's the perfect time to move."

She sighs. "I'd love to, but I don't think I can afford it."

"The landlord's a pretty reasonable guy. I think I can work something out for you."

"Really? Oh, my God, that would be awesome! I'd love to live in your building."

When we hang up, I call Shane.

"Hey, Jamie, what's up?" my brother says.

"Mrs. Powell is moving out of Apt 1A. I want Molly's friend Chloe to move in there. I think Molly would really like that."

"Okay. Both of the downstairs units are opening up. I'm thinking of moving Cameron Stewart into one of the units. I'd feel better if I had one of my guys on the premises."

"Shane." Mentally, I'm rolling my eyes. "Todd Ferguson is no longer a threat, to me or to Molly, and as far as I know, neither one of us has any other nemeses lurking in the background."

Shane laughs. "I know. Just humor me, okay. Mom doesn't like you living alone. Having one of my guys living in your building will go a long way toward alleviating her concerns. And, it would make Elly happy too. She tries not to show it, but she worries about you."

I sigh. "All right, fine." The things we do for family. But Cameron's a good guy. I've met him several times. He's former special forces, a real no-nonsense straight shooter. He'll make a good neighbor.

45

Molly

Jamie picks me up at exactly five o'clock, as promised, and I'm relieved to see him. He comes into the back room and takes off his coat and leans against one of the work tables while I clean up my brushes. It's been a really long day, and I'm exhausted. I haven't had a chance to sit all afternoon.

After clean-up is done, I stand in front of Jamie and tug on the open collar of his flannel shirt. "Would you be too terribly disappointed if we got carryout and took it back to your place? I'm wiped out."

He takes my hands in his and squeezes them gently, then brings them to his lips for a kiss. "That's fine. What would you like?"

"Chinese? I have a craving for Veggie Delight."

"Sounds good to me." He releases one of my hands to pull out his phone and make the call, but he keeps a tight hold on my other hand, lacing our fingers together and rubbing the back of my hand with the pad of his thumb.

I close my eyes and listen to the soothing sound of his baritone voice as he places our order. The physical connection of our hands linked together eases some of my anxiety, and I feel myself starting to relax for the first time all day. Logically, I know Todd is no longer a threat, but I don't think my fight-or-flight system has caught up to current events.

Ten minutes later, the shop is locked up for the evening, and we head back toward our building, stopping just long enough to pick up our carryout order. When we walk inside, I check both my mail box and Jamie's while he holds Gus's harness and the food.

I can't help noticing that Mrs. Powell's welcome mat is gone, as is the little hand-painted Welcome sign that always hung on her door. "Mrs. Powell's decorations are gone."

"She moved out today."

"You're kidding. I didn't know she was leaving."

"I met her granddaughter today. The granddaughter thinks it's no longer safe for her grandmother to live alone, so she's moving Mrs. Powell to her house."

"Then both downstairs units are empty. It's just us in the building now... at least until new people move in."

* * *

After we eat our dinner and clean up the dishes, we cuddle up on the sofa for some much-needed relaxation. Both of us end up reading. I'm reading on my Kindle app on my phone, and Jamie's listening to an audiobook on his. Charlie's curled up on the back of the sofa, and Gus's sleeping on the floor at our feet. I could definitely get used to this.

My apartment has been cleaned up and cleared for occupancy again, but Jamie hasn't said anything about me moving back to my place. I'm in no hurry to move back, but I don't want to wear out my welcome either.

Jamie pulls out his ear buds and sets his phone on the coffee table. "I have some news for you," he says. "I think you'll like it."

I put my phone down too. "What's that?"

"Come here," he says, sitting up and reaching for me. He pulls me onto his lap so that I'm facing him, straddling his lap. "I asked Chloe if she wanted to move into Mrs. Powell's apartment," he says. "She said yes."

"What!" I say, grasping his shoulders. I'm both surprised and elated that he would think of asking Chloe to move in here. "Are you serious?"

"Yes." He laughs at my exuberant response. "I take it you like the idea? I was afraid I'd overstepped my bounds by not asking you first. I should have."

"Oh, my God, of course I like the idea! I would love having her in our building."

"Good. Her lease is up soon, so I told her to move in anytime. I'm sure the guys wouldn't mind spending a few hours helping her move."

"Jamie." I cup his handsome face in my hands and kiss him gently. "Thank you."

"And one of Shane's employees is going to move into the other downstairs apartment. Cameron Stewart, former special forces. He's a good guy. You'll like him."

I'm absolutely thrilled that Chloe's going to move into our building, and I'm glad that the other downstairs apartment will be occupied by someone Jamie knows. Even though Todd's out of the picture, it makes me feel better knowing we'll have two friendly parties living downstairs.

"So, you're okay with both Chloe and Cameron moving in?" he says.

I kiss him again, just a light, teasing kiss. "I think it's wonderful."

His hands come around me and settle on my rear end, gently kneading my butt cheeks through my jeans. "Good," he says.

I sink my fingers into his hair and seal my mouth over his. He makes me so damn happy I could cry.

Jamie opens his mouth and licks his way inside mine, stroking his tongue against mine. His hands tighten on my butt cheeks, kneading me firmly, which makes my girly parts tingle. He pulls me closer so that I'm pressed up against his erection, which is straining at the zipper of his jeans. I rock forward, pressing my cleft against the firm ridge of his cock, and moan in delight. Suddenly, I'm aching for him to be inside me.

His hands have moved up and he's rubbing my back, and it feels so incredibly good.

I grip the waistband of his jeans and kiss him. "I want you. Right now. Right here."

He laughs again as he unbuckles his belt. "Yes, ma'am. You won't get any argument from me."

As he removes his belt and unzips his jeans, I brush my thumbs gently over his lowered eyelids, then lean forward to place a feather-light kiss on each one. This precious man lost an important part of himself serving our country. He made a huge sacrifice, but he's not bitter about it, and he came out of his ordeal strong and whole. I'll be his eyes. I'll be his guide whenever and wherever he needs me. My throat tightens as the depths of my feelings for him rush through me.

He guides me to stand in front of him and unsnaps my jeans and works them and my panties down my legs. After I kick off my jeans and panties, he lifts his hips off the sofa cushion and shoves his jeans and boxers down to his ankles, and I pull them off. Then he pulls of his shirt and tosses it onto the floor with the rest of our clothes.

Jamie grabs a fleece blanket off the back of the sofa and lays it on the seat, then sits down, pulling me back onto his lap.

"Shit, condom!" he says, laughing.

"I'll get it." I hop up, feeling ridiculous standing there in my top and socks, bare assed. "Where are they?"

"In my nightstand drawer." Jamie leans forward to remove his sneakers and socks while I race down the hallway to grab a condom. When I return, he's sitting impatiently, bare naked.

He pats his thighs, then pulls me back down onto him, taking the condom in hand. He rips open the packet and rolls the condom onto his erection. I stare, fascinated by the sight of him fully erect and by the sight of his hands smoothing the condom in place.

Oh, my God, I get to have some of that.

When I settle myself on his lap again, straddling him and ready to take him inside me, he reaches for the hem of my shirt and starts to lift it. I grab his hands to still his movement.

"What's wrong?" he says.

"Can't we just leave it on?" I really don't want to be topless. "I mean, what's the point?" There aren't any breasts for him to nuzzle. There aren't any nipples for him to lick or suckle.

His shoulders fall. "Molly."

"Please. I just don't feel comfortable being shirtless like this, in a brightly-lit room."

"Charlie won't care," he says. "Neither will Gus. And if you think I mind for one second, then you're dead wrong, and I'll prove it to you."

He never once let go of the hem of my shirt. He leans forward. "Kiss me."

"Jamie – "

"Kiss me and trust me."

I'm shaking, and I know he can feel it. Reluctantly, I release his hands and suck in a deep breath as he lifts my T-shirt over my head and drops it on the seat cushion beside us. Then he reaches behind my back and unclips my bra. As the heavy, weighted breast forms fall into his hands, I feel suddenly very chilled, and I cover my bare chest.

He carefully sets my bra aside. Then his hands return to cover mine, and he grips my hands firmly. "Lower your hands, Molly," he says, his voice gentle.

When I don't, he says, "You realize I can't even see your chest, right?"

I laugh nervously. "I know."

"Then why the shyness?"

"It just feels weird, being exposed like this."

He blinks. "I let you see my eyes."

"I know, but that's different."

"How so?"

"Your eyes look normal – they're beautiful. No one would even know they're prosthetic unless you told them. My chest... doesn't look normal. Far from it."

He bites back a chuckle as he tries valiantly to remain serious. "Molly, you have to trust me."

"I do trust you."

"I mean with your body."

"I do," I insist.

He shakes his head. "Trust means letting go of your fear. Letting go of your insecurities."

I make a sound that's part frustration and part growl, and Jamie laughs. He encircles both of my wrists with his fingers and tugs gently.

"Okay, fine! Have it your way!" I drop my arms and sit rigidly on his lap.

When he lays his warm hands on my chest, I flinch. Slowly, his hands slide across my skin, his thumbs brushing along the path of my scars, over my sternum and across my ribs.

He gives me a moment to get used to his touch. Then he says, "Do you know what I feel?"

"Nothing. Because there's nothing there."

"Wrong. I feel the body of a survivor. I feel the courage and determination of a woman who took her health and future into her own hands." He lays his hands over the ribs that cover my heart. "Your heart is inches beneath my fingers, just beneath your ribs."

He leans forward and presses a gentle kiss to my sternum, making me shiver. "I love your body, Molly, because it's yours. I love every inch of it. Every scar. Can you trust in that? Can you trust your body to me?"

Hot tears prick my eyes, and my throat tightens. I'm afraid if I say a word, I'll start bawling like a baby. All I can manage is a vague, "Mmm-hmm."

He smiles. "Is that a yes?"

"Mmm-hmm."

"I'm taking that to mean yes."

Jamie wraps his arms around my back, drawing my body against his. Our chests are touching, his muscular, with a light furring of dark hair, mine pale and flat and scarred. I swallow so hard it's audible, and he smiles again.

"That's not so bad, right?" he says.

"Mmm-hmm." I still can't trust myself to speak.

He leans forward and gives me a gentle, almost reverent kiss. I don't even realize I'm crying until I taste the salt on his lips.

Jamie reaches up and brushes my tears away. "Tonight is a new beginning, all right? You're safe, you're going to remain safe, and we have each other."

I nod, my throat still tight. I don't know what I did to deserve this second chance at happiness – to deserve Jamie. He's exactly what I need, and I've never been so happy. I wrap my hands around his neck, threading my fingers through his thick hair, and lean forward to kiss him. "A new beginning."

The End… for now

Epilogue

Molly

It's only been two weeks since the night Todd broke into my apartment. The police investigation into Todd's death is over, and Jamie has been cleared of any wrong-doing. I never doubted that would happen, but I certainly breathed a sigh of relief once we had the official report in our hands, and Troy assured us Jamie had nothing to worry about.

The coroner performed an autopsy on Todd, as part of normal procedure. As next of kin, Todd's parents received the report, and his mom shared the findings with me. His parents had been just as confused as I was by the changes in Todd's behavior and personality over the past couple of years, and it turns out he had a tumor in the front lobe of his brain. It was benign, but it was impacting the parts of his brain responsible for personality and behavior.

I didn't know what to think of that bombshell. Todd's increasingly erratic and violent behavior never made any sense to me. He'd become someone I no longer recognized – he certainly wasn't the same young man I fell in love with in college. In the past year, all of his good traits had been erased, replaced with narcissism and aggression.

Since the night Todd died in my bedroom, I haven't slept in my own apartment again. I've been sleeping with Jamie in his place, and it feels like home.

To celebrate the end of my nightmare, Shane and Beth have organized a dinner at their place tonight, and we're heading there now in an Uber ride. We invited Chloe to come with us. She moved into her new apartment on the ground floor just a few days ago. Cameron Stewart moved in just this morning, so the building's full again. Chloe will come join us at Shane and Beth's place as soon as she gets off work. Cameron offered to wait and ride over to the dinner with Chloe.

"Do you know if Cameron has a girlfriend?" I ask.

Jamie shakes his head. "Not one I'm aware of. Why?"

"Why? I saw the way she was looking at him at dinner last night. And I saw the way he was looking at her when she wasn't looking at him. I think I saw some sparks there."

Jamie takes my hand in his and links our fingers together. "Are you matchmaking?"

"Well, it doesn't hurt for them to get to know each other. After all, they're neighbors now."

As Jamie's thumb absently rubs the back of my hand, I glance up at him and indulge myself for a moment, admiring his handsome profile. I reach up and brush his hair back, and he leans into my touch, turning his face so he can kiss the palm of my hand.

We arrive at Shane's building, which is a towering architectural masterpiece. It's a beautiful building with lots of glass and lights, situated in a prime location on Lake Shore Drive overlooking Lake Michigan.

As I gaze out the car window and look up at the massive structure, I shake my head in disbelief. "I can't even begin to imagine what a building like this costs."

"Some of the apartments are reserved for his employees, and the rest are leased out to the public. Lia and Jonah have an apartment here. So does Jake and also Liam."

As we walk through the front lobby doors, an elderly doorman dressed in a fine uniform smiles when he sees Jamie.

"Jamie!" the elderly man says, his dark eyes lighting up. He reaches out for Jamie's hand, and the two men shake. "How's it going, man?"

"Hi, Frank," Jamie says. "It's going well. How about you?"

"Fine, fine," Frank says. "You must be here to see Mr. McIntyre. Did you know his missus is going to have a baby? Well, of course you do. You're family."

"Frank, this is Molly Ferguson. Molly, this is Frank. He runs this place."

Frank laughs as he slaps Jamie on the back. Then the old gentleman smiles at me. "Don't listen to a word he says, Miss Molly. The only reason Mr. McIntyre keeps me around this place is because I'm too old to fire."

Frank glances down at our hands, which are linked together, and grins. "It's a pleasure to meet you, Miss Molly."

After we take our leave, Jamie summons the private penthouse elevator with a top-secret code. When the elevator arrives, we step inside the car, and the doors close.

I glance around at the posh interior, with its thick burgundy carpeting, mirrored walls, and fine gold trim. "I can't believe your brother lives in the penthouse apartment and has his own elevator."

"There are certain advantages to having a private elevator." He backs me up against one of the mirrored walls, tips my chin up, and lowers his mouth to mine. He nudges my lips apart so he can slip his tongue inside to play with mine.

I sigh into the kiss, loving the feel of him, the taste. I unzip his jacket so I can slip my arms inside and wrap them around his torso. Jamie looks absolutely edible in a pair of distressed blue jeans and a white button-down shirt. And with his dark glasses on, he looks sexy and mysterious. But as much as I like the look, I prefer him without the glasses. He no longer wears them when it's just the two of us at home, so I don't begrudge him wearing the glasses when we're out in public.

It feels like I have a delicious secret – and that's seeing him without any barriers between us. He's getting more comfortable letting me see his beautiful eyes, and I'm working on getting more comfortable letting him touch my chest. We're both working on our insecurities.

Jamie releases me when the elevator stops at our destination. I peek briefly at my reflection in the mirror to check out the scar on my cheek. The adhesive dissolved just as the doctor said it would, and the scar is healing nicely. It's just a faint pink line now. I can live with that. I shudder when I think how much worse it could have been.

When the elevator door opens, we step out into an elegant foyer with a marble floor and a massive crystal chandelier hanging overhead. I reach for Jamie's hand and lead him across the room to the door that presumably leads to his brother's apartment.

Jamie and I have developed our own protocol. When it's just the two of us going out, he often leaves Gus at home and relies on me to be his eyes. I suspect we both enjoy this arrangement because it keeps us close to each other.

We walk through the door to find a great room filled with familiar faces. "Wow, everyone's here," I say, scanning the room. "Lia, Jonah, Jake, Liam. Shane and Beth are on the sofa. Cooper. Miguel. Your sister Sophie. Beth's friend... what's her name? The redhead?"

"Gabrielle."

"Right. Gabrielle. Oh, and your parents."

I lead Jamie further into the room, our hands linked together, and give him a narrative run down on the inhabitants of the room. "Most of the guys are at the bar... your brothers, Jonah, Miguel, and your dad. Your mom just went into the kitchen with someone wearing a catering uniform. Beth's on the sofa with Shane, and it looks like he's giving her a back rub. Let's go say hi to our hosts."

"Hi, Molly! Hi, Jamie!" Beth says when she sees us.

She starts to get up, but Shane catches her hand and pulls her back down. "No, you need to rest," he says. He looks at us with a suffering expression. "She's been on her feet all day."

Beth rolls her eyes at us. "If he's this bad now, I can't imagine what he'll be like when I'm as big as a house."

Jamie's mother hands Beth a glass of water and gently brushes her hair back. "Here, drink this, honey. You need to stay hydrated."

Shane smiles at us. "Make yourselves at home. Drinks are at the bar – alcoholic as well as non-alcoholic. Dinner will be served in about thirty minutes."

Jamie and I walk over to the bar and take our seats. After taking our orders, Jake hands Jamie a cold beer and me a bottle of Pepsi.

While Jamie's giving his family an update on the investigation into the break-in and Todd's death, I casually study Cooper, who's standing behind the bar with his arms crossed over his chest, looking rather formidable. Other than giving us a polite nod hello, Cooper hasn't said a word. Jamie did mention something about Cooper's boyfriend, Sam, abruptly leaving town the morning after the wedding, but I don't know the whole story. All I know is Cooper seems distant and unhappy, and glancing around, I see no sign of Sam.

Chloe and Cameron arrive shortly after we finish our drinks. When they walk through the foyer door, all eyes turn their way. They make a striking pair. Chloe, with her long, dark hair and dark eyes, and beautiful café au lait complexion, is the perfect complement to Cameron, who's a blond, blue-eyed mountain of a man.

"Chloe!" I wave her over to the bar, and she takes the empty bar seat beside mine.

Cameron follows her over and shakes hands with Jake and Jamie.

"Can I get you a drink?" Jake asks Chloe, after I make all the introductions.

"Sure, I'll take a beer. Whatever's on tap."

I lean close to her, whispering, "That was nice of Cameron to wait for you to get off work and ride over with you."

"You mean Thor?" she says.

Of course Cameron overhears her. He looks my way and rolls his eyes. Thankfully, he seems amused by the comparison. Not that being compared to Chris Hemsworth could *ever* be considered an insult.

"Oh, come on!" Chloe says, taking a sip of her beer. "He looks just like Thor, don't you think? In the movie when his hair was cut short. He's certainly built like him. All he needs is a hammer."

I try not to laugh.

"Here you go, Thor," Jake says as he hands Cameron a beer.

"I told you!" Chloe says. "Even the bartender thinks so!"

Cameron maintains a straight face as he accepts a bottle of beer from Jake. Chloe does have a point. Cameron's a big guy, tall and muscular. He's probably the tallest man here, and that's saying a lot. He must be at least six-and-a-half feet tall. I have to admit, his short, dirty-blond hair, scruffy beard, and blue eyes do remind me of the actor in question.

Cameron seems completely unfazed by Chloe's teasing. If she's trying to get a rise out of him, it's not working.

But I do catch him watching her when she's not looking, and I think maybe he's not as unaffected as he appears.

* * *

Dinner is a lavish affair, with multiple courses, from potato soup and salad, to baked chicken breasts marinated in a delicious lemon and mustard sauce, roasted sweet potatoes, and warm dinner rolls with butter. The catering staff serves everyone at the table, and it's all very fancy.

Several bottles of red wine are passed around the table, and there are also local craft beers available. Although I'm not a big beer drinker, I opt for one of the local brews, and Beth has water. For dessert, there's a pumpkin cheesecake topped with real whipped cream.

I can't remember the last time I had such a delicious meal.

There's lively conversation at the table that lasts long after the dishes have been cleared away by the catering staff. Jamie and I happen to be sitting directly across the table from his parents, and his mother asks me all sorts of questions about my art studio, while Jamie and his dad chat about Chicago basketball.

Bridget's pretty blue eyes light up whenever Jamie leans close to me and whispers in my ear, or he reaches over to fiddle with my hair or touch my hand. She smiles warmly at me, and I'm relieved to have her tacit approval.

A couple of times, I glance around the long table. Chloe's sitting on my other side, and Cameron's seated at the far end of the table beside Shane's gorgeous sister Sophie, who is a curvaceous, brunette bombshell. A couple of times, I catch Chloe watching Cameron, who's conversing easily with Sophie.

After everyone's finished eating, Shane invites everyone to gather in the rec room, where there's a pool table and pinball games, along with a bar, dance floor, and boxing ring.

The boxing ring takes center stage, in the middle of the room, up on an elevated platform. I remember seeing Jamie spar with Jake at the house in Kenilworth, and being amazed at his capabilities.

Lia and Jonah pick up pool cues and start a game of 8 ball. Cooper mans the bar, and Jake and Liam climb into the boxing ring and start messing around.

"What do you want to do?" I ask Jamie. There's really not much he can do here. He can't play pool or pinball games.

"What I'd like to do we can't do here. At least not without an audience."

I laugh and nudge him with my elbow. "Not with your parents watching! Eew!"

Jake and Liam start a wrestling match in the ring, and a small crowd develops. Beth gets comfortable on one of the several black leather sofas positioned against the walls around the room.

When Liam manages to pin Jake to the mat, Jake steps down and taunts Shane to take his place.

Jamie and I join Beth on the sofa.

"Are you feeling okay?" I ask her. She doesn't look happy at the moment.

She shrugs. "I'm fine."

"You don't look fine."

She turns to me, a frown marring her lovely face. "I miss Sam. He should be here."

"How's he doing?"

"He's okay. He's staying with his mom right now, getting physical therapy, gaining his strength back." Her blue-green eyes mist with tears. "I just miss him so much." Her gaze travels across the room to the bar on the far wall, where Cooper is dispensing drinks. "And Cooper – well, he's not been the same since Sam left."

"Have you spoken to Sam?" I ask.

She nods. "We've Skyped a few times. He seems pretty subdued right now. I think he's hurting."

I'm not sure if she means he's hurting physically or emotionally. I think it might be both.

I pat Beth's knee. "I'm sure he'll be back soon. Don't worry. He just needs some time to recuperate."

"He'd better come back. He promised me he would. And Shane promised me he'd go down to Dayton and drag Sam back here by his hair if he refused."

After Shane's turn in the ring, Miguel has a turn, and Liam remains the champion at hand-to-hand.

"Well, hell, what do you expect?" Jake says. "He's a master in Jiu

Jitsu. Plus, he fights dirty."

Liam remains alone in the ring, offering to take on any remaining contenders.

Jake gently kicks Jamie's boot. "How about you, cowboy? You're the only one besides Jonah who hasn't tried to dethrone the boy wonder."

I look at Jamie, my heart suddenly in my throat. I don't want him fighting. It's not fair. Especially not against Liam. Liam has an unfair advantage.

I tighten my grip on Jamie's hand, and he smiles at his brother. "No, thanks. I'm good."

"What, are you losing your edge?" Jake says, clearly taunting his brother.

"No," Jamie says. "I just don't feel the need to show off."

"Come on, man! Somebody's got to put Liam in his place. You're the only one who can."

Jamie sighs as he releases my hand and rises to his feet. He takes off his glasses and hands them to me. "Fine. Let's make it quick."

As Jamie walks toward the ring, I get up and follow him, wanting a front row seat.

"What are you doing, honey?" Bridget says.

I look over by the pool table, where Bridget and Calum are watching Lia and Jonah in their game. Bridget's gaze is locked on her son as he stands next to the ring and removes his boots.

"Jamie, honey, what are you doing?"

"It's okay, Mom," Jamie says as he climbs through the ropes. "We're just playing around."

Bridget's eyes narrow and she comes toward the ring. "I don't think this is a good idea, boys."

"Mom, it's fine," Liam says, standing with his hands on his hips.

Clearly, he's a little worse for wear, with the beginnings of a few bruises on his face and arms. "I'm not going to hurt him."

"And I promise not to hurt your baby boy," Jamie says, to a roomful of laughter.

Jamie walks to the middle of the ring and takes a stance. His eyelids are closed as he listens for any tell-tale sound that will give Liam away.

Liam circles his brother, looking for an opening.

"Watch this," Jake says. "If Jamie gets his hands on Liam, it's over for Liam. Liam's only chance is to come in fast and hard and drop Jamie to the mat before Jamie can react."

"I don't like this, boys," Bridget says, standing beside the ring with her hands on her hips. "Somebody could get hurt."

"Bridget, honey, leave the boys alone," Calum says, laying his hands on his wife's shoulders. He leans forward and kisses the top of her head. "They know what they're doing."

"I know they do, but Jamie's at a disadvantage. It's not fair."

"More like Liam will get his ass handed to him," Shane says, chuckling. "Mom, don't worry."

The room grows quiet in anticipation. Someone even turns off the sound system, which had been piping in pop music. The only sound that can be heard now is the soft shuffling of Liam's bare feet as he circles his brother.

"Oh, he's toast," Jake mutters from somewhere nearby. "He's making way too much noise."

Liam makes his move, coming in hard and fast. He's probably hoping to catch Jamie off guard, but it's as if Jamie anticipated Liam's every move and meets him halfway. I gasp when Jamie catches Liam, twisting them both as they fall to the mat. Jamie lands on top of his brother and wraps his legs around Liam's. His arms go around Liam's shoulders and neck, and he immobilizes his brother. Liam struggles against the hold, but Jamie already has the upper hand as he pins Liam squarely on the mat.

"I told you," Jake says, admiration clear in his voice.

Jamie releases Liam and the two men bounce back to their feet, neither worse for wear. They shake hands, clapping each other on the back the way guys do. Then Jamie climbs down from the ring. I meet him there, reaching for his hand.

He surprises me by pulling me into his arms and kissing me soundly in front of everyone.

The music comes back on.

"I need something to drink," Jamie says.

We head toward the bar, serenaded by hoots and hollers.

"Nice job, Jamie," Cooper says. "What can I get you two to drink?"

Seeing Cooper reminds me of what Beth said about missing Sam. I hope Sam does indeed come back, and I hope he and Cooper can work things out. Life's too short not to be with the one you love.

Jamie and I stand at the bar with our cold drinks. He pulls me in front of him and loops his arm across my chest, holding me against him.

I feel utterly sheltered in his embrace, and I don't think it's a coincidence that his arm is positioned protectively across my chest.

The song changes from a popular rap tune to a romantic hit by Sam Hunt.

Everyone starts laughing when Beth drags a reluctant Shane onto the dance floor.

"I love this song," Lia says, pulling Jonah out onto the dance floor.

Several other couples join them.

I turn in Jamie's arms and say, "Will you dance with me?"

I'm reminded of the wedding reception, when Jamie asked me to dance, and I repaid him for his kindness by walking away from him after the dance finished. I regret that moment more than I can ever express.

After setting both of our drinks on the bar, he gives me a beautiful smile. "I would be honored."

Coming Next

Stay tuned for more books in the McIntyre Security, Inc. series! I have lots of exciting new books planned for this series, including stories for Cooper and Sam, Jake, Erin and Mack, Tyler, Liam, and lots more!

Here are the next few books on my
publishing schedule for 2018:

Ruined #6 (Sam and Cooper's book), 2018
Hostage #7 (Beth and Shane, Lia and Jonah), 2018
Redemption #8 (Jake's book), 2018
... with lots more to follow!

Author's Diary

Molly's story has special meaning for me. In June of 2009, I was diagnosed with an aggressive form of breast cancer. Fortunately for me, it was caught very early – stage 0 – which means it hadn't left the breast tissue yet. As a single (divorced) mother of a 9-year-old daughter at that time, my only thought was to maximize my chances for survival in the long term so I could be there for my daughter. Knowing what I knew from my own grandmother's two-decade bout with breast cancer (she survived it, but battled it twice), I chose to have a double mastectomy immediately. I also chose *not* to have breast reconstruction surgery... because like Molly, I prefer to go *au natural.*

It wasn't until after my surgery that I realized how prominently breasts feature in romance novels. Before, I hadn't given it much thought. Now that I didn't have breasts, I was more attuned to the role of breasts in romance novels. Immediately, I started brainstorming an idea for a romance novel featuring a female protagonist who'd had a double mastectomy and whose chest was "flat," like mine. And from that idea, eight years later, Molly's story was born.

Molly considers herself defective after her surgery, especially in light of her husband's negative reaction to her post-surgery body, and it seemed appropriate to pair her with a romantic hero who was also "defective." Hence the title: *Imperfect. Imperfect* is the story of two physically damaged people who come together and heal each other emotionally through unconditional love and acceptance.

Part of Molly's story is autobiographical for me, but some of it is purely fictional. I had been divorced for many years before I was diagnosed with breast cancer and made my treatment decisions. My ex-husband, who is still a close friend of mine today, was very supportive of my choices and actions. (Todd is a completely fictitious character.)

I truly hope that readers respond well to Molly's story. I imagine it might be a painful subject for some women to read – for those who have experienced breast cancer first-hand, or those who know someone who has. There are many women who've had mastectomies, and they long for romance too. They deserve heroes who find them beautiful just the way they are. This story is for them.

Please Leave a Review

I hope you'll take a moment to leave a brief review for me on Amazon. It doesn't have to be long... just leave a brief comment saying whether you liked the book or not. Reviews are vitally important to authors! I'd be incredibly grateful to you if you'd leave one.

Stay in Touch

Follow me on Facebook or subscribe to my newsletter for up-to-date information on the schedule for new releases. I'm active daily on Facebook, and I love to interact with my readers. Come talk to me on Facebook by leaving me a message or a comment, or share my book posts with your friends. I also have a very active fan group on Facebook where I post excerpts often and do giveaways. Come join us!

Many of my readers have become familiar names and faces greeting me daily on Facebook, and I feel so blessed to have made so many new friends. I thank you all, from the bottom of my heart, for every Facebook like, share, and comment. You have no idea how thrilled I am to read your comments each day. I wouldn't be able to do the thing that I love to do most – share my characters and their stories – without your amazing support. Every day, I wake up and thank my lucky stars for you all!

Acknowledgements

Books aren't written in a vacuum. Authors are often greatly indebted to the support and kindness of friends and associates. I'm no different. Here are some of the people I'd like to thank.

First and foremost, I want to thank my darling daughter for her unending patience as she puts up with her mom's crazy work schedule.

I am deeply indebted to my sister and best friend, Lori Holmes, for her unending support. I couldn't do this without her.

I'd like to thank my beta readers Tiffany Mann, who's always ready with a kind word and brilliant insight; and Keely Knutton, who is always there with a kind word of support.

Thank you to Becky Morean, a dear friend and colleague (not to mention an amazing author who teaches me so much).

I'm so grateful for the friendship and support of the amazing Samantha Christy, author extraordinaire! I'd be lost without you, girlfriend! You're the best writing buddy a girl could ever have.

Thank you to Laura Williams of the romance writing duo J&L Wells, for your tireless support and friendship. You make every day more fun!

But most importantly, I want to thank all my fans around the world who support me by reading my books, posting their kind comments on Facebook, sharing my posts, recommending my books to their friends, and writing reviews on Amazon. Every one of you helped make my writing career a great success, and I'd be nowhere without you all. I thank my lucky stars for you every single day!

With much love to you all… April

92644025R00208

Made in the USA
Middletown, DE
10 October 2018